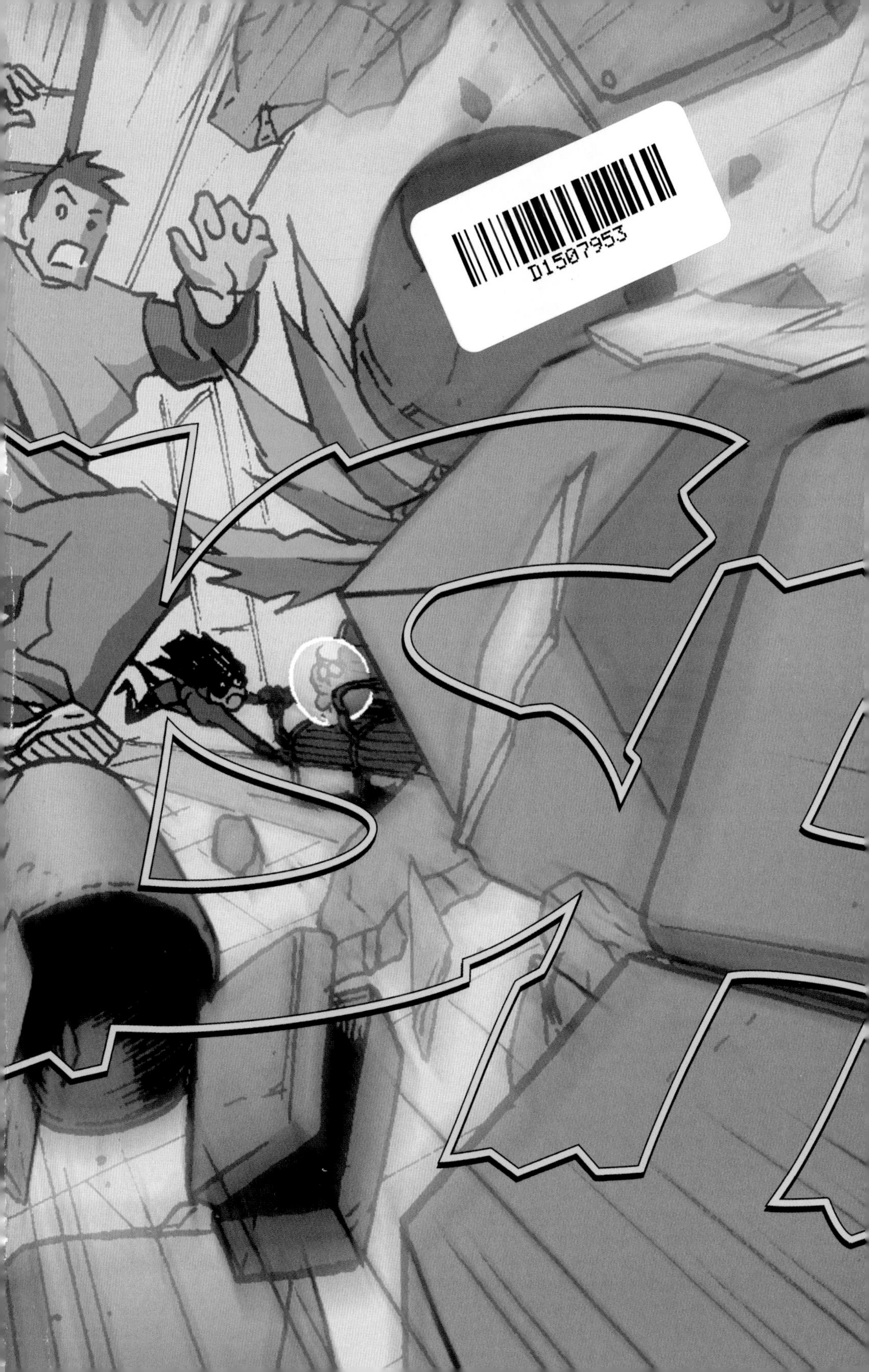

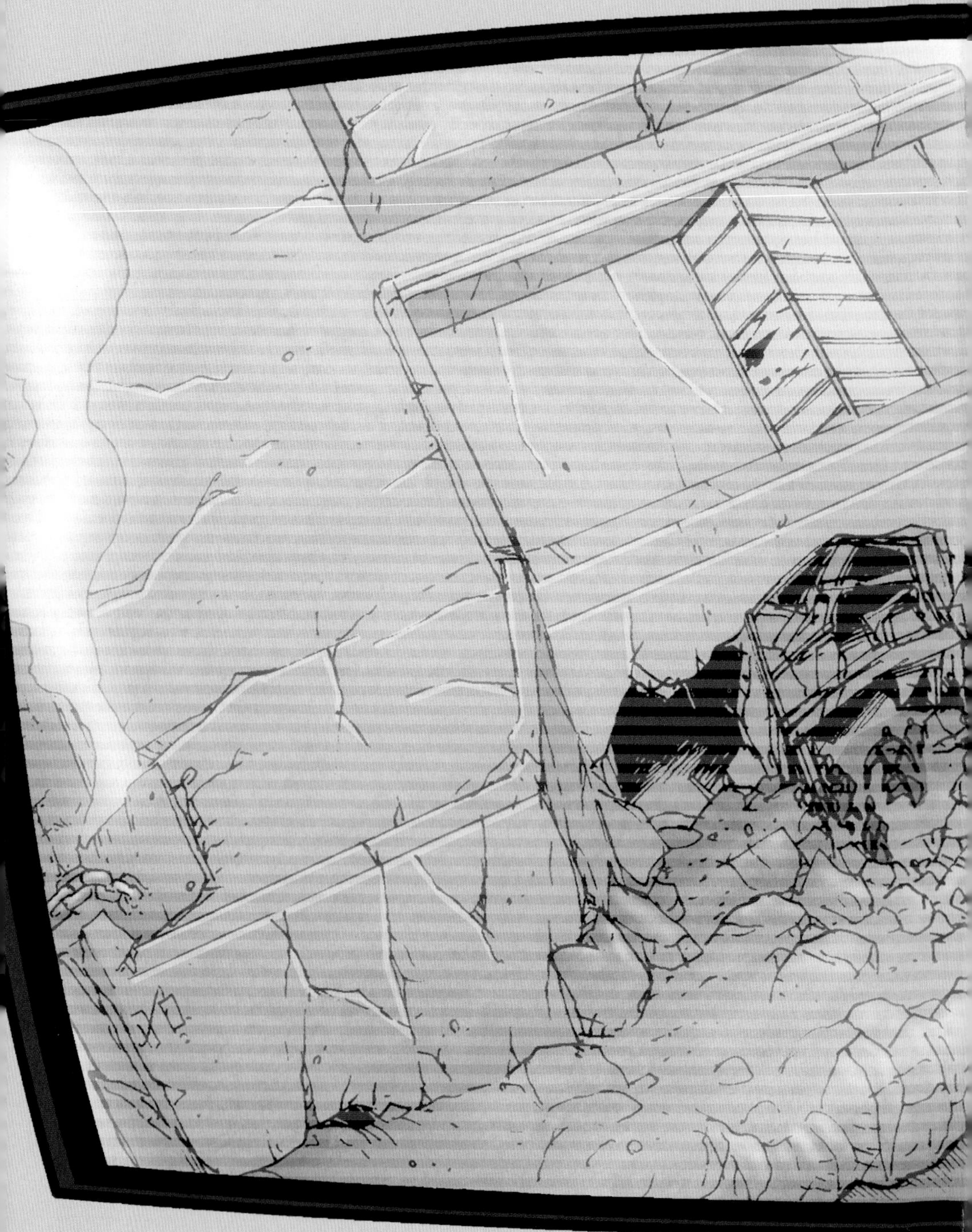

Disney · PIXAR

THE INCREDIBLES

CITY OF INCREDIBLES

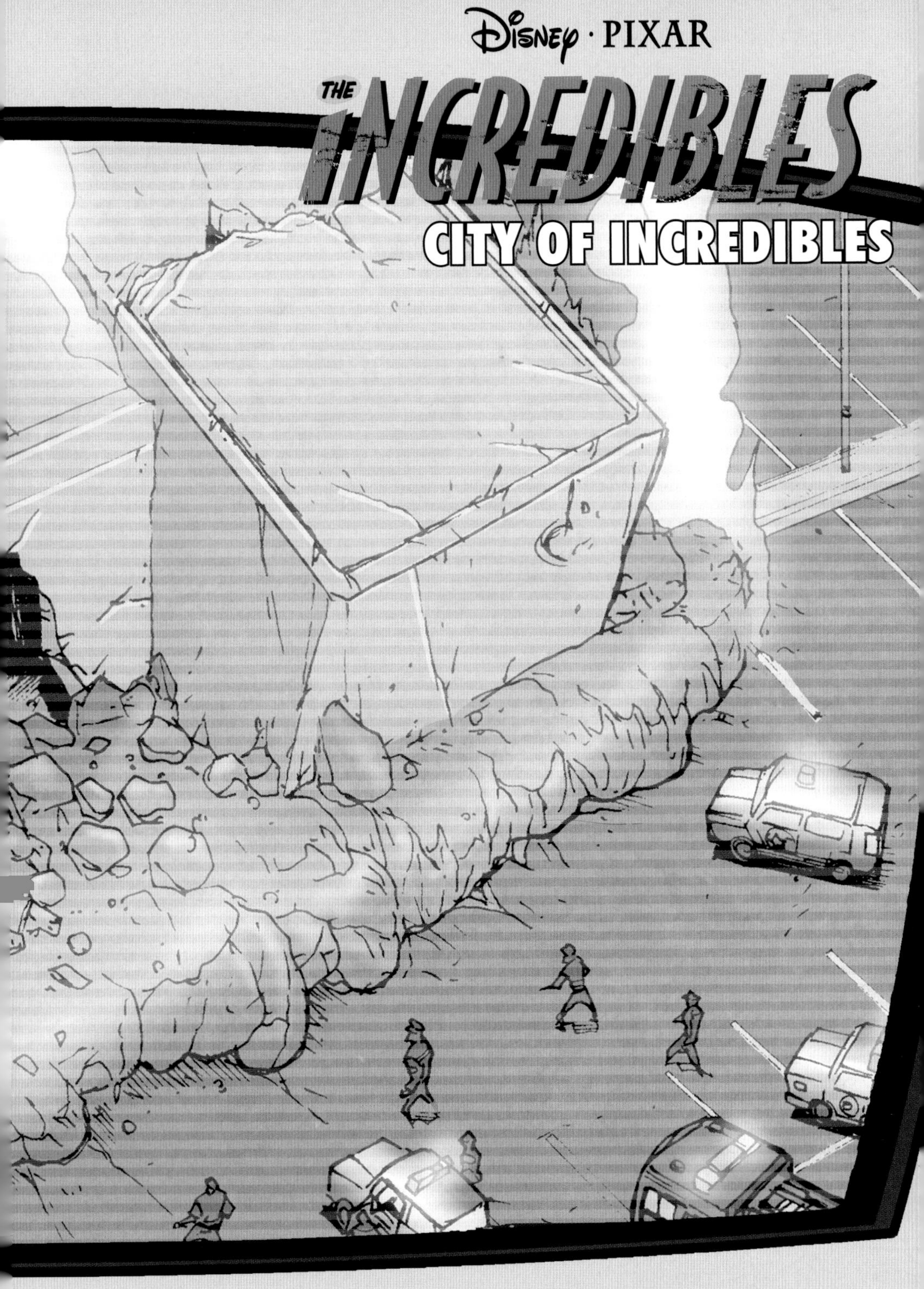

Disney · PIXAR

THE INCREDIBLES

CITY OF INCREDIBLES

BOOM KIDS!

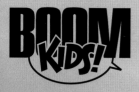

ROSS RICHIE
chief executive officer

MARK WAID
editor-in-chief

ADAM FORTIER
vice president, publishing

CHIP MOSHER
marketing director

MATT GAGNON
managing editor

JENNY CHRISTOPHER
sales director

FIRST EDITION: DECEMBER 2009

10 9 8 7 6 5 4 3 2 1
PRINTED BY WORLD COLOR PRESS, INC., ST-ROMUALD, QC., CANADA.

Office of publication: 6310 San Vicente Blvd Ste 404, Los Angeles, CA 90048.

A catalog record for this book is available from the Library of Congress and on our website at www.boom-kids.com on the Librarian Resource Page.

WRITERS:

MARK WAID
PROLOGUE

MARK WAID AND LANDRY WALKER
CHAPTERS 1-3

ART BY:

MARCIO TAKARA AND RAMANDA KAMARGA
PROLOGUE & CHAPTER 2   *CHAPTERS 1 &3*

COLORS: ANDREW DALHOUSE
LETTERS: TROY PETERI

DESIGNER: ERIKA TERRIQUEZ
EDITOR: AARON SPARROW

COVER ARTIST: MARCIO TAKARA
COLORS BY: ANDREW DALHOUSE

PROLOGUE

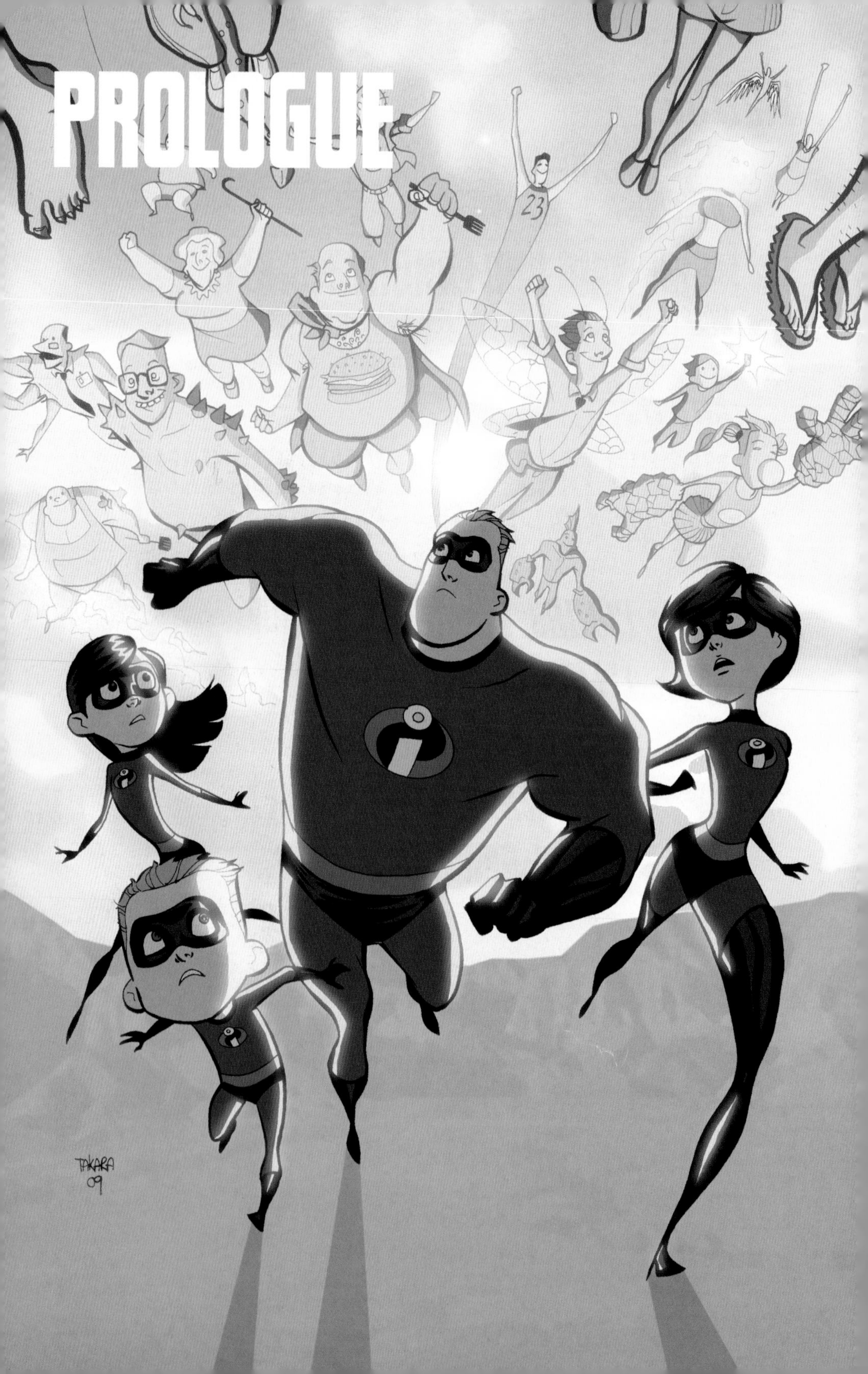
23
TAKARA 09

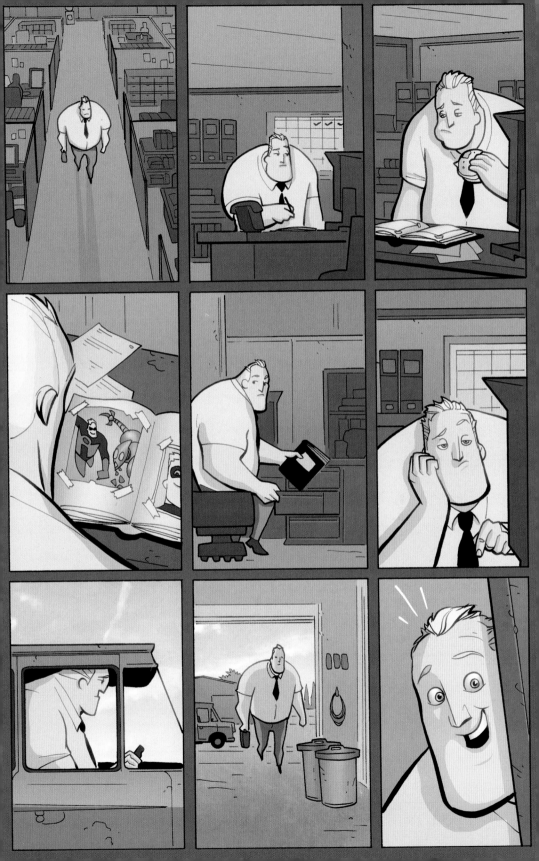

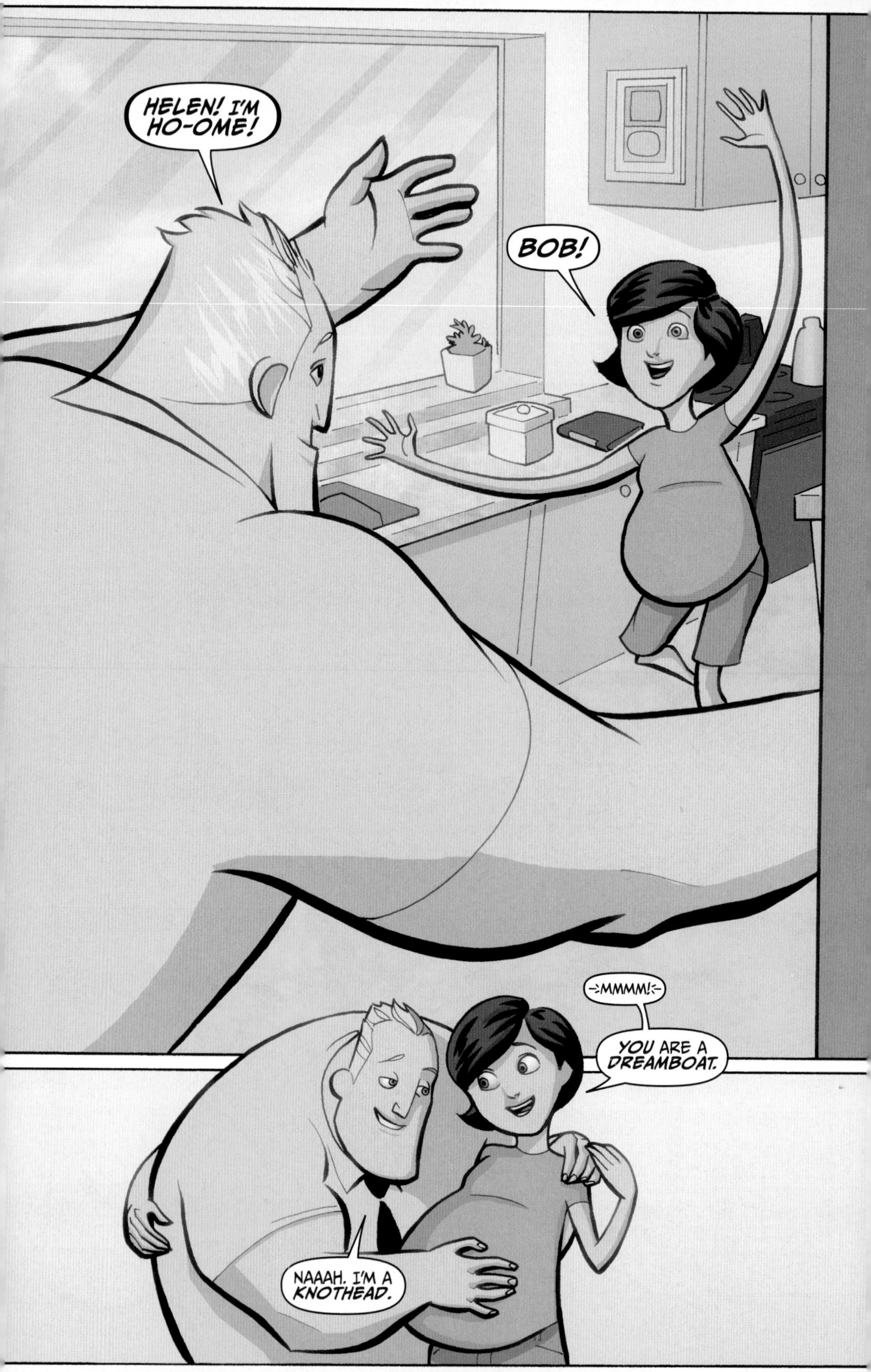
HELEN! I'M HO-OME!
BOB!
MMMM!
YOU ARE A DREAMBOAT.
NAAAH. I'M A KNOTHEAD.

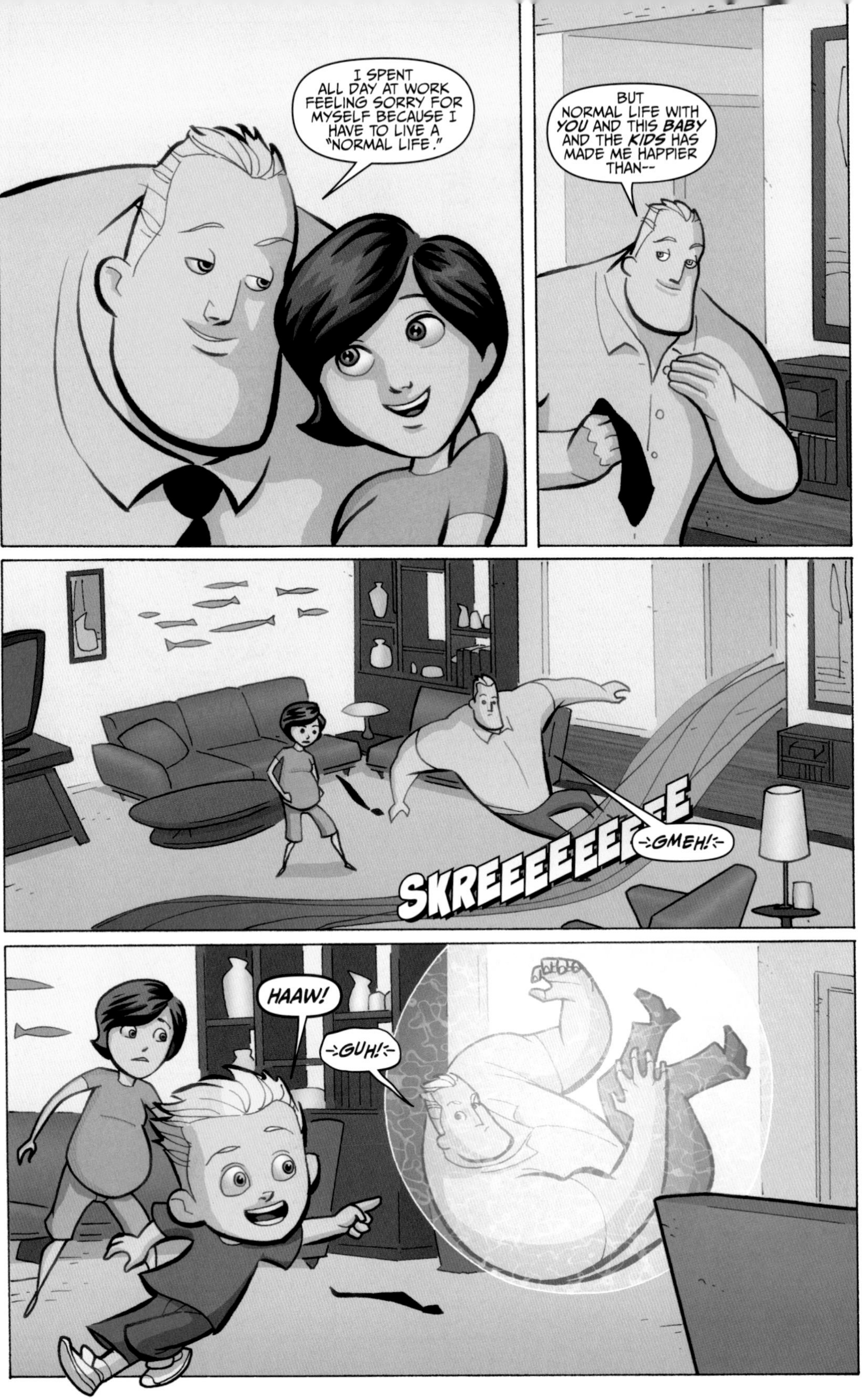
I SPENT ALL DAY AT WORK FEELING SORRY FOR MYSELF BECAUSE I HAVE TO LIVE A "NORMAL LIFE."
BUT NORMAL LIFE WITH *YOU* AND THIS *BABY* AND THE *KIDS* HAS MADE ME HAPPIER THAN--
SKREEEEEEEEEE
-GMEH!-
HAAW!
-GUH!-

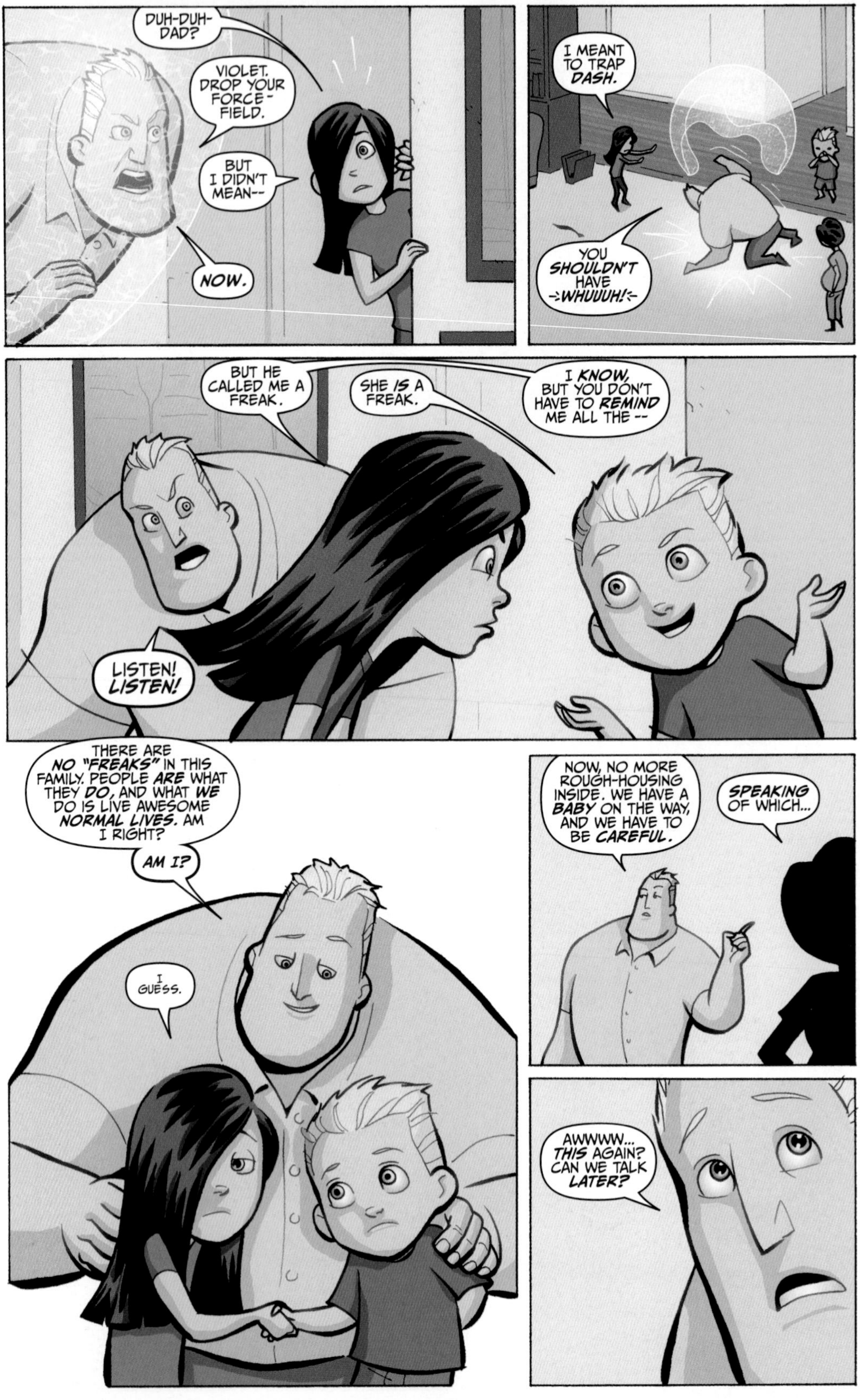

DUH-DUH-DAD?
VIOLET. DROP YOUR FORCE-FIELD.
BUT I DIDN'T MEAN--
NOW.
I MEANT TO TRAP DASH.
YOU SHOULDN'T HAVE -WHUUUH!-
BUT HE CALLED ME A FREAK.
SHE IS A FREAK.
I KNOW, BUT YOU DON'T HAVE TO REMIND ME ALL THE --
LISTEN! LISTEN!
THERE ARE NO "FREAKS" IN THIS FAMILY. PEOPLE ARE WHAT THEY DO, AND WHAT WE DO IS LIVE AWESOME NORMAL LIVES. AM I RIGHT?
AM I?
I GUESS.
NOW, NO MORE ROUGH-HOUSING INSIDE. WE HAVE A BABY ON THE WAY, AND WE HAVE TO BE CAREFUL.
SPEAKING OF WHICH...
AWWWW... THIS AGAIN? CAN WE TALK LATER?

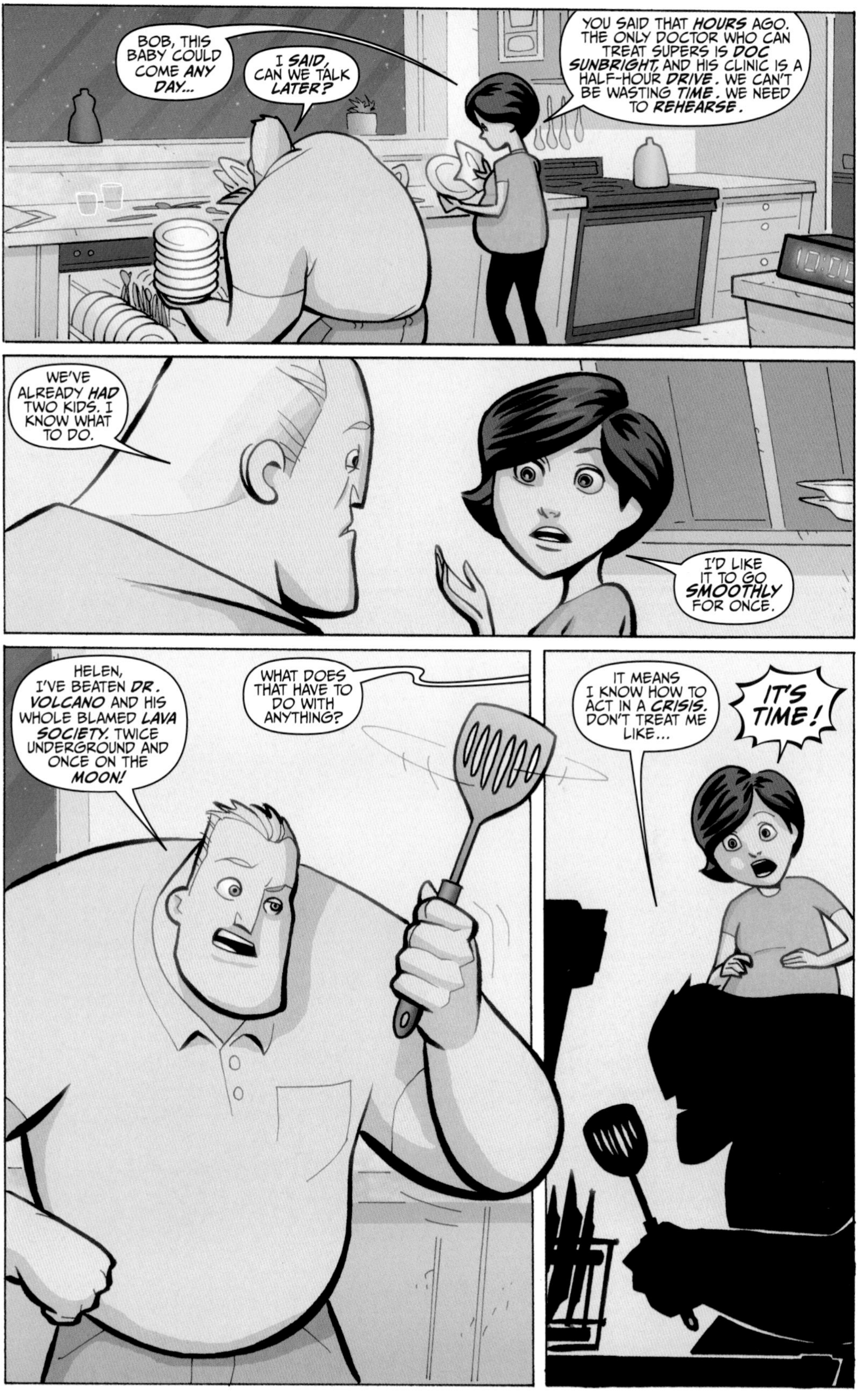
BOB, THIS BABY COULD COME ANY DAY...
I SAID, CAN WE TALK LATER?
YOU SAID THAT HOURS AGO. THE ONLY DOCTOR WHO CAN TREAT SUPERS IS DOC SUNBRIGHT, AND HIS CLINIC IS A HALF-HOUR DRIVE. WE CAN'T BE WASTING TIME. WE NEED TO REHEARSE.
WE'VE ALREADY HAD TWO KIDS. I KNOW WHAT TO DO.
I'D LIKE IT TO GO SMOOTHLY FOR ONCE.
HELEN, I'VE BEATEN DR. VOLCANO AND HIS WHOLE BLAMED LAVA SOCIETY. TWICE UNDERGROUND AND ONCE ON THE MOON!
WHAT DOES THAT HAVE TO DO WITH ANYTHING?
IT MEANS I KNOW HOW TO ACT IN A CRISIS. DON'T TREAT ME LIKE...
IT'S TIME!

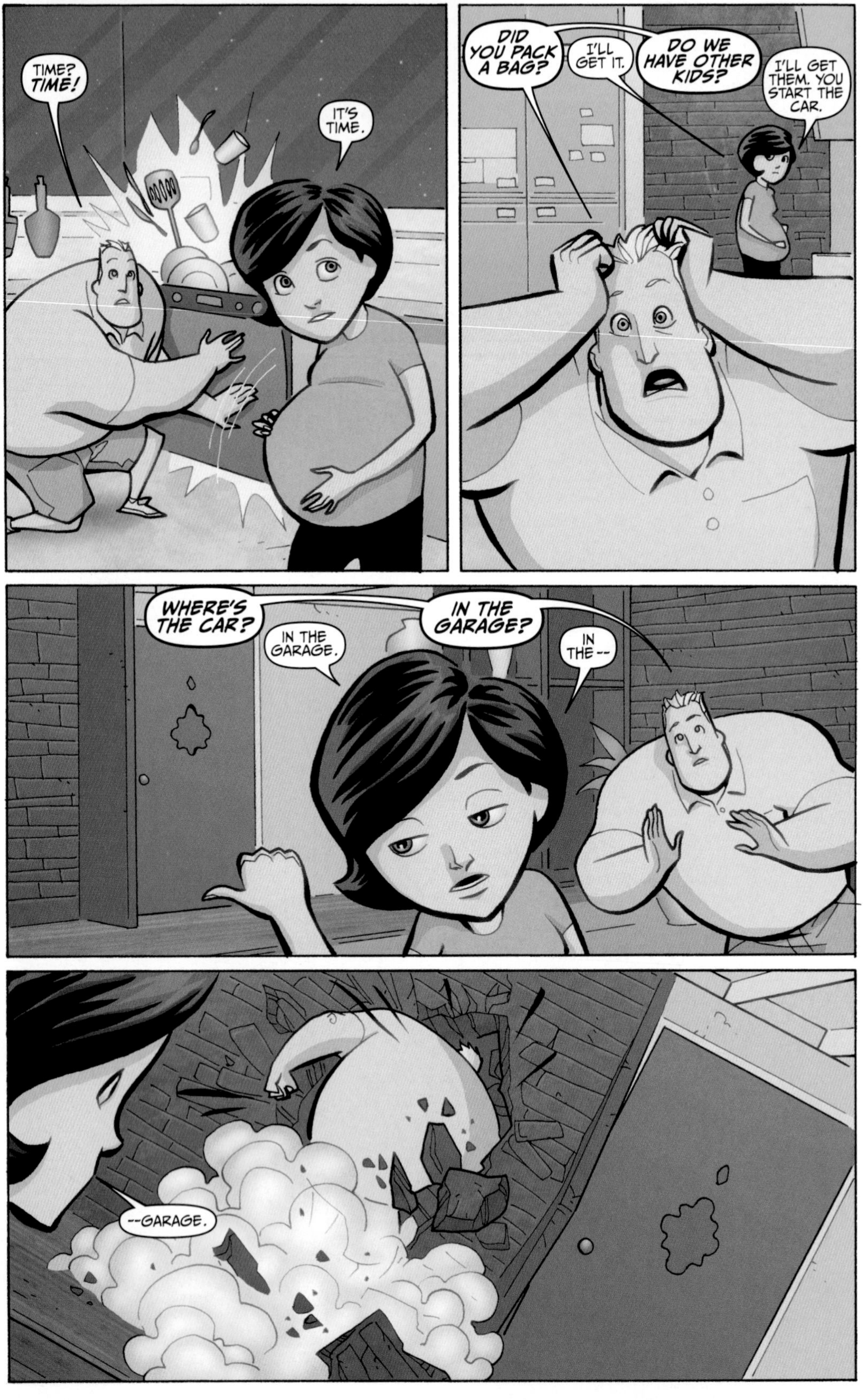
TIME? TIME!
IT'S TIME.
DID YOU PACK A BAG?
I'LL GET IT.
DO WE HAVE OTHER KIDS?
I'LL GET THEM. YOU START THE CAR.
WHERE'S THE CAR?
IN THE GARAGE.
IN THE GARAGE?
IN THE--
--GARAGE.

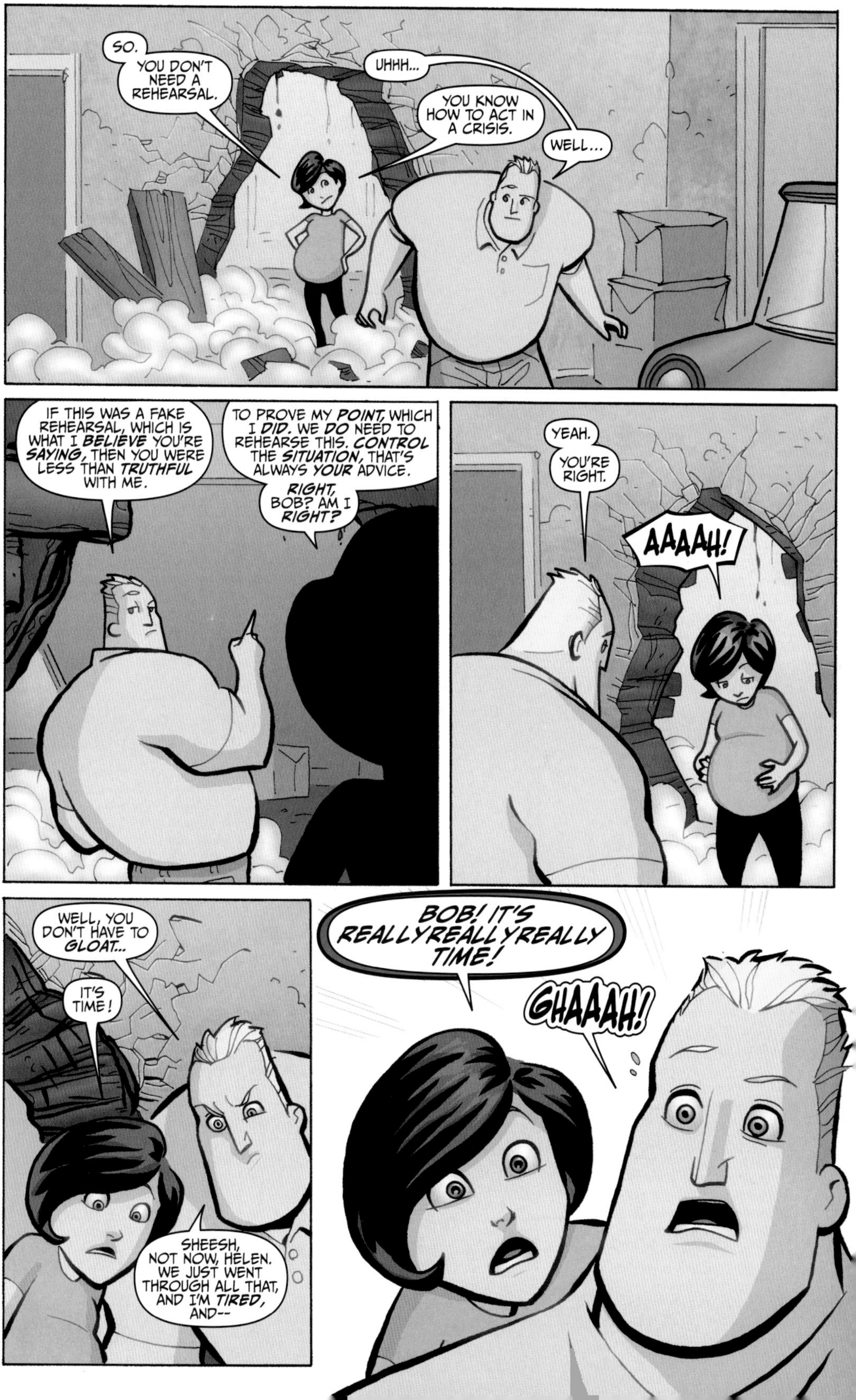
SO.
YOU DON'T NEED A REHEARSAL.
UHHH...
YOU KNOW HOW TO ACT IN A CRISIS.
WELL...
IF THIS WAS A FAKE REHEARSAL, WHICH IS WHAT I BELIEVE YOU'RE SAYING, THEN YOU WERE LESS THAN TRUTHFUL WITH ME.
TO PROVE MY POINT, WHICH I DID. WE DO NEED TO REHEARSE THIS. CONTROL THE SITUATION, THAT'S ALWAYS YOUR ADVICE.
RIGHT, BOB? AM I RIGHT?
YEAH.
YOU'RE RIGHT.
AAAAH!
WELL, YOU DON'T HAVE TO GLOAT...
IT'S TIME!
SHEESH, NOT NOW, HELEN. WE JUST WENT THROUGH ALL THAT, AND I'M TIRED, AND--
BOB! IT'S REALLYREALLYREALLY TIME!
GHAAAH!

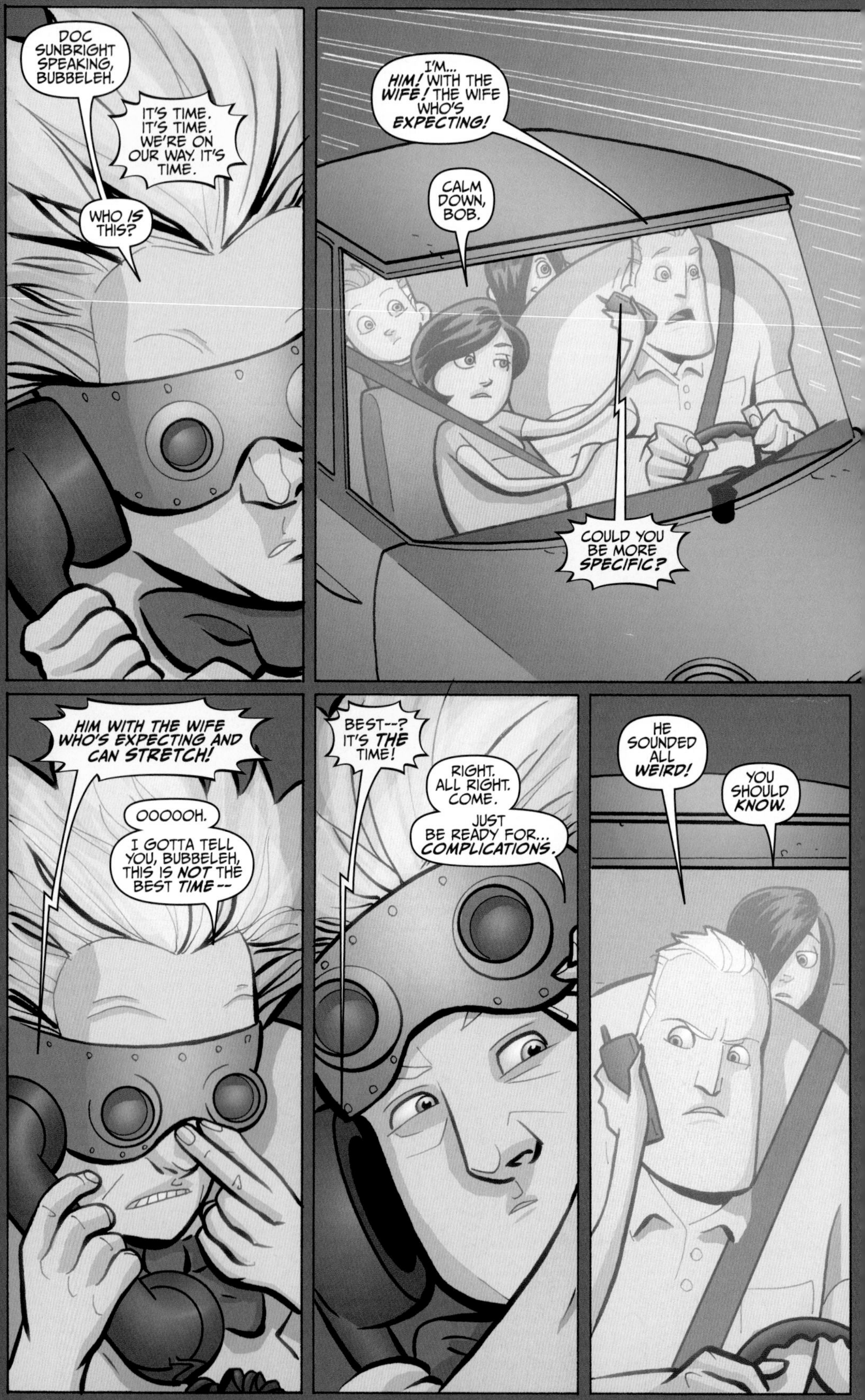
DOC SUNBRIGHT SPEAKING, BUBBELEH.
IT'S TIME. IT'S TIME. WE'RE ON OUR WAY. IT'S TIME.
WHO *IS* THIS?
I'M... *HIM!* WITH THE *WIFE!* THE WIFE WHO'S *EXPECTING!*
CALM DOWN, BOB.
COULD YOU BE MORE *SPECIFIC?*
HIM WITH THE WIFE WHO'S EXPECTING AND CAN STRETCH!
OOOOOH.
I GOTTA TELL YOU, BUBBELEH, THIS IS *NOT* THE BEST *TIME* --
BEST--? IT'S *THE* TIME!
RIGHT. ALL RIGHT. COME.
JUST BE READY FOR... *COMPLICATIONS*.
HE SOUNDED ALL *WEIRD!*
YOU SHOULD *KNOW.*

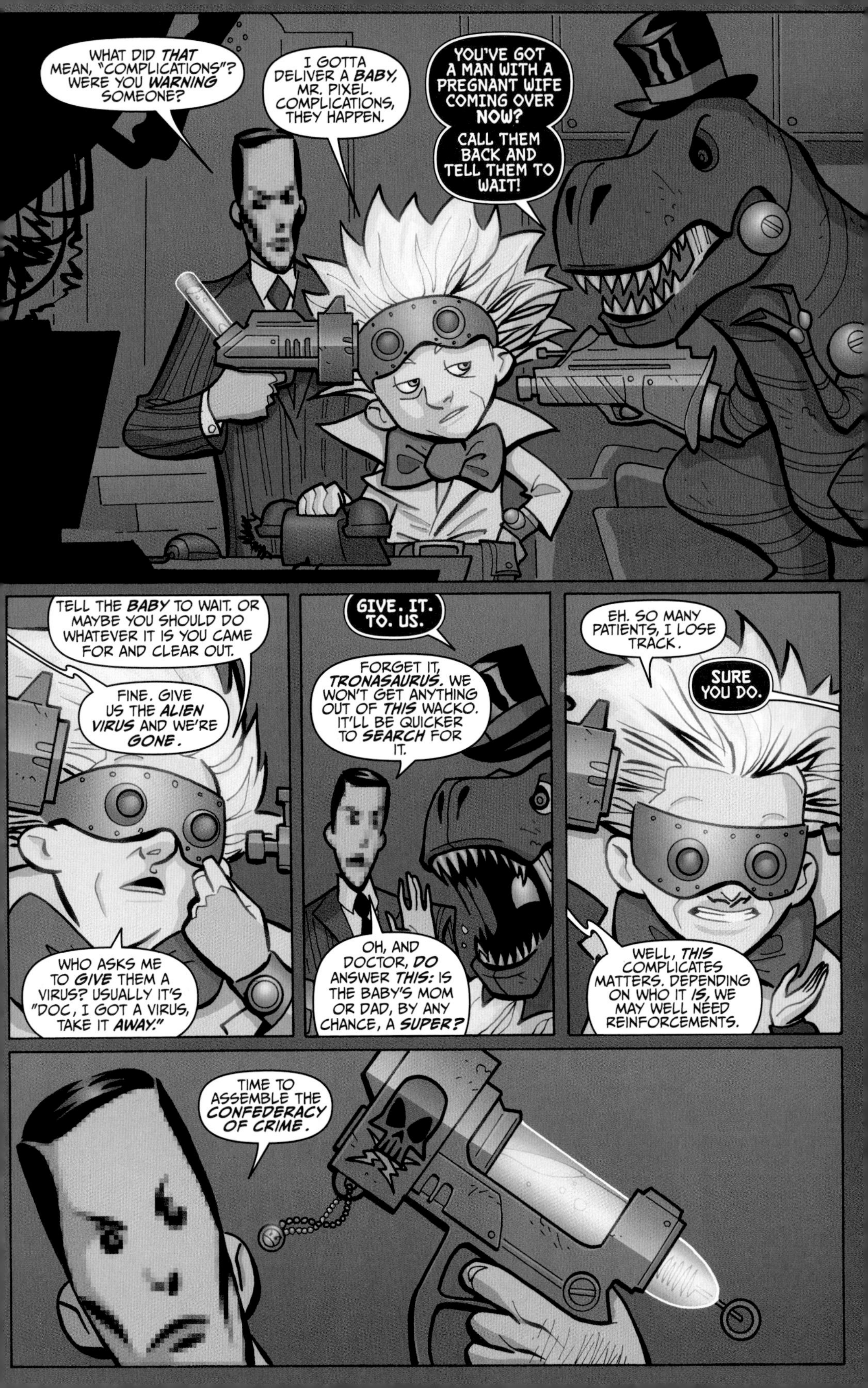
WHAT DID *THAT* MEAN, "COMPLICATIONS"? WERE YOU *WARNING* SOMEONE?
I GOTTA DELIVER A *BABY,* MR. PIXEL. COMPLICATIONS, THEY HAPPEN.
YOU'VE GOT A MAN WITH A PREGNANT WIFE COMING OVER **NOW?**
CALL THEM BACK AND TELL THEM TO WAIT!
TELL THE *BABY* TO WAIT. OR MAYBE YOU SHOULD DO WHATEVER IT IS YOU CAME FOR AND CLEAR OUT.
FINE. GIVE US THE *ALIEN VIRUS* AND WE'RE *GONE*.
WHO ASKS ME TO *GIVE* THEM A VIRUS? USUALLY IT'S "DOC, I GOT A VIRUS, TAKE IT *AWAY.*"
GIVE. IT. TO. US.
FORGET IT, *TRONASAURUS*. WE WON'T GET ANYTHING OUT OF *THIS* WACKO. IT'LL BE QUICKER TO *SEARCH* FOR IT.
OH, AND DOCTOR, *DO* ANSWER *THIS:* IS THE BABY'S MOM OR DAD, BY ANY CHANCE, A *SUPER?*
EH. SO MANY PATIENTS, I LOSE TRACK.
SURE YOU DO.
WELL, *THIS* COMPLICATES MATTERS. DEPENDING ON WHO IT *IS,* WE MAY WELL NEED REINFORCEMENTS.
TIME TO ASSEMBLE THE *CONFEDERACY OF CRIME*.

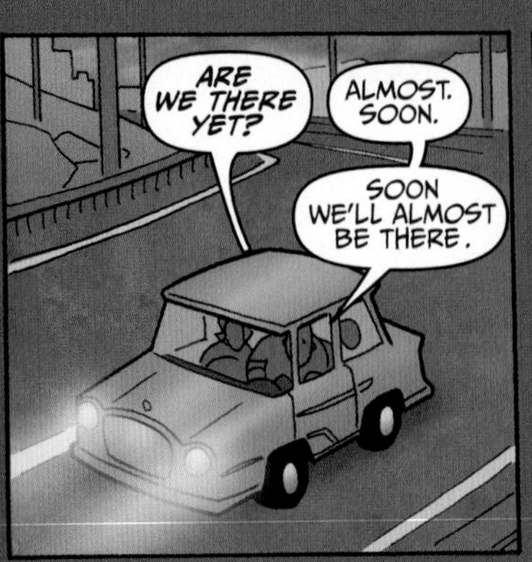
ARE WE THERE YET?
ALMOST. SOON.
SOON WE'LL ALMOST BE THERE.
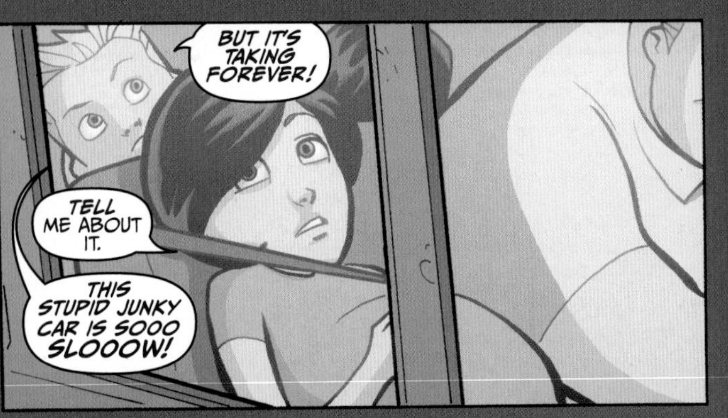
BUT IT'S TAKING FOREVER!
TELL ME ABOUT IT.
THIS STUPID JUNKY CAR IS SOOO SLOOOW!
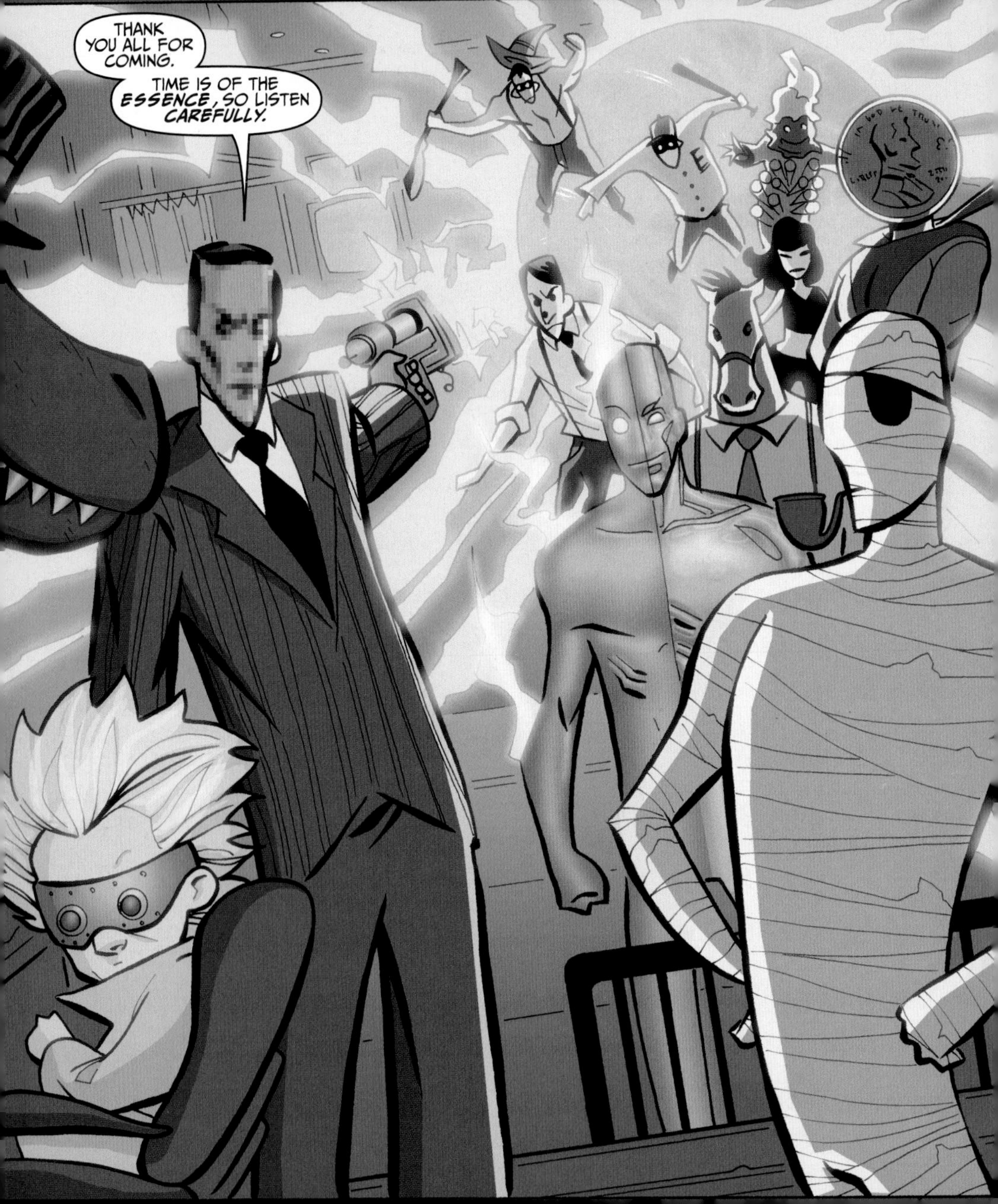
THANK YOU ALL FOR COMING.
TIME IS OF THE ESSENCE, SO LISTEN CAREFULLY.

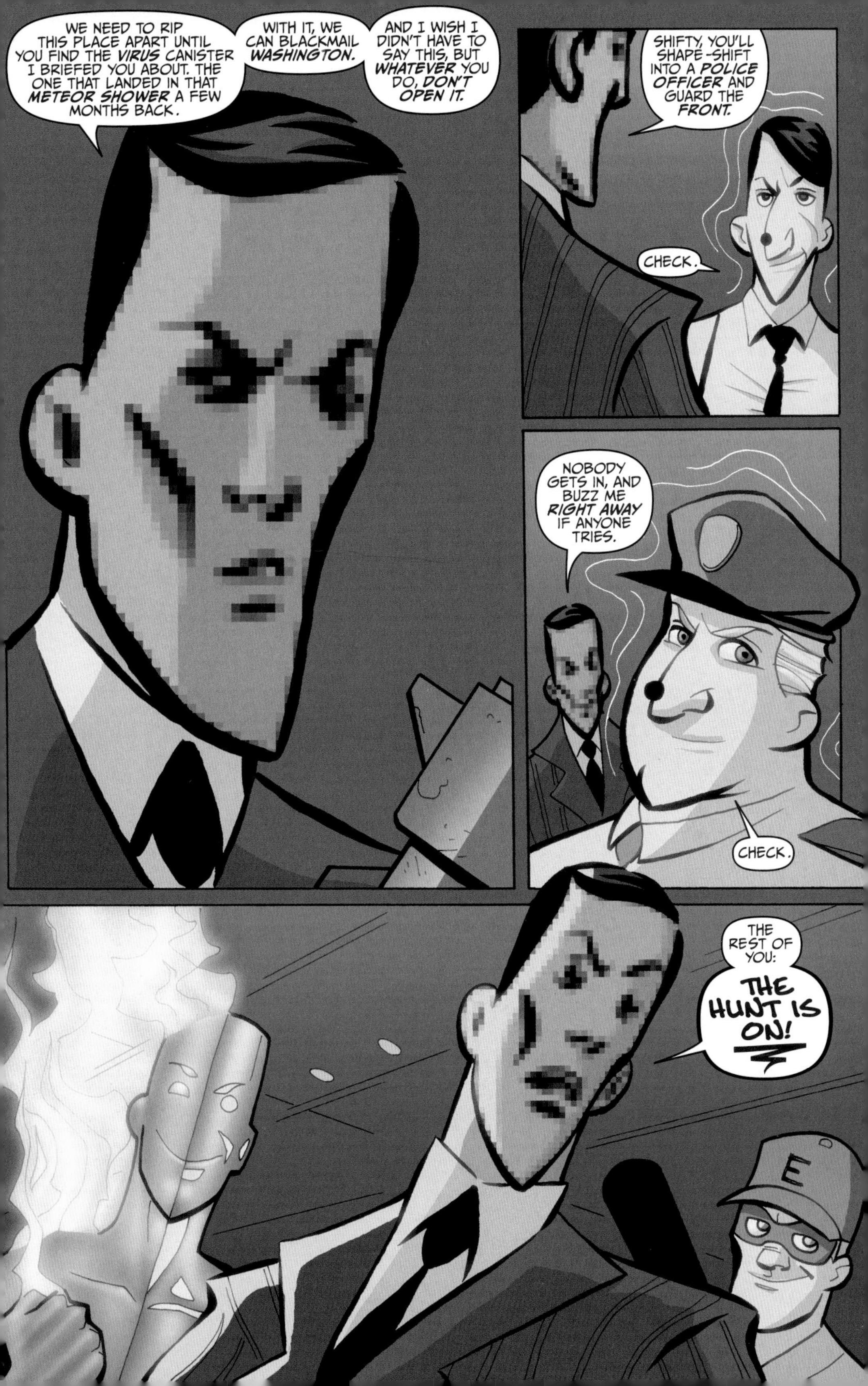
WE NEED TO RIP THIS PLACE APART UNTIL YOU FIND THE VIRUS CANISTER I BRIEFED YOU ABOUT. THE ONE THAT LANDED IN THAT METEOR SHOWER A FEW MONTHS BACK.
WITH IT, WE CAN BLACKMAIL WASHINGTON.
AND I WISH I DIDN'T HAVE TO SAY THIS, BUT WHATEVER YOU DO, DON'T OPEN IT.
SHIFTY, YOU'LL SHAPE-SHIFT INTO A POLICE OFFICER AND GUARD THE FRONT.
CHECK.
NOBODY GETS IN, AND BUZZ ME RIGHT AWAY IF ANYONE TRIES.
CHECK.
THE REST OF YOU:
THE HUNT IS ON!
E

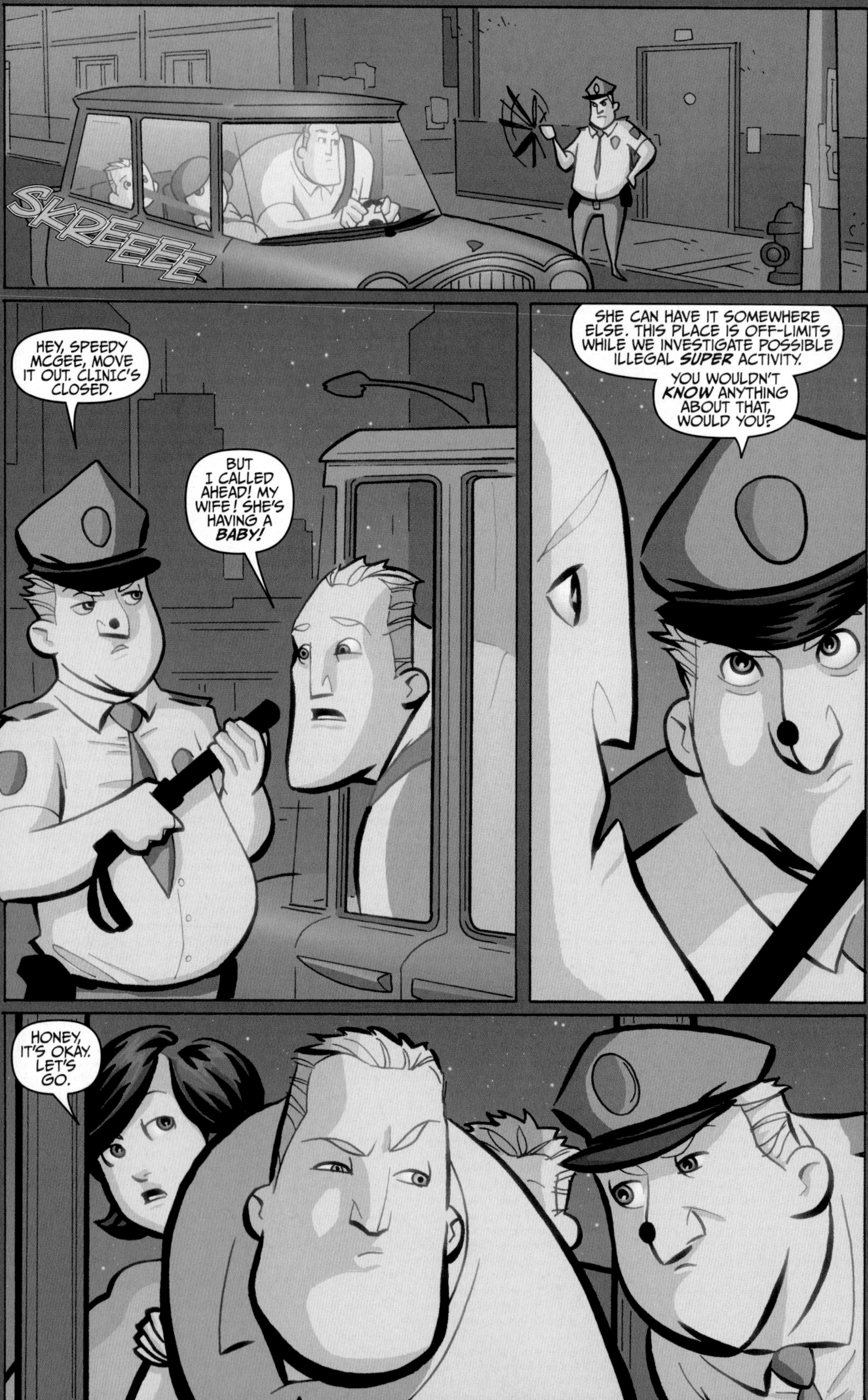
SKREEEEE
HEY, SPEEDY MCGEE, MOVE IT OUT. CLINIC'S CLOSED.
BUT I CALLED AHEAD! MY WIFE! SHE'S HAVING A BABY!
SHE CAN HAVE IT SOMEWHERE ELSE. THIS PLACE IS OFF-LIMITS WHILE WE INVESTIGATE POSSIBLE ILLEGAL SUPER ACTIVITY.
YOU WOULDN'T KNOW ANYTHING ABOUT THAT, WOULD YOU?
HONEY, IT'S OKAY. LET'S GO.

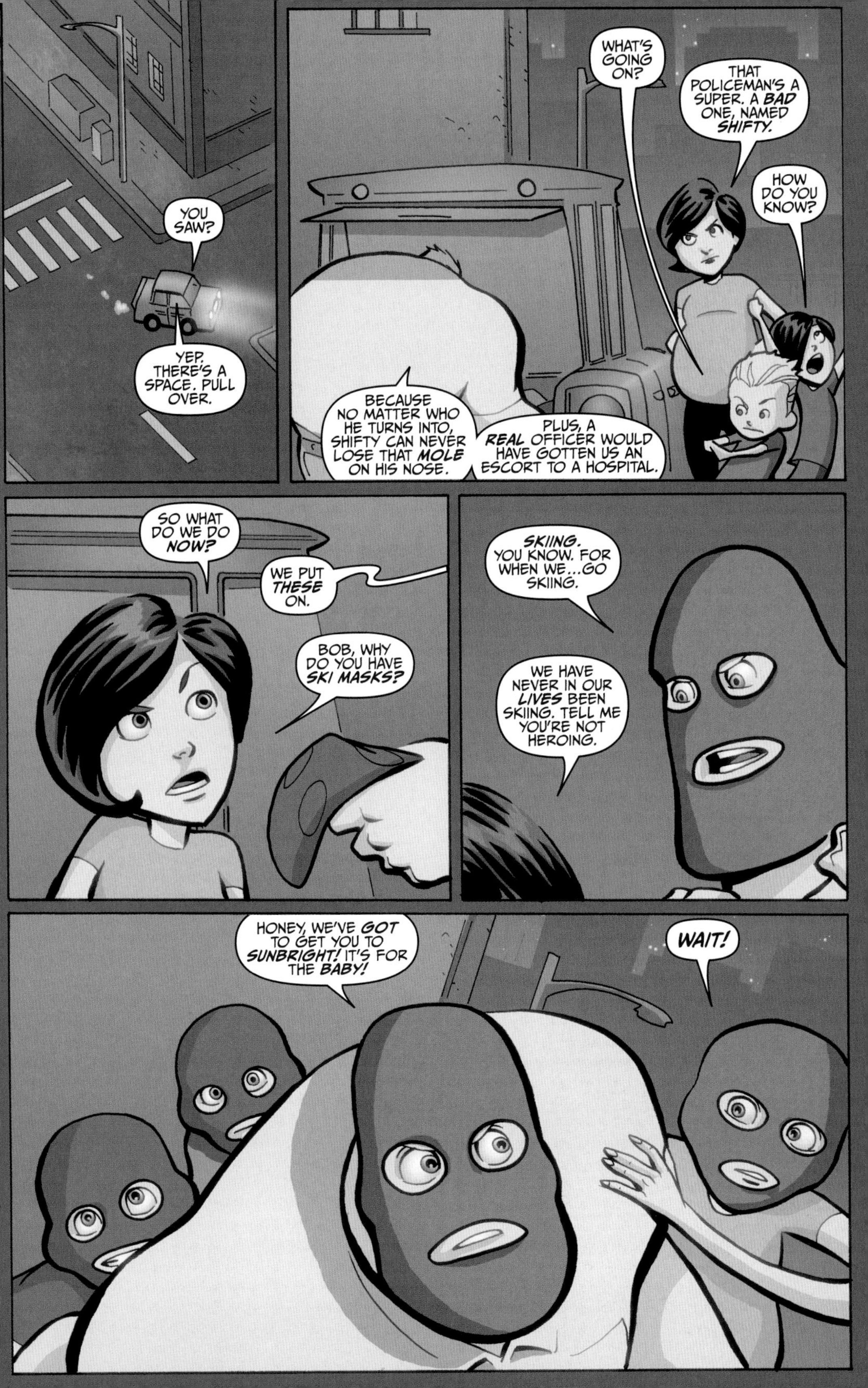
YOU SAW?
YEP. THERE'S A SPACE. PULL OVER.
WHAT'S GOING ON?
THAT POLICEMAN'S A SUPER. A BAD ONE, NAMED SHIFTY.
HOW DO YOU KNOW?
BECAUSE NO MATTER WHO HE TURNS INTO, SHIFTY CAN NEVER LOSE THAT MOLE ON HIS NOSE.
PLUS, A REAL OFFICER WOULD HAVE GOTTEN US AN ESCORT TO A HOSPITAL.
SO WHAT DO WE DO NOW?
WE PUT THESE ON.
BOB, WHY DO YOU HAVE SKI MASKS?
SKIING. YOU KNOW. FOR WHEN WE...GO SKIING.
WE HAVE NEVER IN OUR LIVES BEEN SKIING. TELL ME YOU'RE NOT HEROING.
HONEY, WE'VE GOT TO GET YOU TO SUNBRIGHT! IT'S FOR THE BABY!
WAIT!

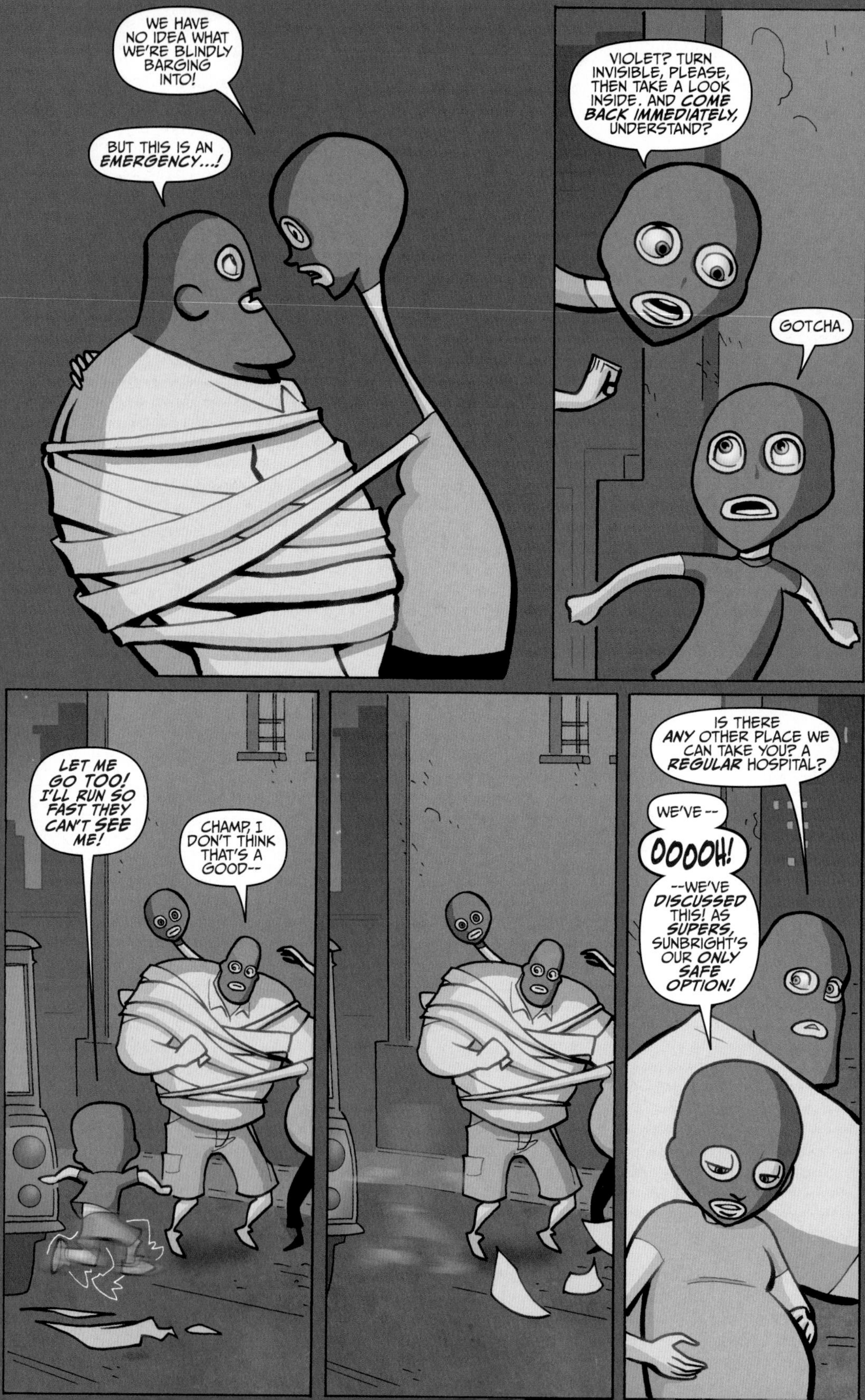

WE HAVE NO IDEA WHAT WE'RE BLINDLY BARGING INTO!
BUT THIS IS AN *EMERGENCY...!*
VIOLET? TURN INVISIBLE, PLEASE, THEN TAKE A LOOK INSIDE. AND *COME BACK IMMEDIATELY,* UNDERSTAND?
GOTCHA.
LET ME GO TOO! I'LL RUN SO FAST THEY CAN'T SEE ME!
CHAMP, I DON'T THINK THAT'S A GOOD--
IS THERE *ANY* OTHER PLACE WE CAN TAKE YOU? A *REGULAR* HOSPITAL?
WE'VE --
OOOOH!
--WE'VE *DISCUSSED* THIS! AS *SUPERS,* SUNBRIGHT'S OUR *ONLY SAFE OPTION!*

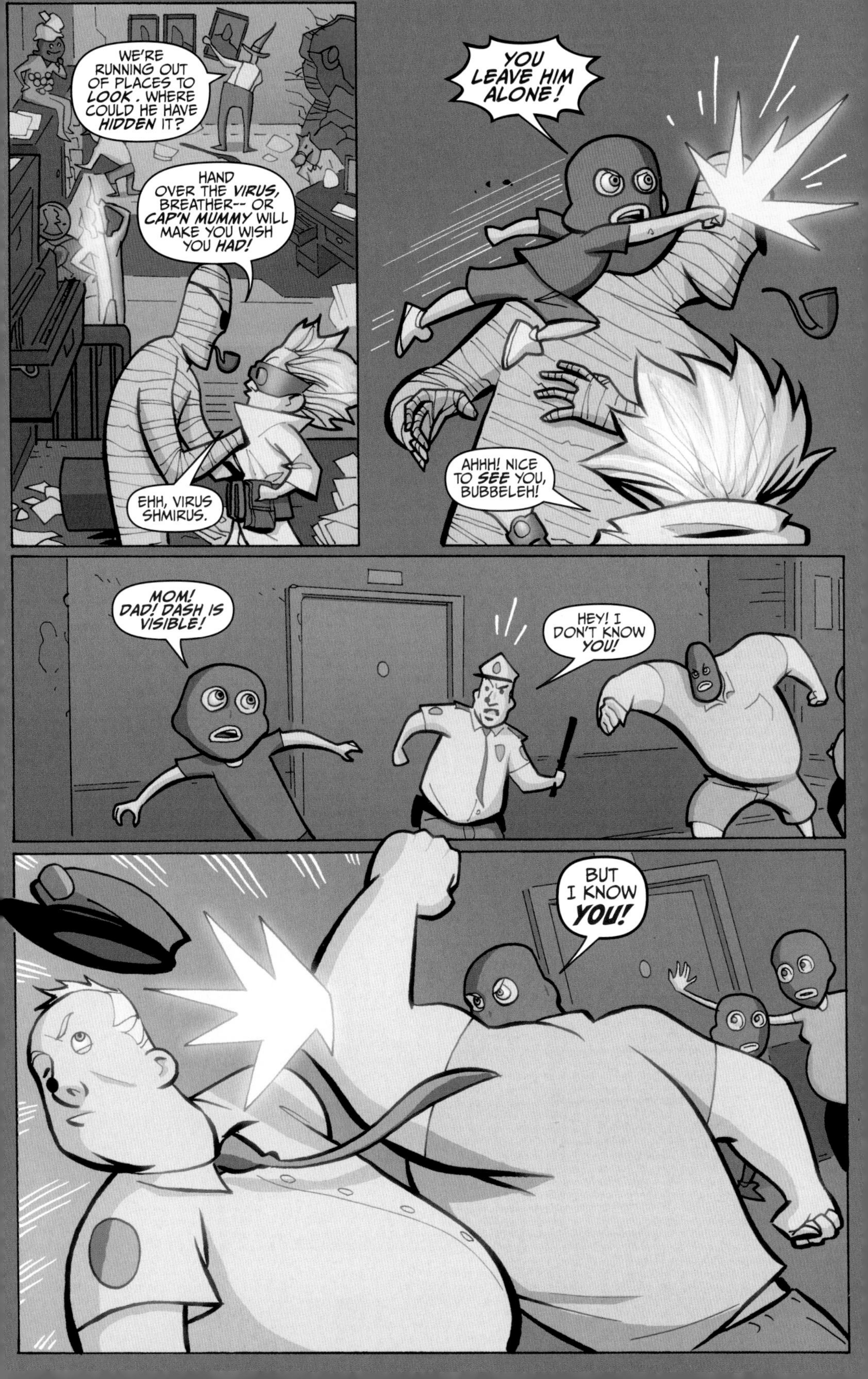
WE'RE RUNNING OUT OF PLACES TO LOOK. WHERE COULD HE HAVE HIDDEN IT?
HAND OVER THE VIRUS, BREATHER-- OR CAP'N MUMMY WILL MAKE YOU WISH YOU HAD!
EHH, VIRUS SHMIRUS.
YOU LEAVE HIM ALONE!
AHHH! NICE TO SEE YOU, BUBBELEH!
MOM! DAD! DASH IS VISIBLE!
HEY! I DON'T KNOW YOU!
BUT I KNOW YOU!

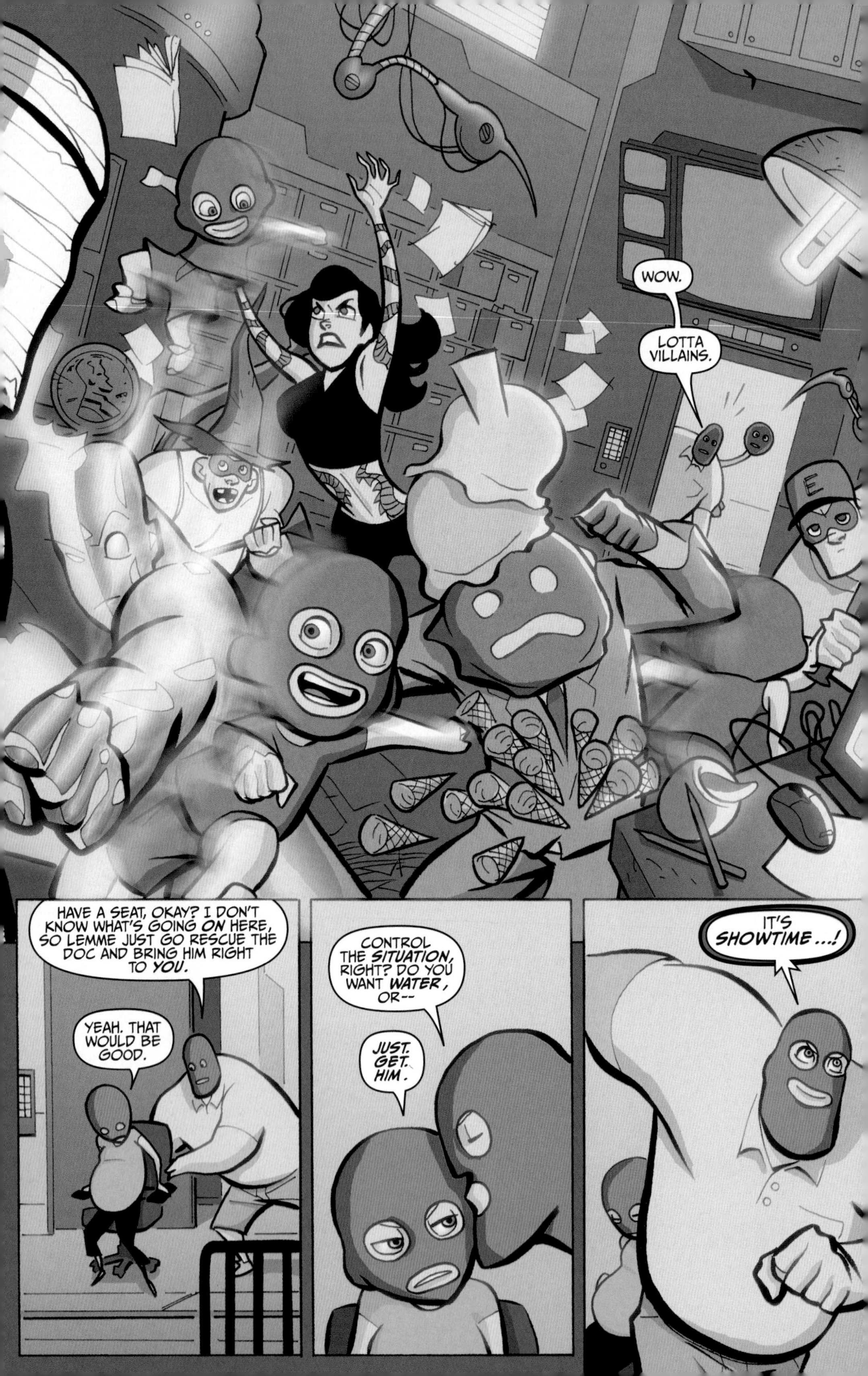
WOW.
LOTTA VILLAINS.
HAVE A SEAT, OKAY? I DON'T KNOW WHAT'S GOING ON HERE, SO LEMME JUST GO RESCUE THE DOC AND BRING HIM RIGHT TO YOU.
YEAH. THAT WOULD BE GOOD.
CONTROL THE SITUATION, RIGHT? DO YOU WANT WATER, OR--
JUST. GET. HIM.
IT'S SHOWTIME ...!

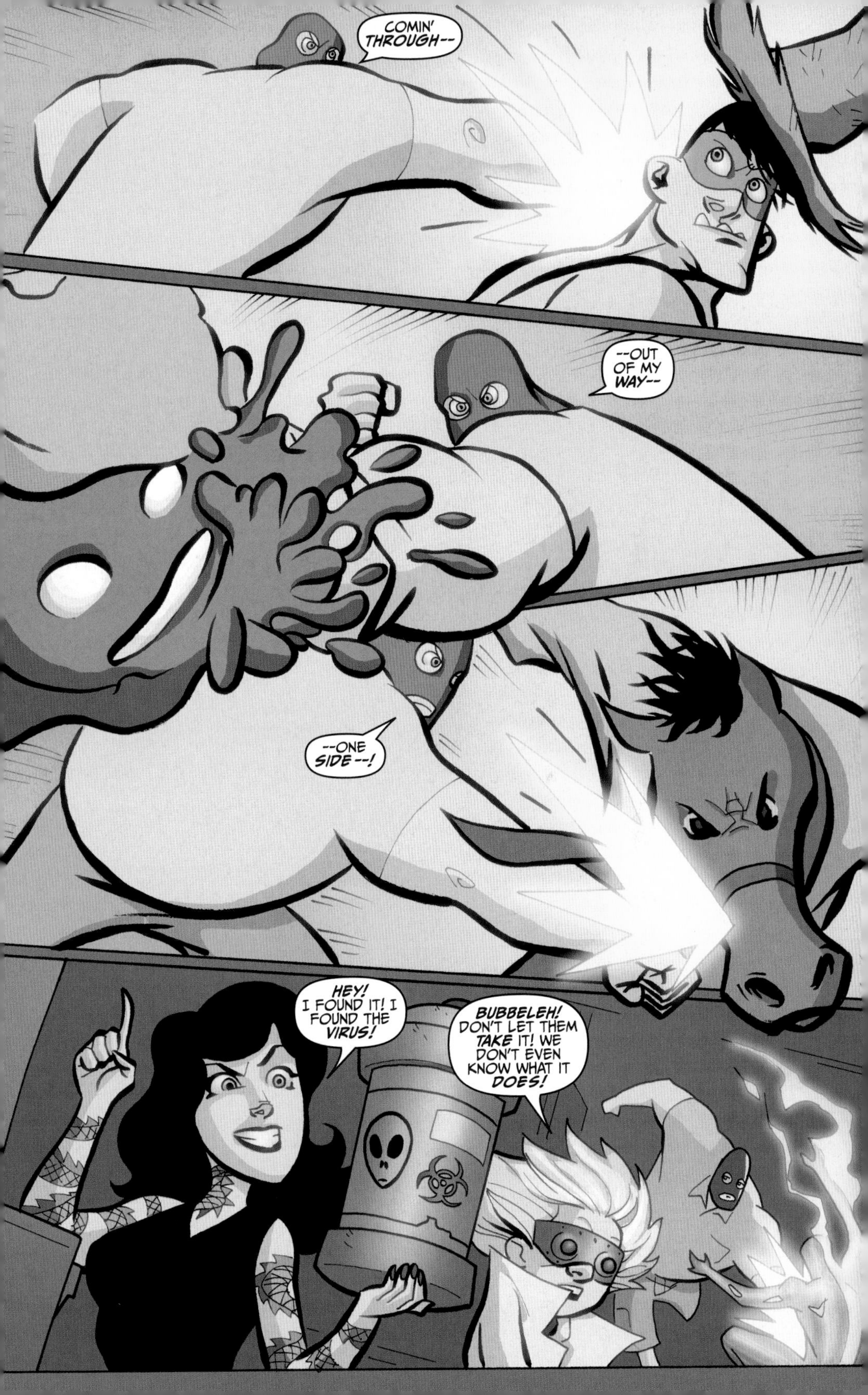
COMIN' THROUGH--
--OUT OF MY WAY--
--ONE SIDE--!
HEY! I FOUND IT! I FOUND THE VIRUS!
BUBBELEH! DON'T LET THEM TAKE IT! WE DON'T EVEN KNOW WHAT IT DOES!

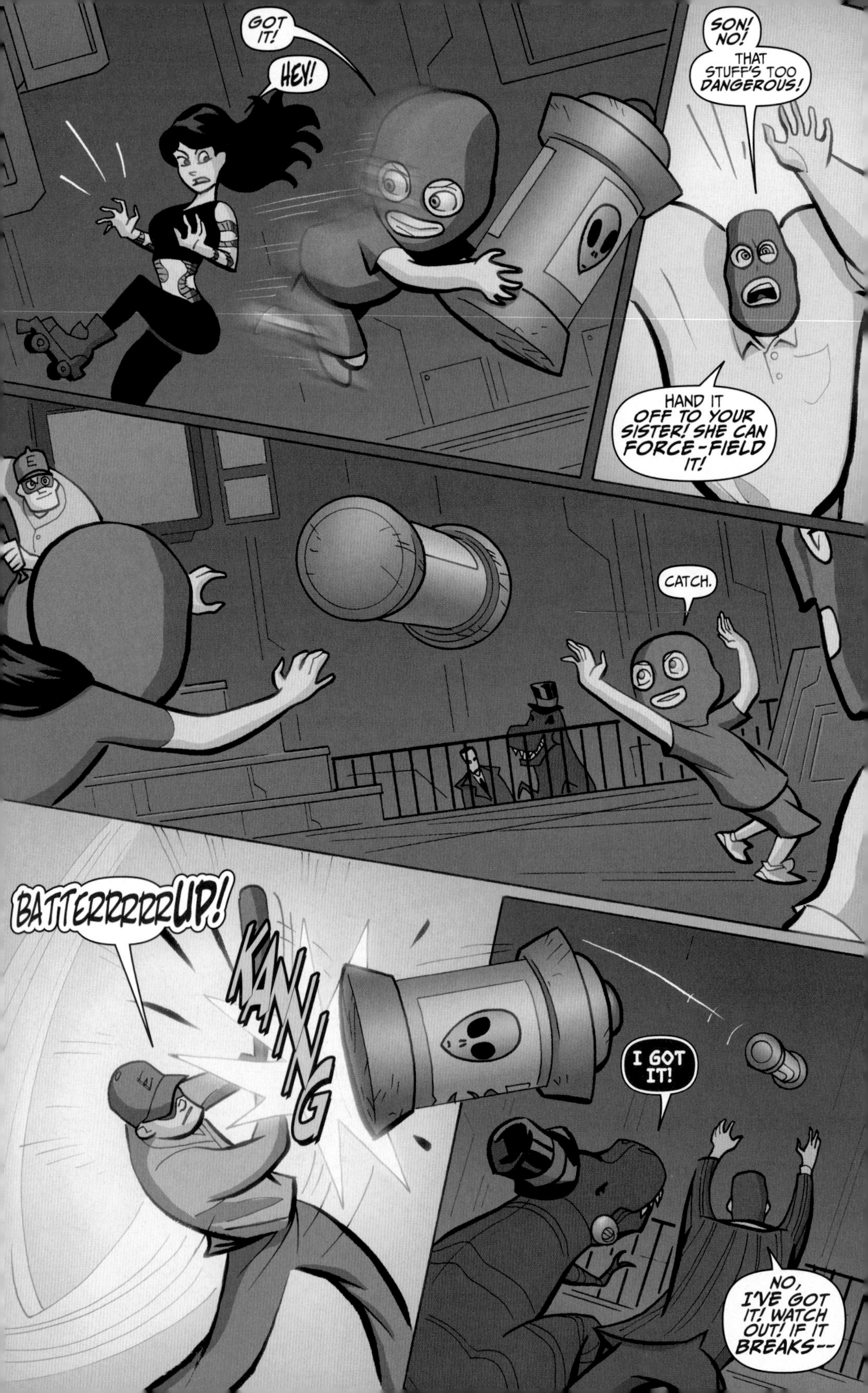
GOT IT!
HEY!
SON! NO! THAT STUFF'S TOO DANGEROUS!
HAND IT OFF TO YOUR SISTER! SHE CAN FORCE-FIELD IT!
CATCH.
BATTERRRRRUP!
KANNNG
I GOT IT!
NO, I'VE GOT IT! WATCH OUT! IF IT BREAKS--

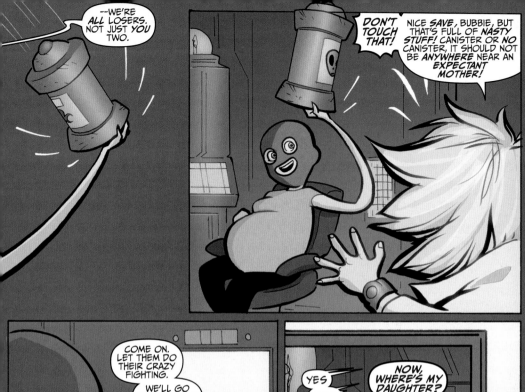

--WE'RE ALL LOSERS. NOT JUST *YOU* TWO.

DON'T TOUCH THAT!

NICE *SAVE*, BUBBIE, BUT THAT'S FULL OF *NASTY STUFF!* CANISTER OR *NO* CANISTER, IT SHOULD NOT BE *ANYWHERE* NEAR AN *EXPECTANT* MOTHER!

COME ON. LET THEM DO THEIR CRAZY FIGHTING.

WE'LL GO BRING A *LIFE* INTO THE WORLD.

SON! GET THE DOC AND YOUR MOM TO SAFETY *FAST!*

YES SIR!

NOW, WHERE'S MY *DAUGHTER?*

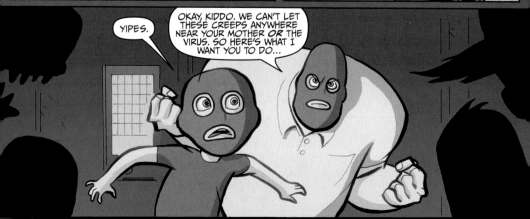

YIPES.

OKAY, KIDDO. WE CAN'T LET THESE CREEPS ANYWHERE NEAR YOUR MOTHER *OR* THE VIRUS. SO HERE'S WHAT I WANT YOU TO DO...

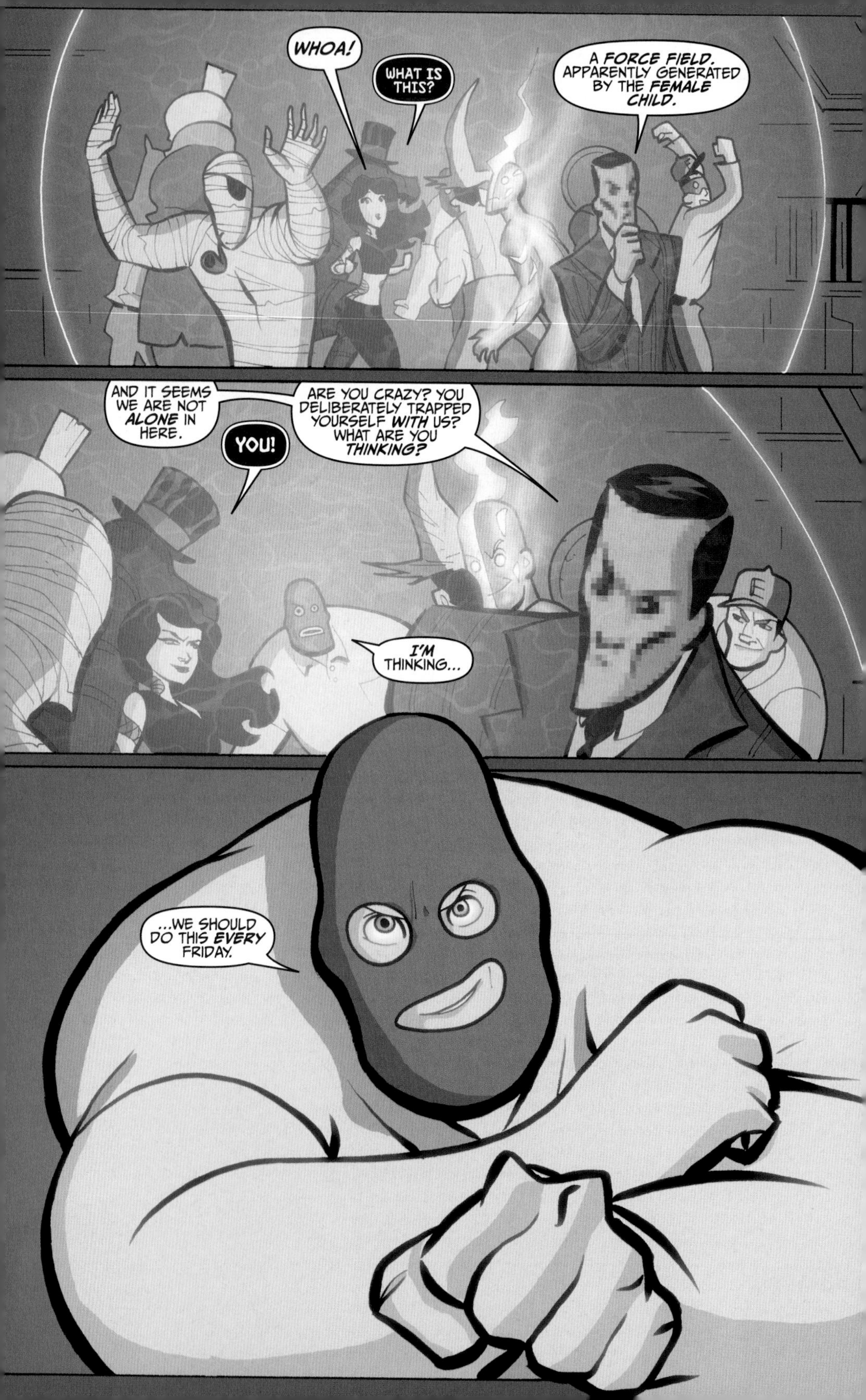
WHOA!
WHAT IS THIS?
A FORCE FIELD. APPARENTLY GENERATED BY THE FEMALE CHILD.
AND IT SEEMS WE ARE NOT ALONE IN HERE.
ARE YOU CRAZY? YOU DELIBERATELY TRAPPED YOURSELF WITH US? WHAT ARE YOU THINKING?
YOU!
I'M THINKING...
...WE SHOULD DO THIS EVERY FRIDAY.

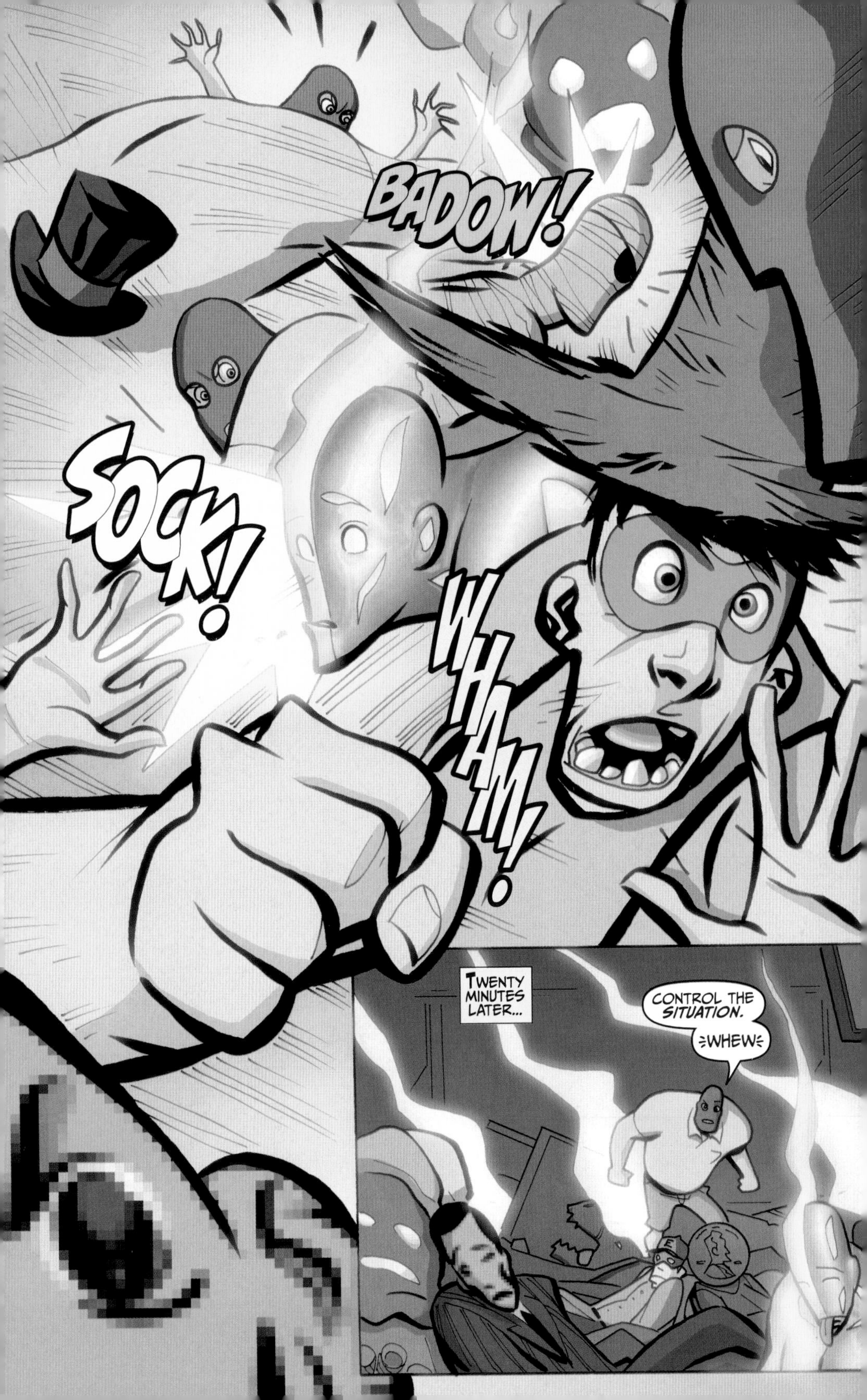
BADOW!
SOCK!
WHHAM!
TWENTY MINUTES LATER...
CONTROL THE SITUATION.
WHEW

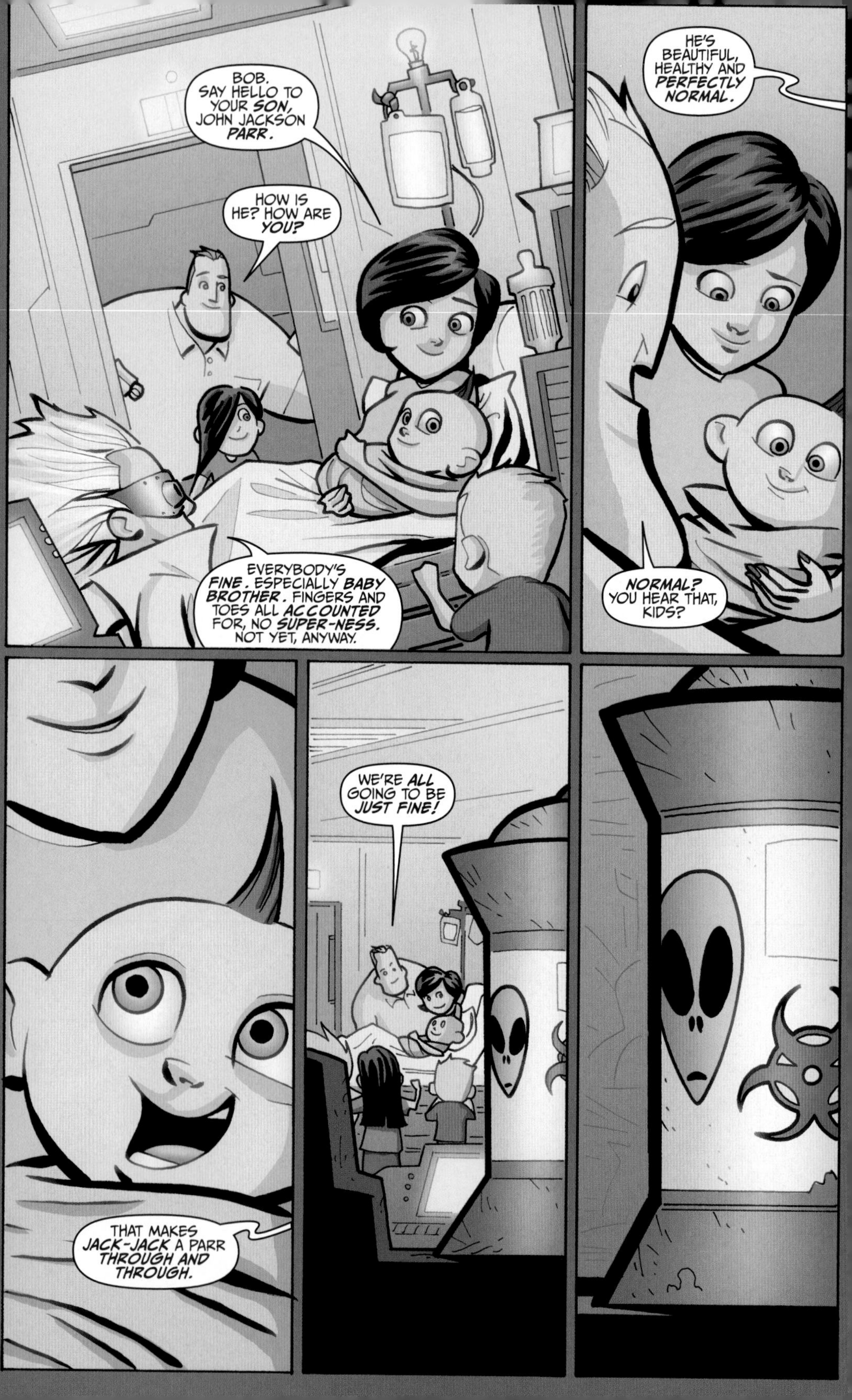
BOB. SAY HELLO TO YOUR SON, JOHN JACKSON PARR.
HOW IS HE? HOW ARE YOU?
EVERYBODY'S FINE. ESPECIALLY BABY BROTHER. FINGERS AND TOES ALL ACCOUNTED FOR, NO SUPER-NESS. NOT YET, ANYWAY.
HE'S BEAUTIFUL, HEALTHY AND PERFECTLY NORMAL.
NORMAL? YOU HEAR THAT, KIDS?
THAT MAKES JACK-JACK A PARR THROUGH AND THROUGH.
WE'RE ALL GOING TO BE JUST FINE!

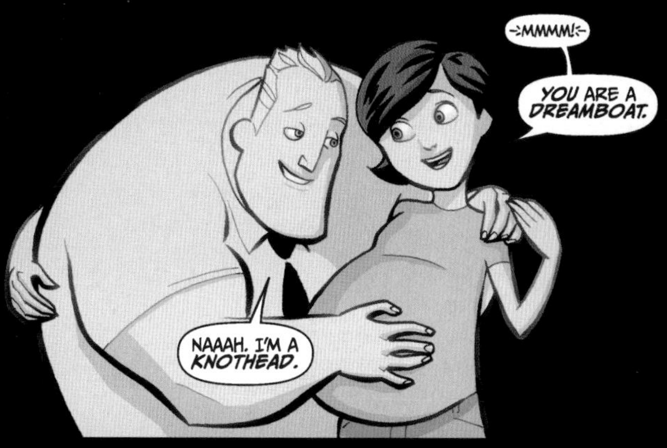
-MMMM!-
YOU ARE A DREAMBOAT.
NAAAH. I'M A KNOTHEAD.

CHAPTER ONE

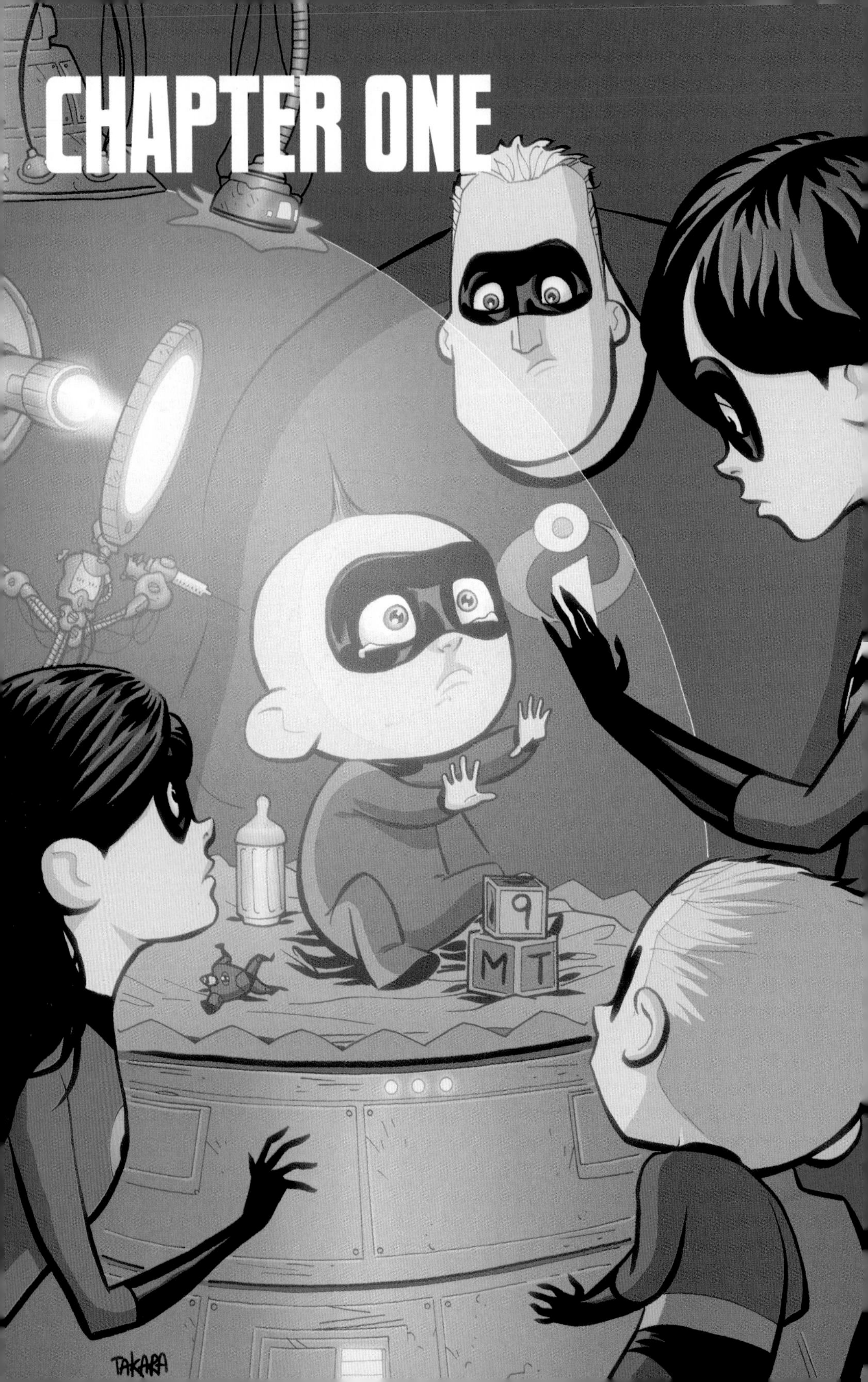
9
M T
TAKARA

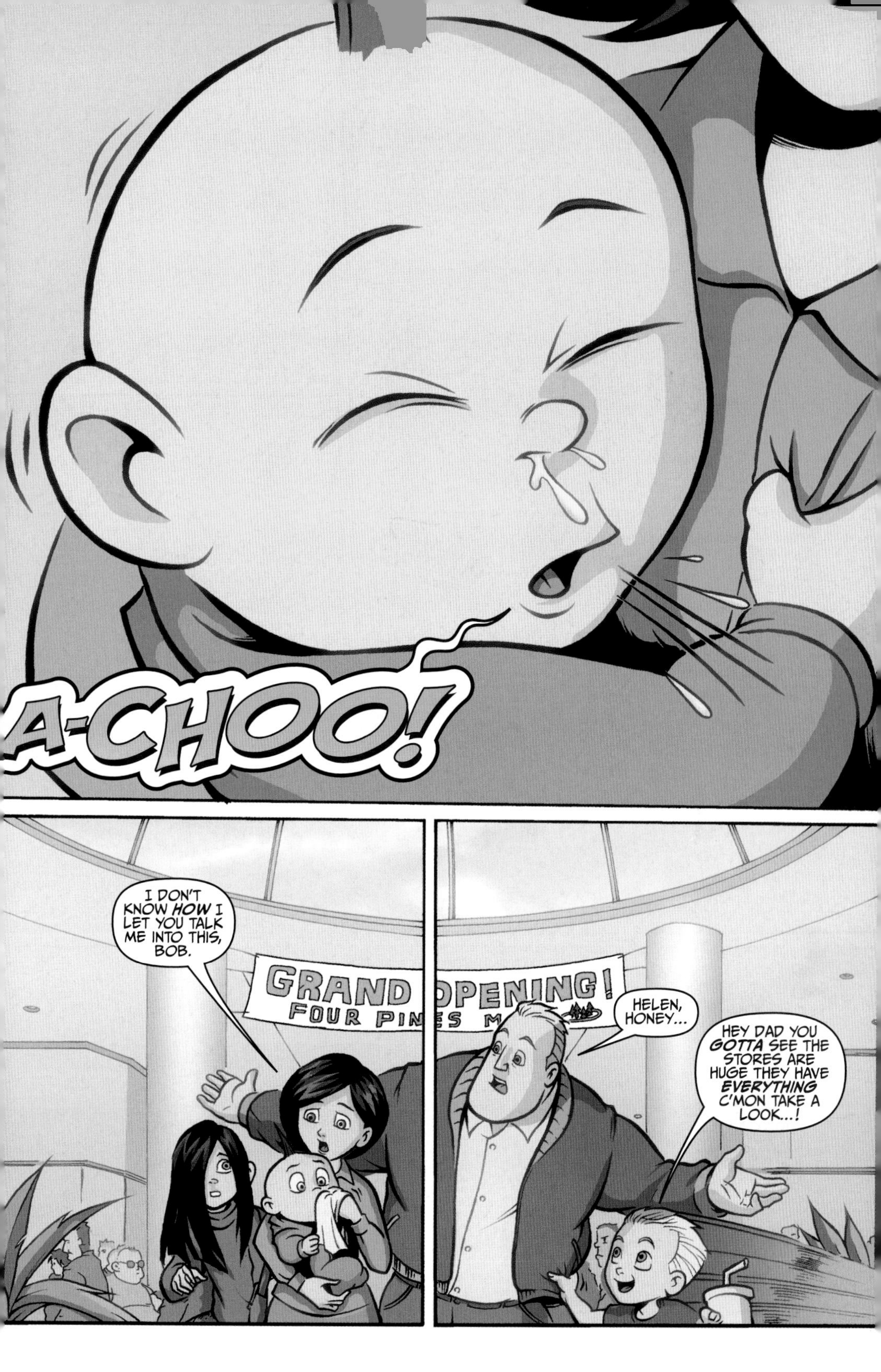
A-CHOO!
I DON'T KNOW *HOW* I LET YOU TALK ME INTO THIS, BOB.
GRAND OPENING!
FOUR PINES M
HELEN, HONEY...
HEY DAD YOU *GOTTA* SEE THE STORES ARE HUGE THEY HAVE *EVERYTHING* C'MON TAKE A LOOK...!

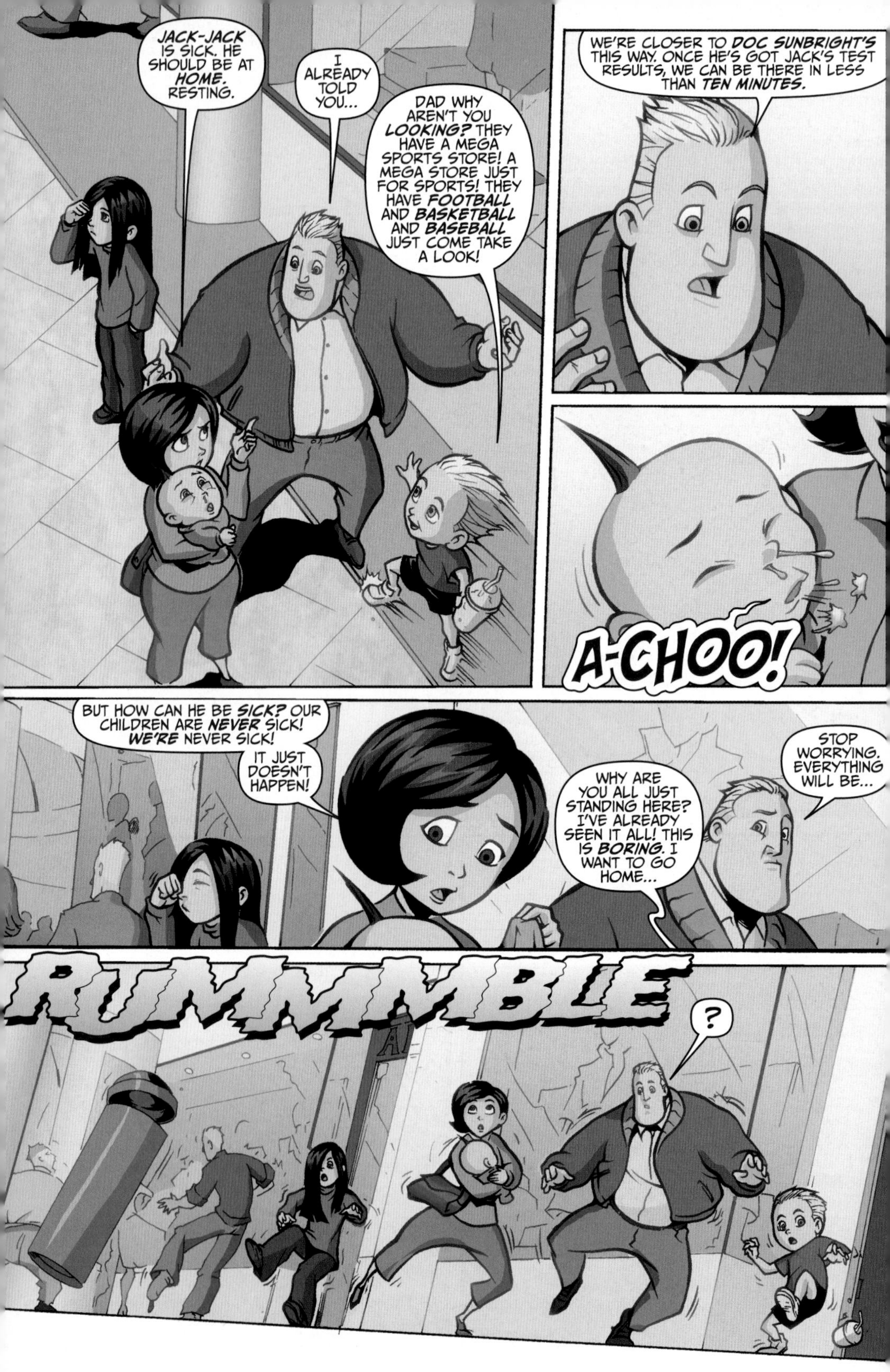
JACK-JACK IS SICK. HE SHOULD BE AT HOME. RESTING.
I ALREADY TOLD YOU...
DAD WHY AREN'T YOU LOOKING? THEY HAVE A MEGA SPORTS STORE! A MEGA STORE JUST FOR SPORTS! THEY HAVE FOOTBALL AND BASKETBALL AND BASEBALL JUST COME TAKE A LOOK!
WE'RE CLOSER TO DOC SUNBRIGHT'S THIS WAY. ONCE HE'S GOT JACK'S TEST RESULTS, WE CAN BE THERE IN LESS THAN TEN MINUTES.
A-CHOO!
BUT HOW CAN HE BE SICK? OUR CHILDREN ARE NEVER SICK! WE'RE NEVER SICK!
IT JUST DOESN'T HAPPEN!
WHY ARE YOU ALL JUST STANDING HERE? I'VE ALREADY SEEN IT ALL! THIS IS BORING. I WANT TO GO HOME...
STOP WORRYING. EVERYTHING WILL BE...
RUMMMBLE
?

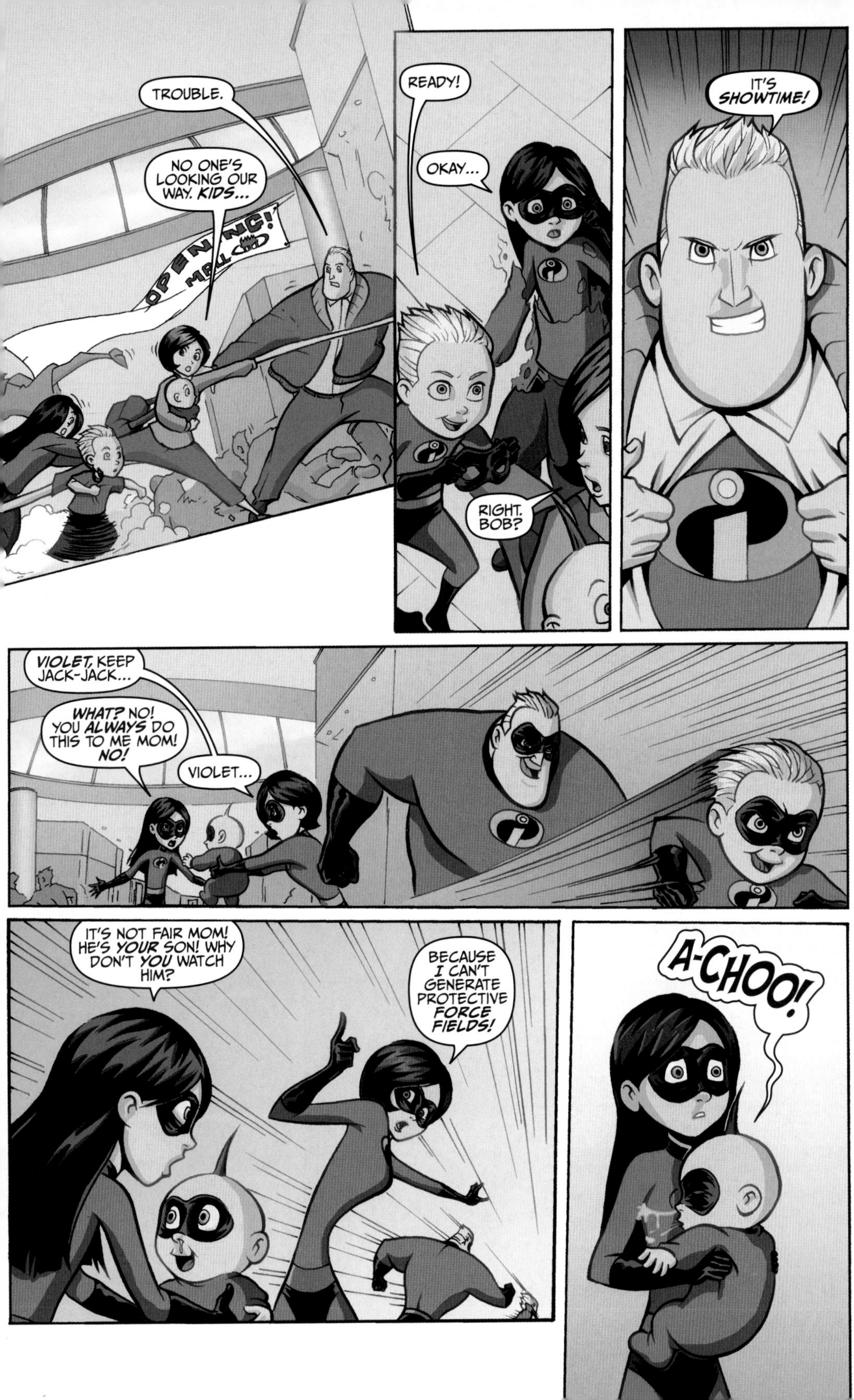
TROUBLE.
NO ONE'S LOOKING OUR WAY. KIDS...
OPENING! MALL
READY!
OKAY...
RIGHT. BOB?
IT'S SHOWTIME!
VIOLET, KEEP JACK-JACK...
WHAT? NO! YOU ALWAYS DO THIS TO ME MOM! NO!
VIOLET...
IT'S NOT FAIR MOM! HE'S YOUR SON! WHY DON'T YOU WATCH HIM?
BECAUSE I CAN'T GENERATE PROTECTIVE FORCE FIELDS!
A-CHOO!

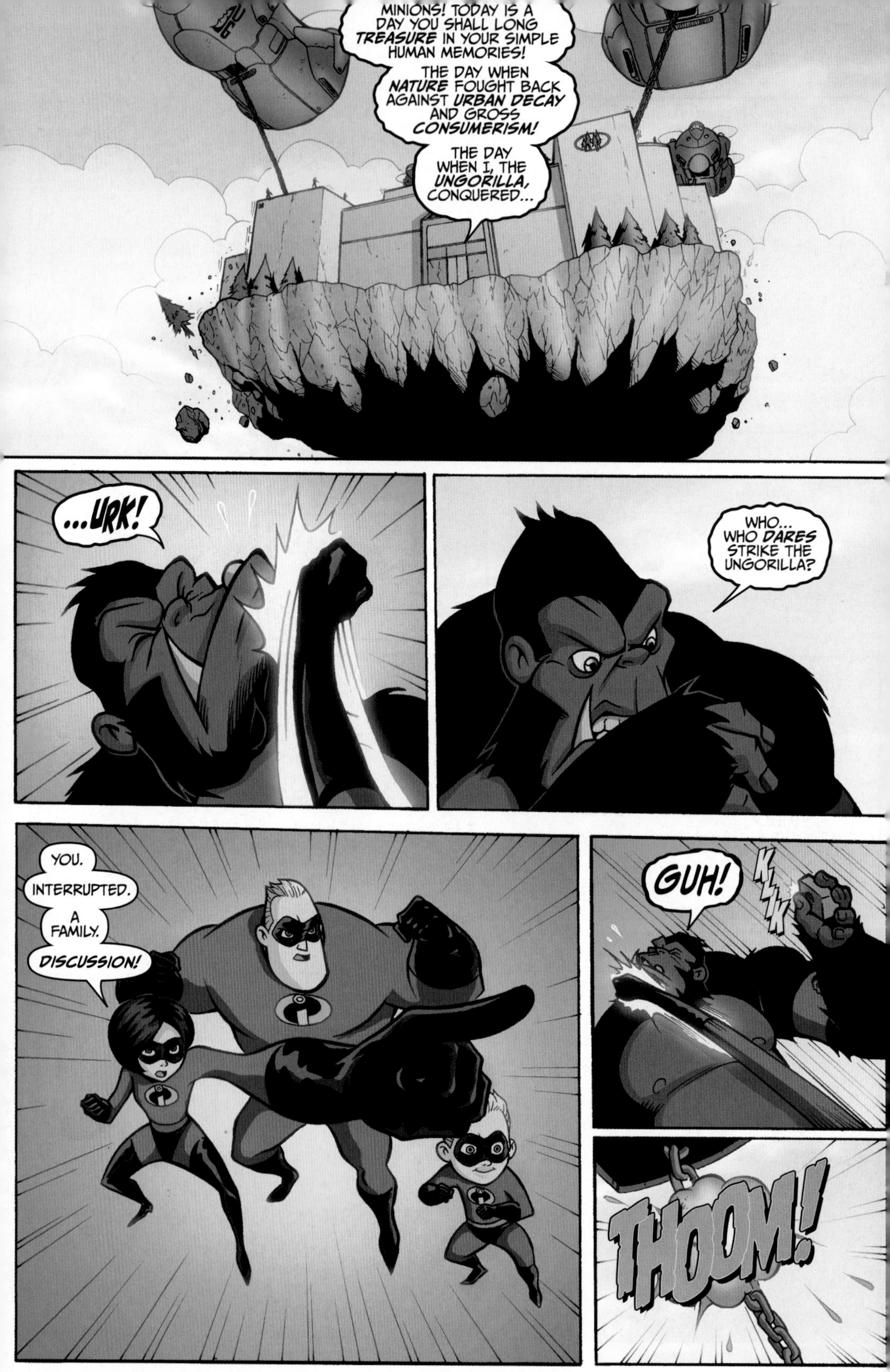
MINIONS! TODAY IS A DAY YOU SHALL LONG TREASURE IN YOUR SIMPLE HUMAN MEMORIES!
THE DAY WHEN NATURE FOUGHT BACK AGAINST URBAN DECAY AND GROSS CONSUMERISM!
THE DAY WHEN I, THE UNGORILLA, CONQUERED...
...URK!
WHO... WHO DARES STRIKE THE UNGORILLA?
YOU.
INTERRUPTED.
A
FAMILY.
DISCUSSION!
GUH!
KLIK
THOOM!

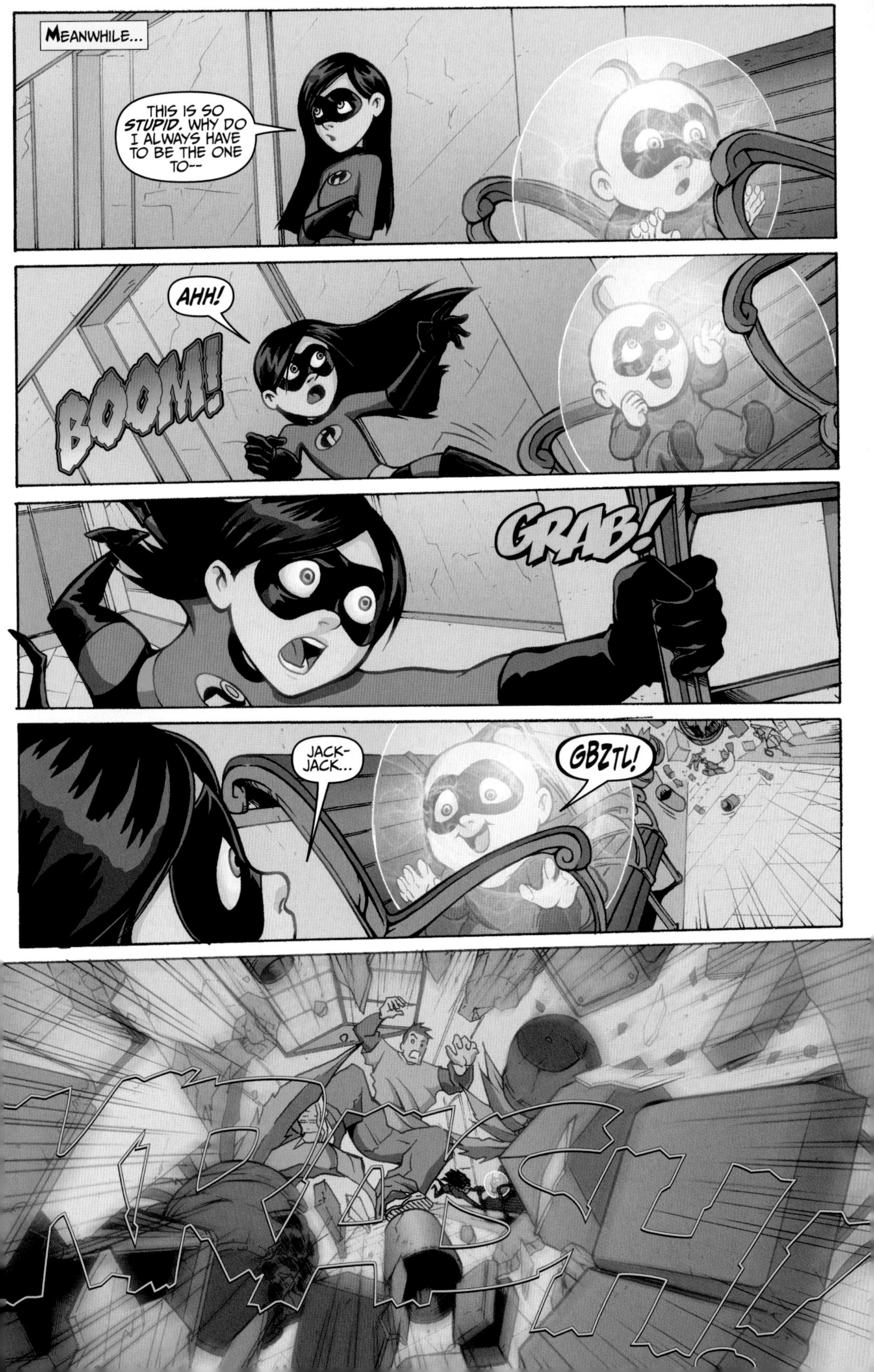
MEANWHILE...
THIS IS SO STUPID. WHY DO I ALWAYS HAVE TO BE THE ONE TO--
AHH!
BOOM!
GRAB!
JACK-JACK...
GBZTL!

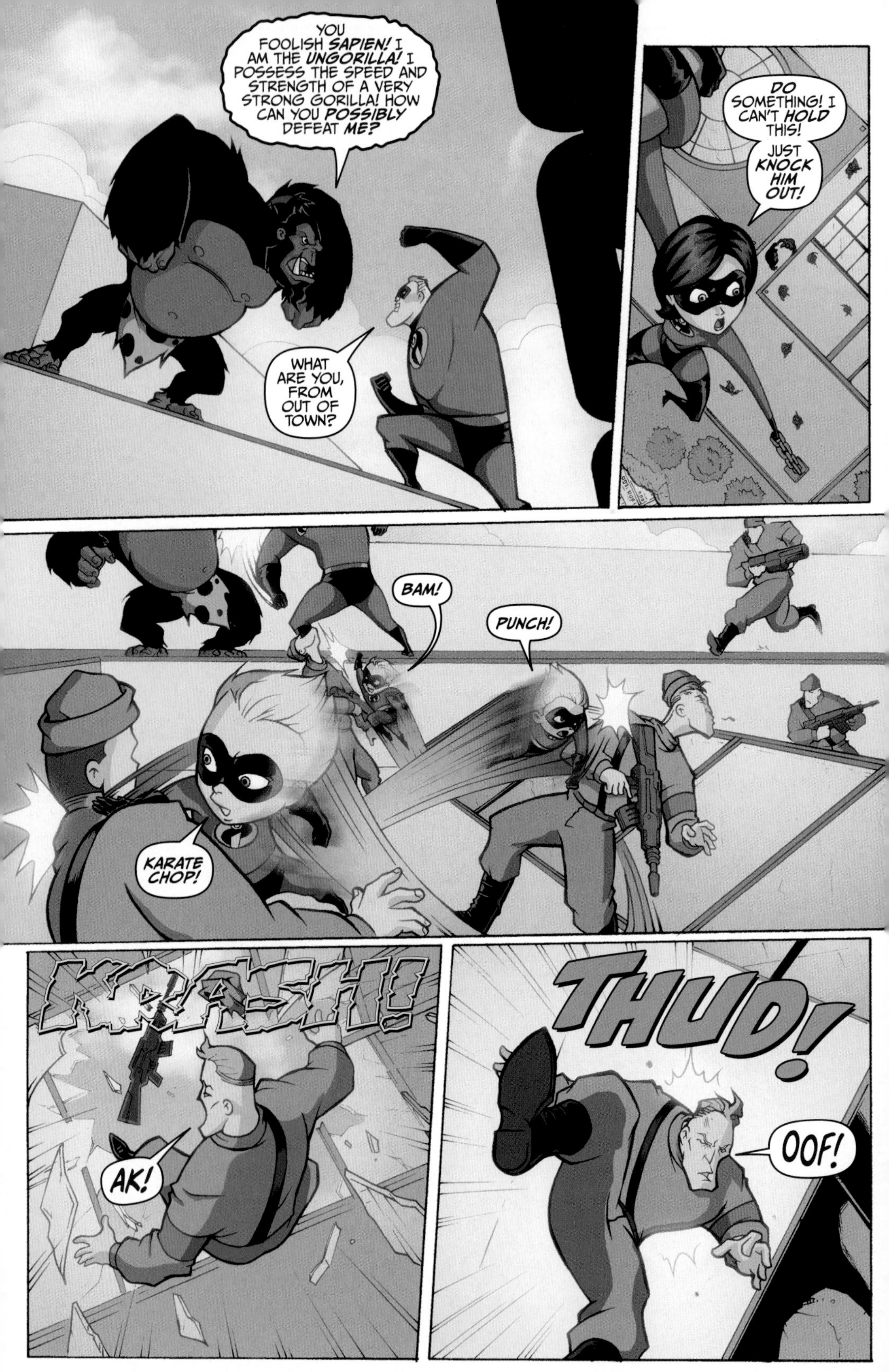
YOU FOOLISH SAPIEN! I AM THE UNGORILLA! I POSSESS THE SPEED AND STRENGTH OF A VERY STRONG GORILLA! HOW CAN YOU POSSIBLY DEFEAT ME?
WHAT ARE YOU, FROM OUT OF TOWN?
DO SOMETHING! I CAN'T HOLD THIS!
JUST KNOCK HIM OUT!
BAM!
PUNCH!
KARATE CHOP!
KRASH!
AK!
THUD!
OOF!

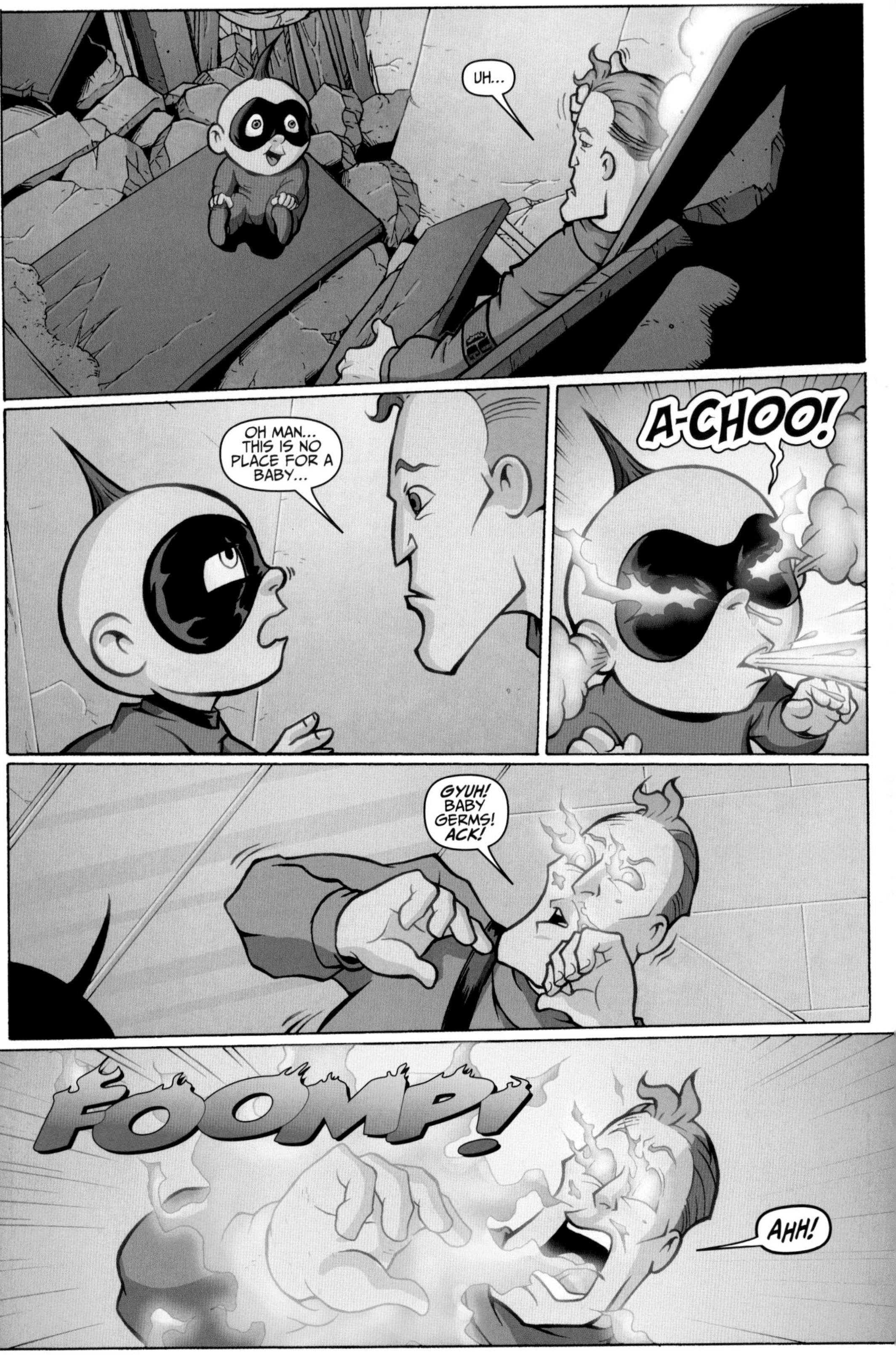
UH...
OH MAN... THIS IS NO PLACE FOR A BABY...
A-CHOO!
GYUH! BABY GERMS! ACK!
FOOMP!
AHH!

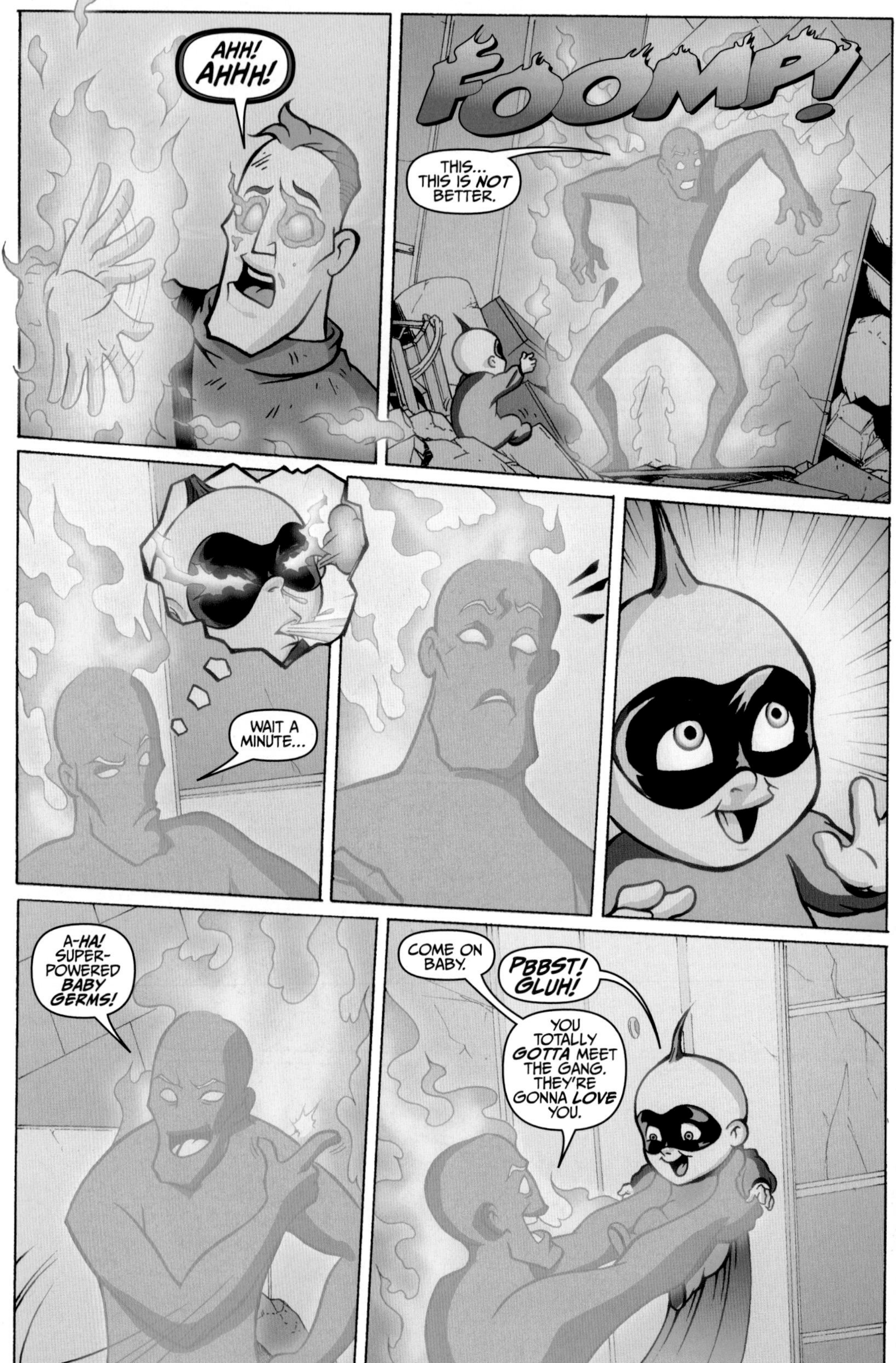
AHH! AHHH!
FOOMP!
THIS... THIS IS NOT BETTER.
WAIT A MINUTE...
A-HA! SUPER-POWERED BABY GERMS!
COME ON BABY.
PBBST! GLUH!
YOU TOTALLY GOTTA MEET THE GANG. THEY'RE GONNA LOVE YOU.

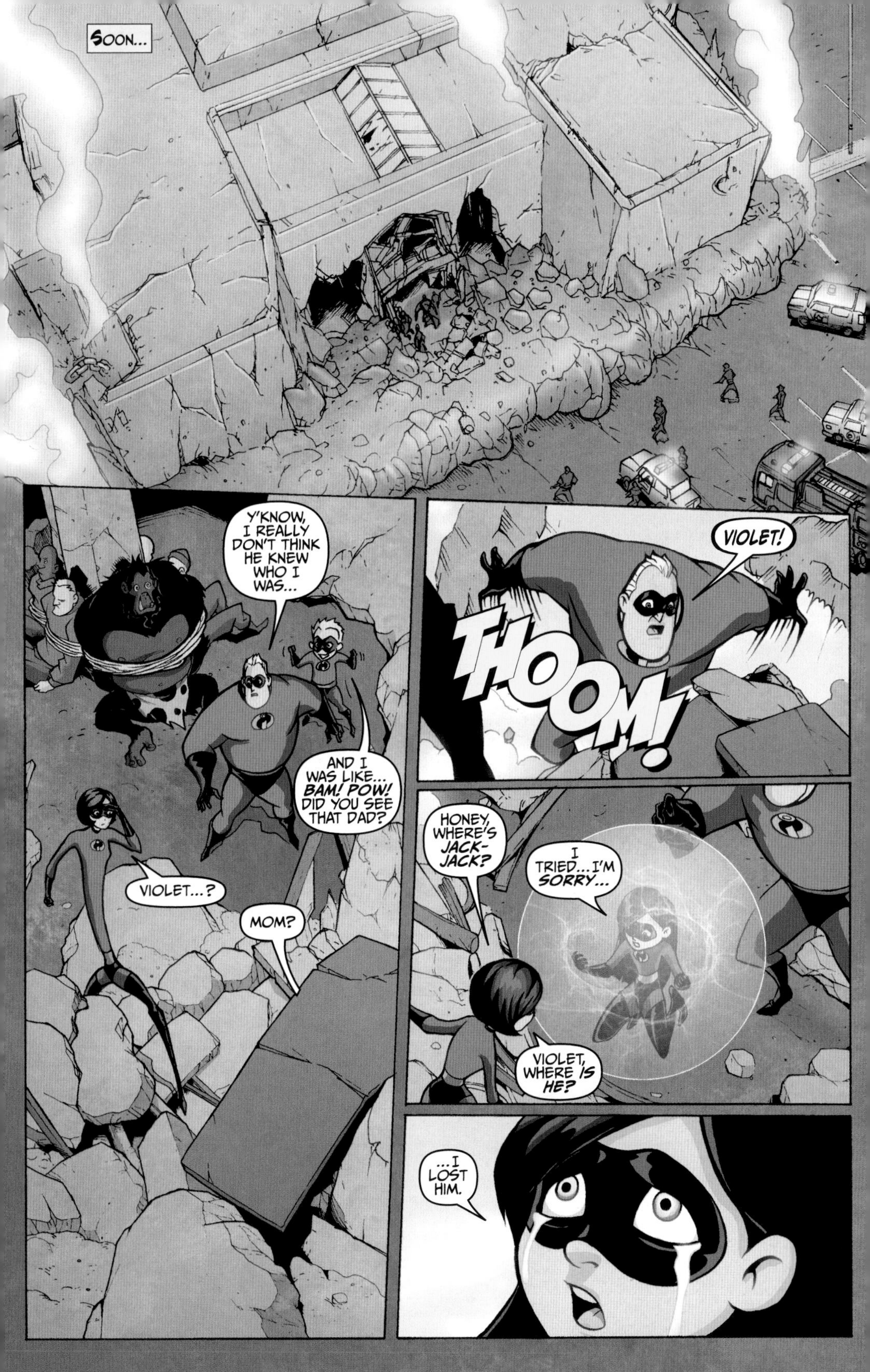
SOON...
Y'KNOW, I REALLY DON'T THINK HE KNEW WHO I WAS...
AND I WAS LIKE... BAM! POW! DID YOU SEE THAT DAD?
VIOLET...?
MOM?
VIOLET!
THOOM!
HONEY, WHERE'S JACK-JACK?
I TRIED... I'M SORRY...
VIOLET, WHERE IS HE?
...I LOST HIM.

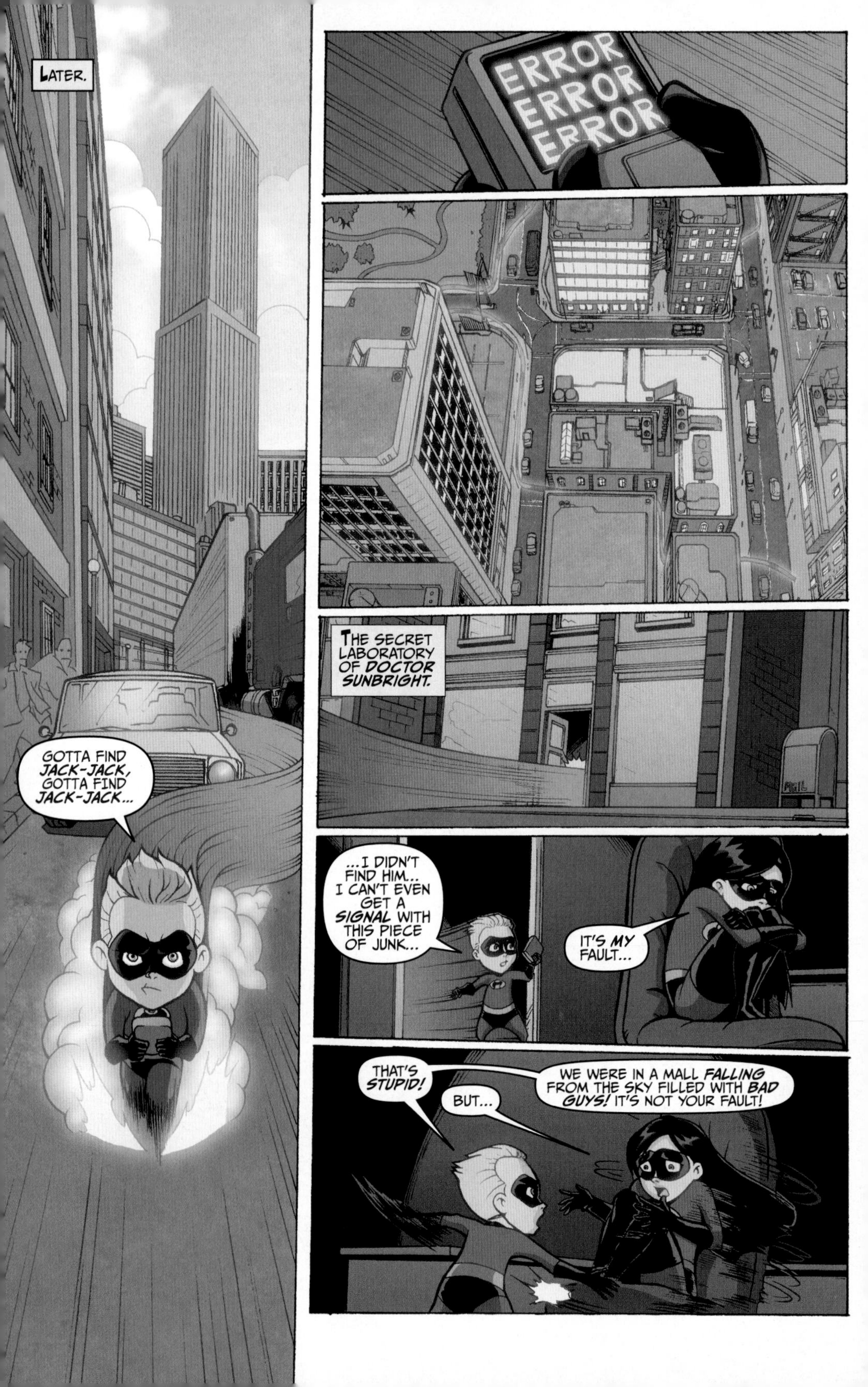
LATER.
GOTTA FIND JACK-JACK, GOTTA FIND JACK-JACK...
ERROR ERROR ERROR
THE SECRET LABORATORY OF DOCTOR SUNBRIGHT.
MAIL
...I DIDN'T FIND HIM... I CAN'T EVEN GET A SIGNAL WITH THIS PIECE OF JUNK...
IT'S MY FAULT...
THAT'S STUPID!
WE WERE IN A MALL FALLING FROM THE SKY FILLED WITH BAD GUYS! IT'S NOT YOUR FAULT!
BUT...

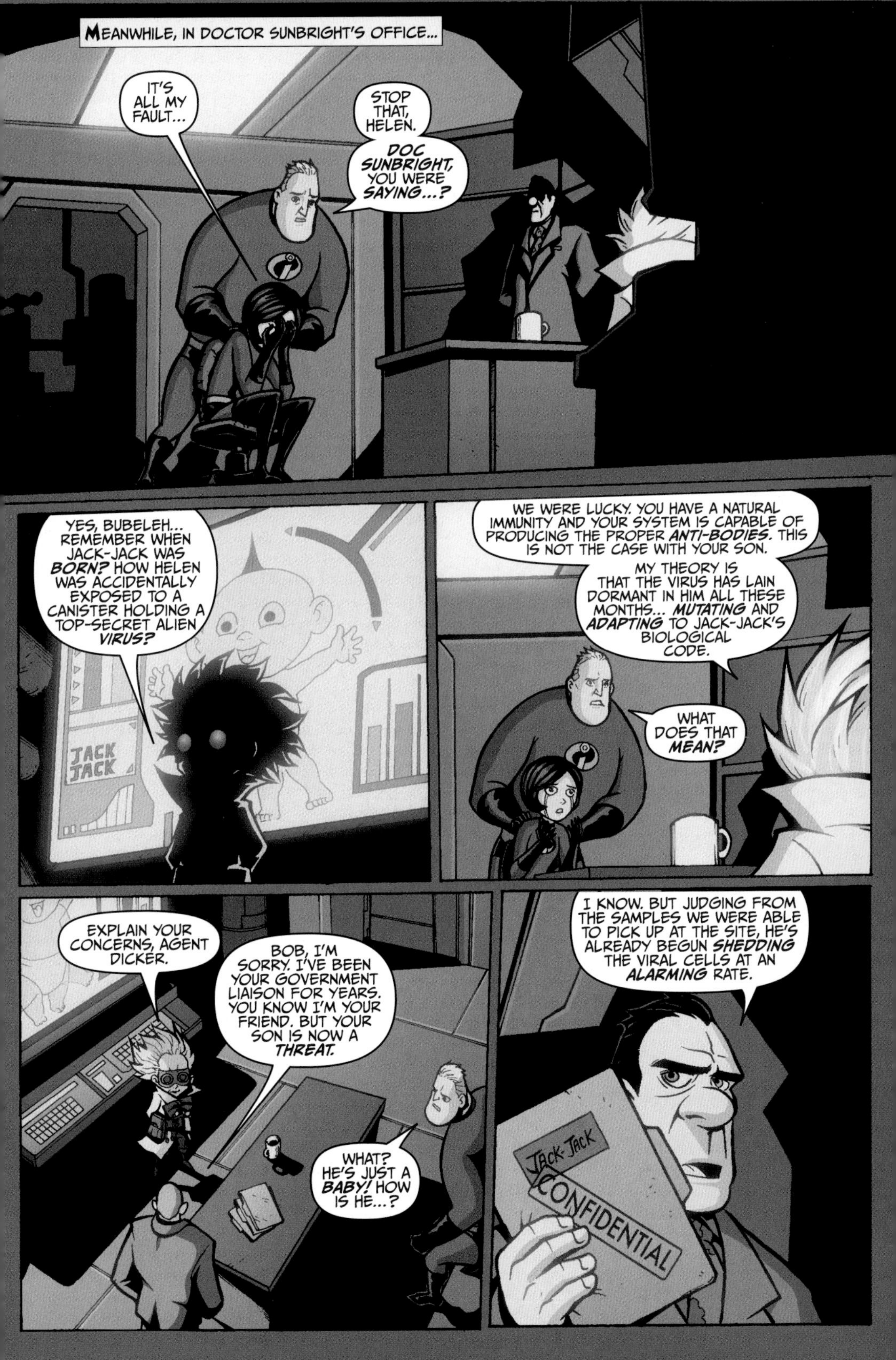

MEANWHILE, IN DOCTOR SUNBRIGHT'S OFFICE...
IT'S ALL MY FAULT...
STOP THAT, HELEN.
DOC SUNBRIGHT, YOU WERE SAYING...?
YES, BUBELEH... REMEMBER WHEN JACK-JACK WAS BORN? HOW HELEN WAS ACCIDENTALLY EXPOSED TO A CANISTER HOLDING A TOP-SECRET ALIEN VIRUS?
JACK JACK
WE WERE LUCKY. YOU HAVE A NATURAL IMMUNITY AND YOUR SYSTEM IS CAPABLE OF PRODUCING THE PROPER ANTI-BODIES. THIS IS NOT THE CASE WITH YOUR SON.
MY THEORY IS THAT THE VIRUS HAS LAIN DORMANT IN HIM ALL THESE MONTHS... MUTATING AND ADAPTING TO JACK-JACK'S BIOLOGICAL CODE.
WHAT DOES THAT MEAN?
EXPLAIN YOUR CONCERNS, AGENT DICKER.
BOB, I'M SORRY. I'VE BEEN YOUR GOVERNMENT LIAISON FOR YEARS. YOU KNOW I'M YOUR FRIEND. BUT YOUR SON IS NOW A THREAT.
WHAT? HE'S JUST A BABY! HOW IS HE...?
I KNOW. BUT JUDGING FROM THE SAMPLES WE WERE ABLE TO PICK UP AT THE SITE, HE'S ALREADY BEGUN SHEDDING THE VIRAL CELLS AT AN ALARMING RATE.
JACK-JACK
CONFIDENTIAL

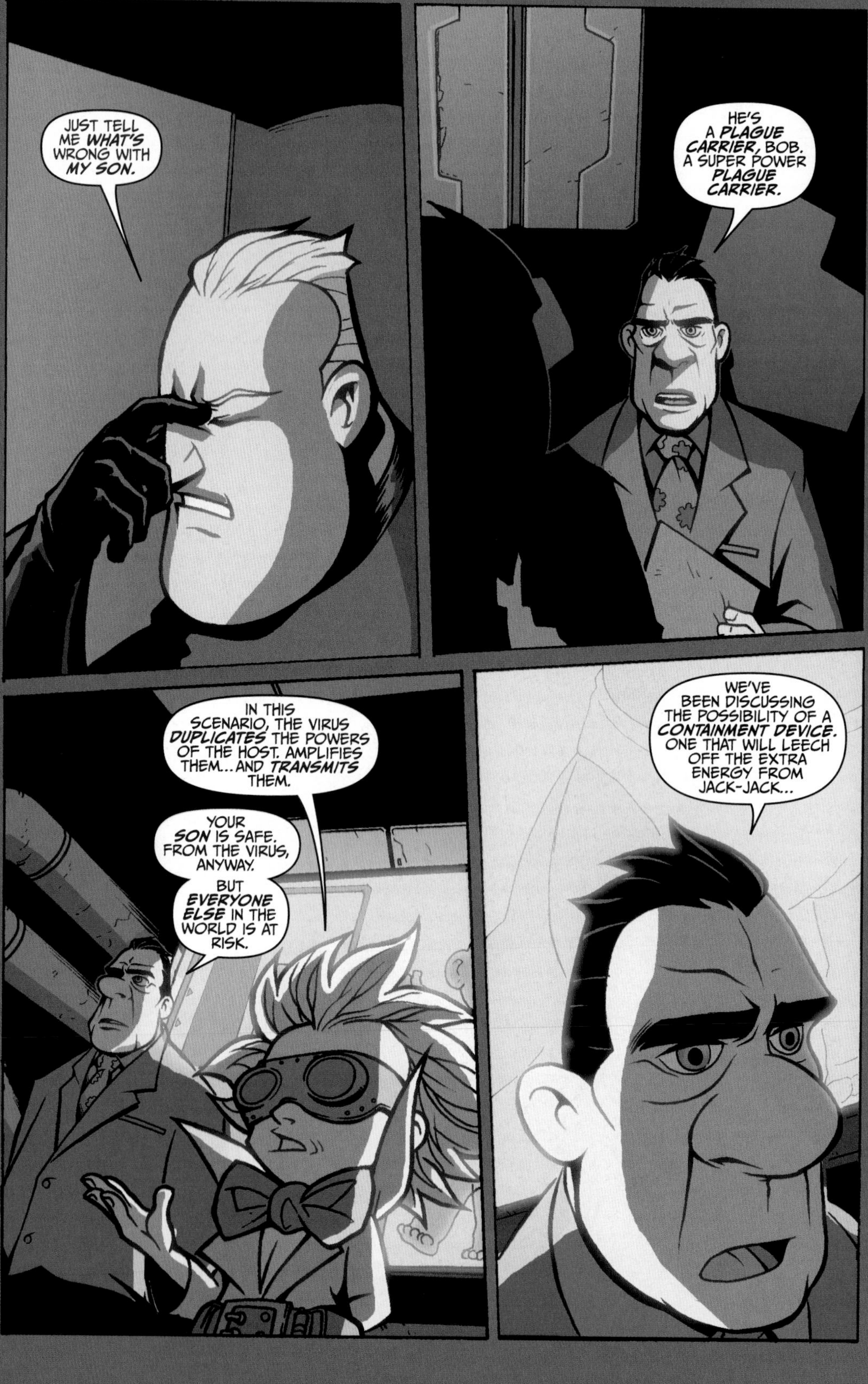
JUST TELL ME WHAT'S WRONG WITH MY SON.
HE'S A PLAGUE CARRIER, BOB. A SUPER POWER PLAGUE CARRIER.
IN THIS SCENARIO, THE VIRUS DUPLICATES THE POWERS OF THE HOST. AMPLIFIES THEM... AND TRANSMITS THEM.
YOUR SON IS SAFE. FROM THE VIRUS, ANYWAY.
BUT EVERYONE ELSE IN THE WORLD IS AT RISK.
WE'VE BEEN DISCUSSING THE POSSIBILITY OF A CONTAINMENT DEVICE. ONE THAT WILL LEECH OFF THE EXTRA ENERGY FROM JACK-JACK...

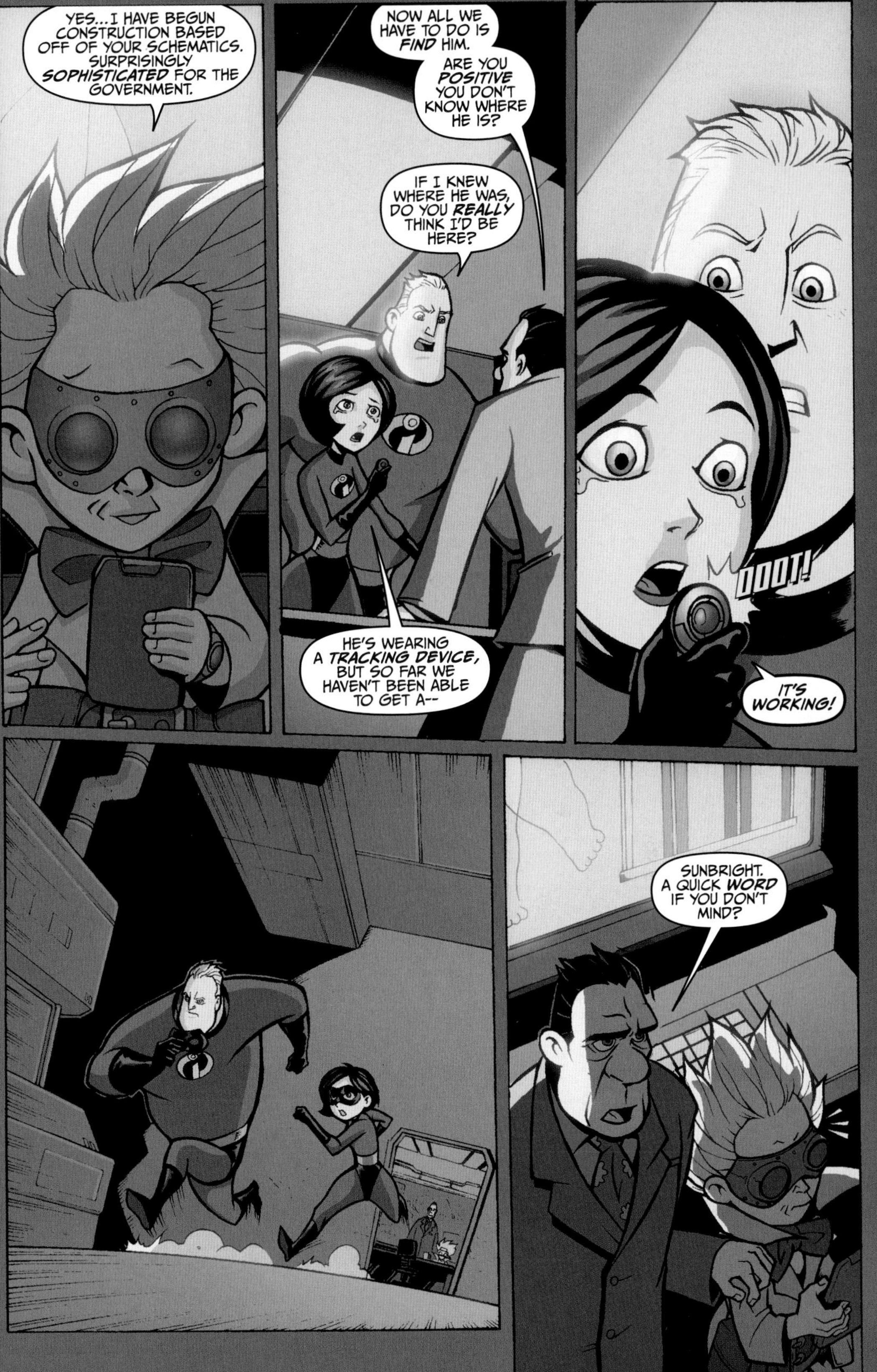
YES...I HAVE BEGUN CONSTRUCTION BASED OFF OF YOUR SCHEMATICS. SURPRISINGLY SOPHISTICATED FOR THE GOVERNMENT.
NOW ALL WE HAVE TO DO IS FIND HIM.
ARE YOU POSITIVE YOU DON'T KNOW WHERE HE IS?
IF I KNEW WHERE HE WAS, DO YOU REALLY THINK I'D BE HERE?
HE'S WEARING A TRACKING DEVICE, BUT SO FAR WE HAVEN'T BEEN ABLE TO GET A--
DOOT!
IT'S WORKING!
SUNBRIGHT. A QUICK WORD IF YOU DON'T MIND?

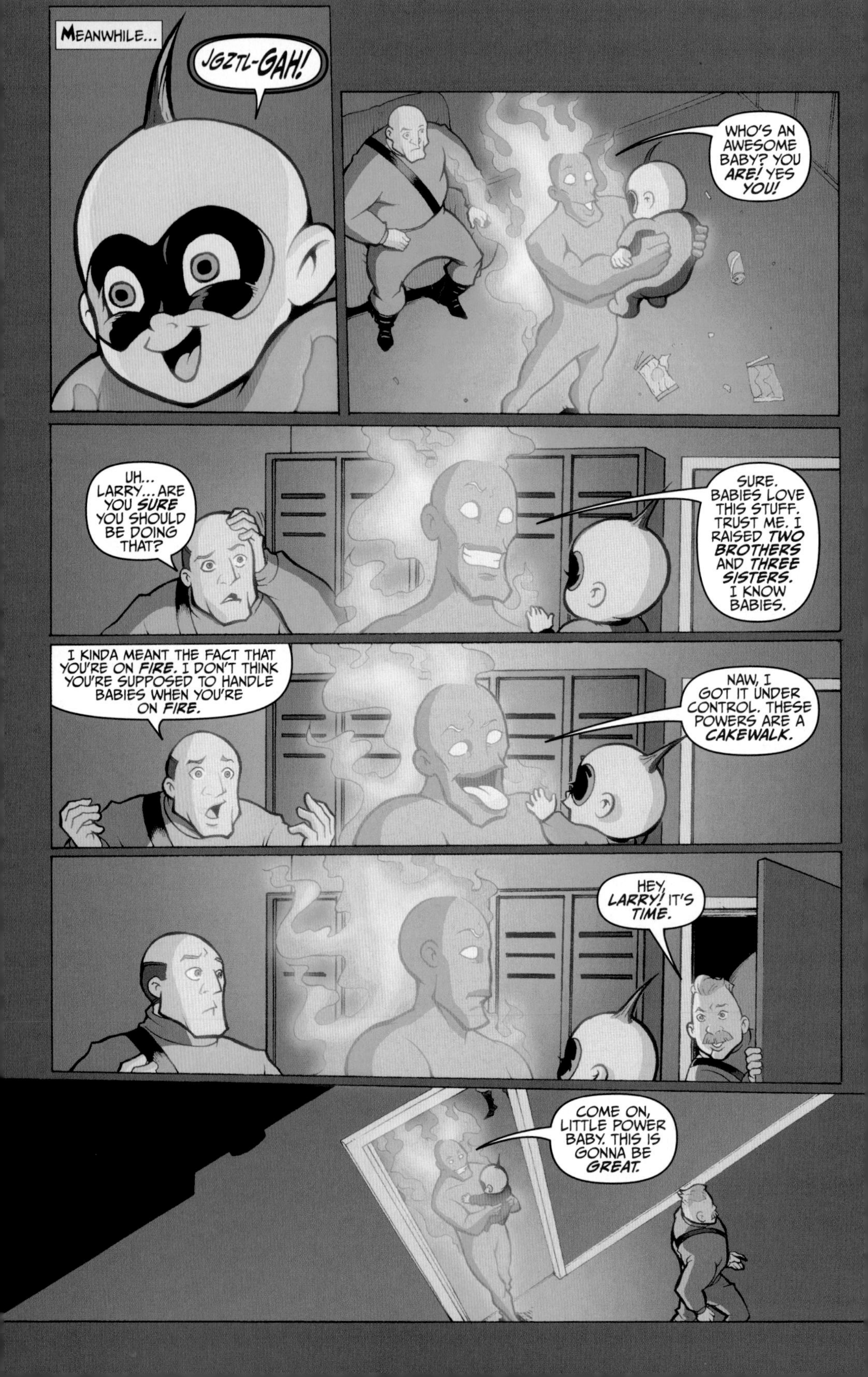
MEANWHILE...
JGZTL-GAH!
WHO'S AN AWESOME BABY? YOU ARE! YES YOU!
UH... LARRY... ARE YOU SURE YOU SHOULD BE DOING THAT?
SURE. BABIES LOVE THIS STUFF. TRUST ME. I RAISED TWO BROTHERS AND THREE SISTERS. I KNOW BABIES.
I KINDA MEANT THE FACT THAT YOU'RE ON FIRE. I DON'T THINK YOU'RE SUPPOSED TO HANDLE BABIES WHEN YOU'RE ON FIRE.
NAW, I GOT IT UNDER CONTROL. THESE POWERS ARE A CAKEWALK.
HEY, LARRY! IT'S TIME.
COME ON, LITTLE POWER BABY. THIS IS GONNA BE GREAT.

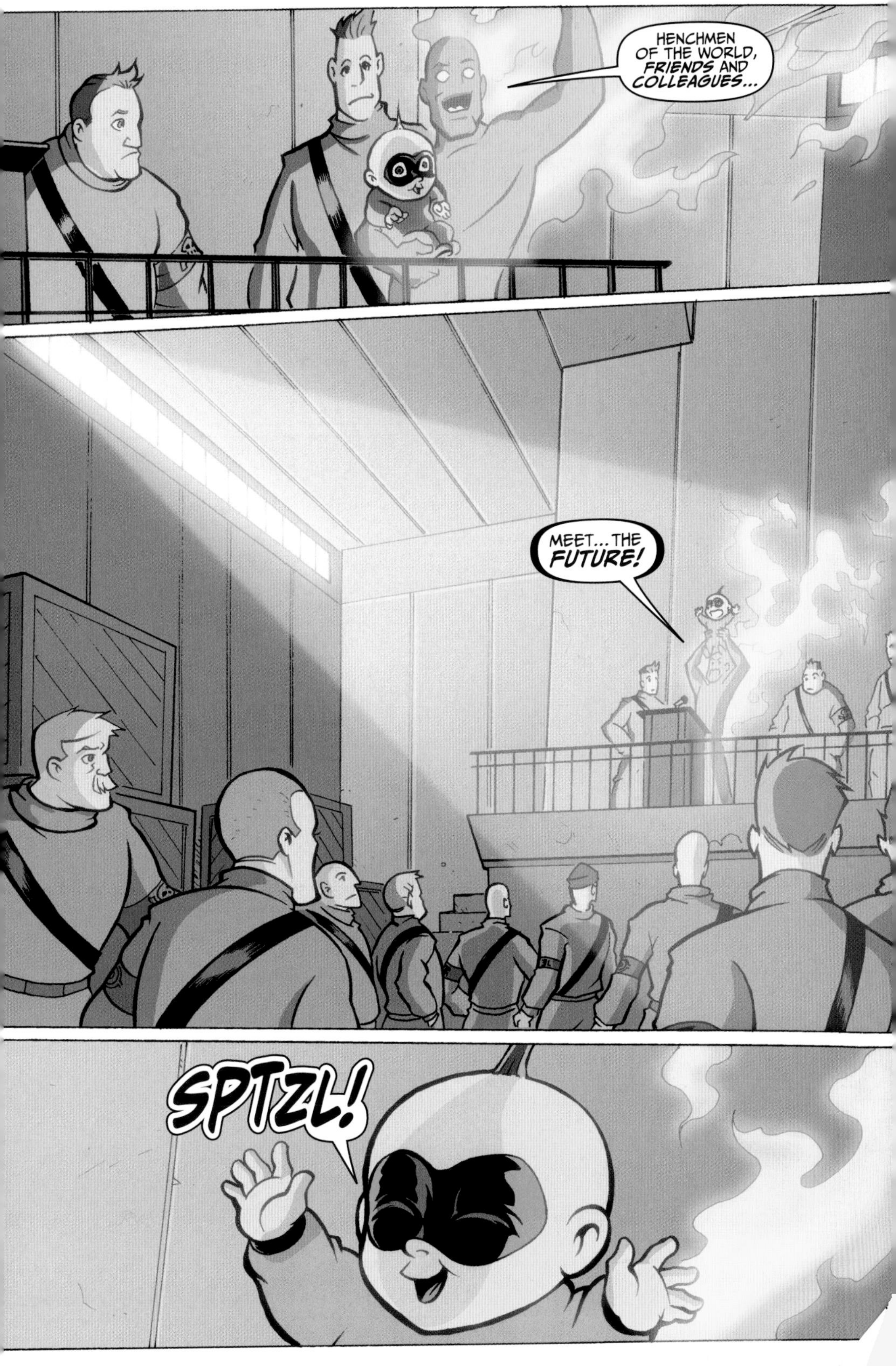
HENCHMEN OF THE WORLD, FRIENDS AND COLLEAGUES...
MEET... THE FUTURE!
SPTZL!

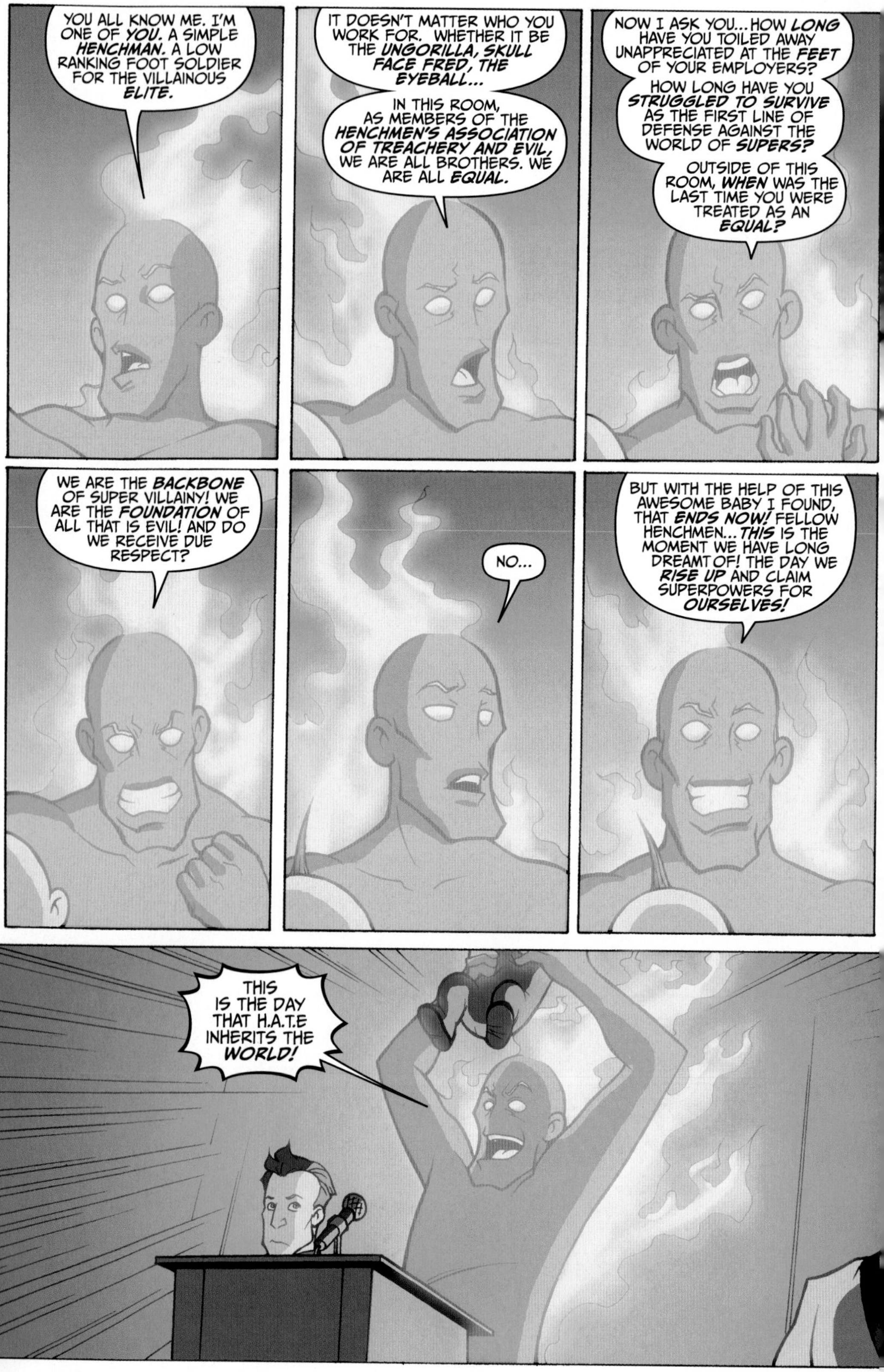

YOU ALL KNOW ME. I'M ONE OF YOU. A SIMPLE HENCHMAN. A LOW RANKING FOOT SOLDIER FOR THE VILLAINOUS ELITE.
IT DOESN'T MATTER WHO YOU WORK FOR. WHETHER IT BE THE UNGORILLA, SKULL FACE FRED, THE EYEBALL...
IN THIS ROOM, AS MEMBERS OF THE HENCHMEN'S ASSOCIATION OF TREACHERY AND EVIL, WE ARE ALL BROTHERS. WE ARE ALL EQUAL.
NOW I ASK YOU... HOW LONG HAVE YOU TOILED AWAY UNAPPRECIATED AT THE FEET OF YOUR EMPLOYERS?
HOW LONG HAVE YOU STRUGGLED TO SURVIVE AS THE FIRST LINE OF DEFENSE AGAINST THE WORLD OF SUPERS?
OUTSIDE OF THIS ROOM, WHEN WAS THE LAST TIME YOU WERE TREATED AS AN EQUAL?
WE ARE THE BACKBONE OF SUPER VILLAINY! WE ARE THE FOUNDATION OF ALL THAT IS EVIL! AND DO WE RECEIVE DUE RESPECT?
NO...
BUT WITH THE HELP OF THIS AWESOME BABY I FOUND, THAT ENDS NOW! FELLOW HENCHMEN... THIS IS THE MOMENT WE HAVE LONG DREAMT OF! THE DAY WE RISE UP AND CLAIM SUPERPOWERS FOR OURSELVES!
THIS IS THE DAY THAT H.A.T.E INHERITS THE WORLD!

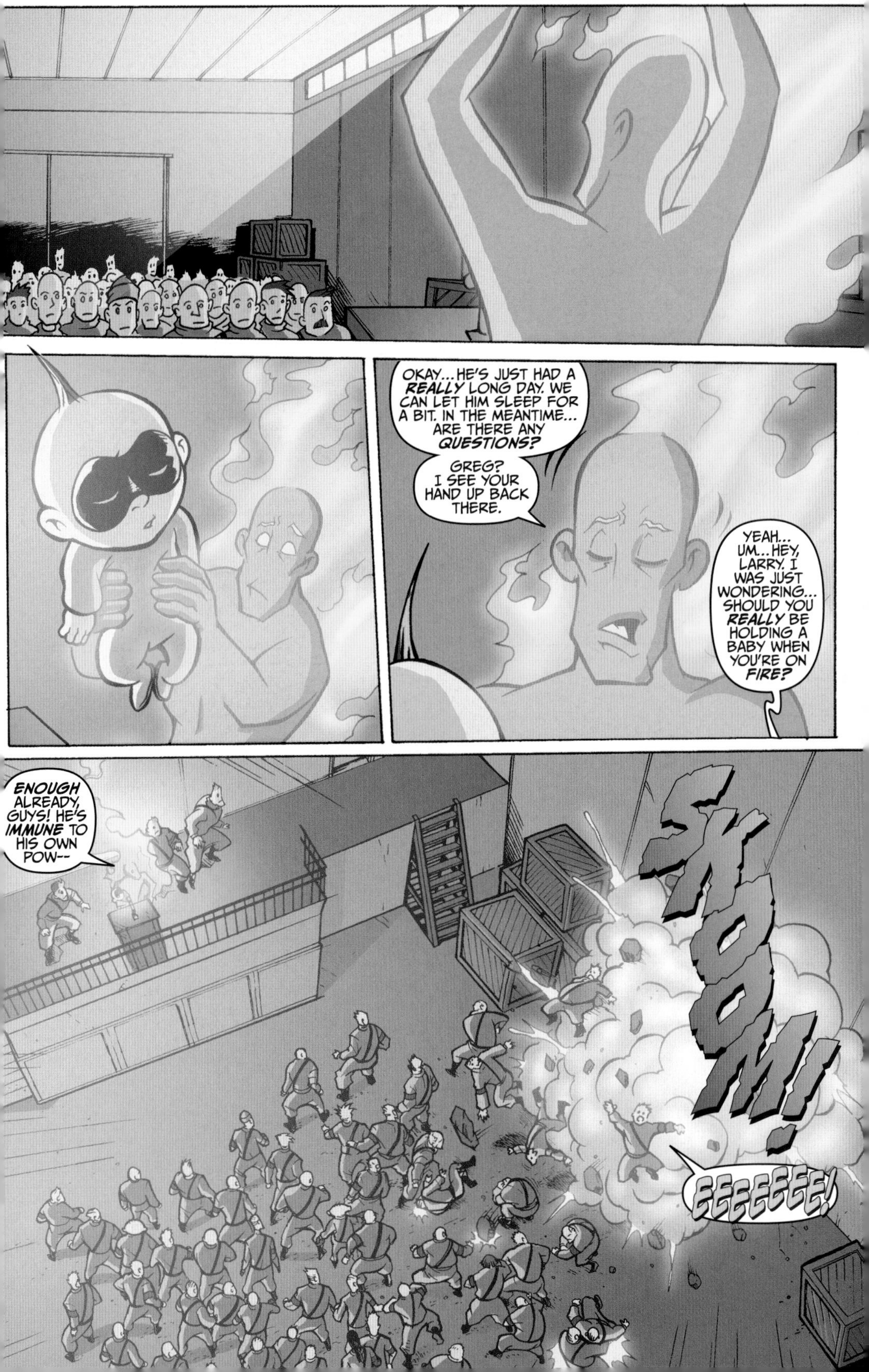

OKAY... HE'S JUST HAD A REALLY LONG DAY. WE CAN LET HIM SLEEP FOR A BIT. IN THE MEANTIME... ARE THERE ANY QUESTIONS?
GREG? I SEE YOUR HAND UP BACK THERE.
YEAH... UM... HEY, LARRY. I WAS JUST WONDERING... SHOULD YOU REALLY BE HOLDING A BABY WHEN YOU'RE ON FIRE?
ENOUGH ALREADY, GUYS! HE'S IMMUNE TO HIS OWN POW--
SKOOM!
EEEEEEE!

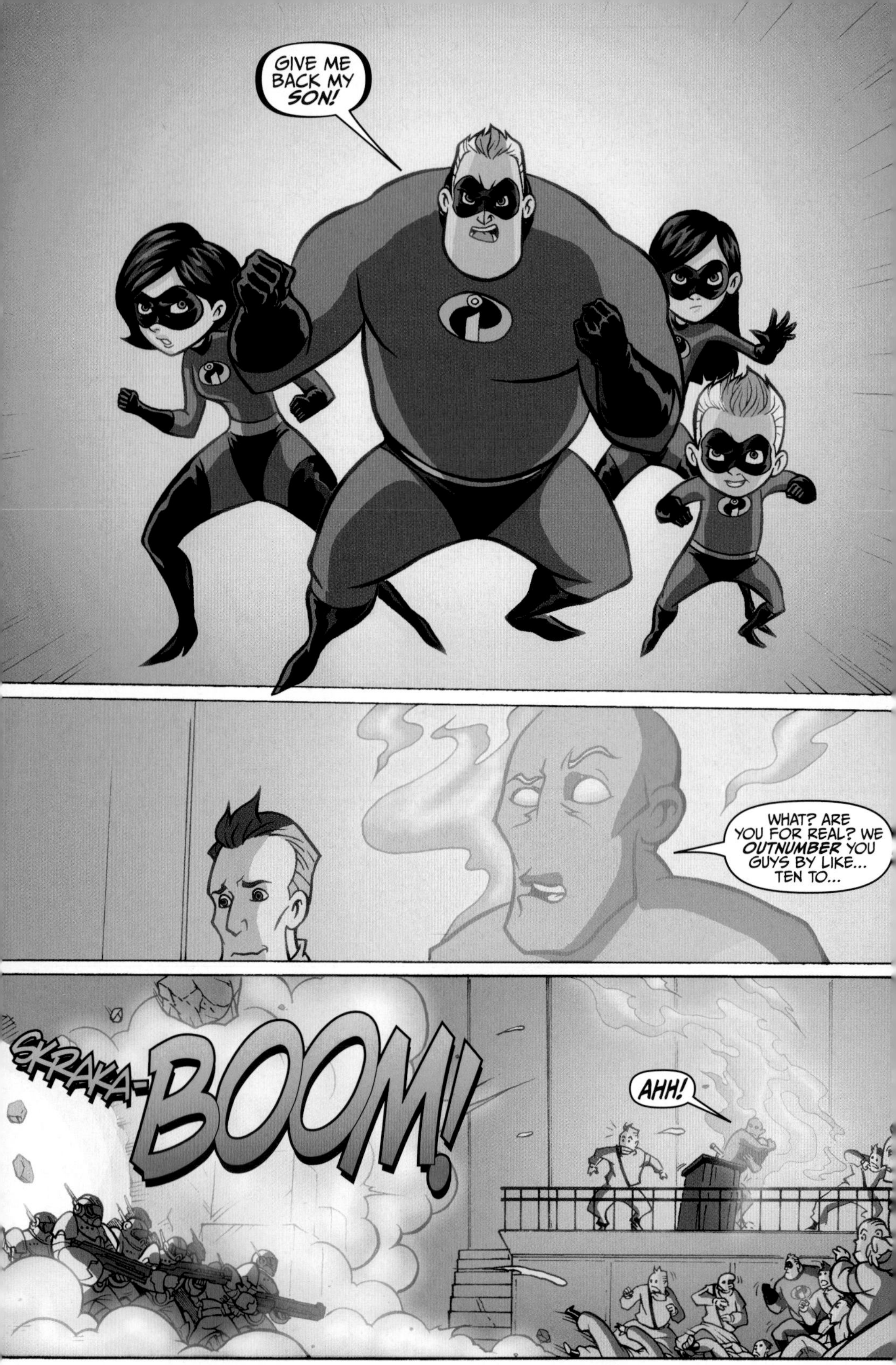
GIVE ME BACK MY SON!
WHAT? ARE YOU FOR REAL? WE OUTNUMBER YOU GUYS BY LIKE... TEN TO...
SKRAKA-BOOM!
AHH!

OKAY... UM...

I GUESS *NOW* WOULD BE A REALLY GOOD TIME TO *GIVE UP.*

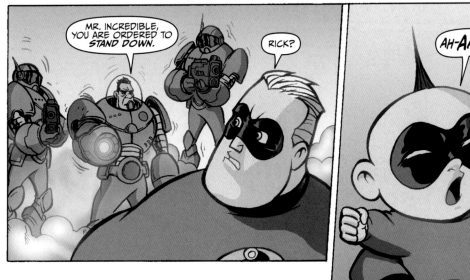

MR. INCREDIBLE, YOU ARE ORDERED TO *STAND DOWN.*

RICK?

AH-AA!

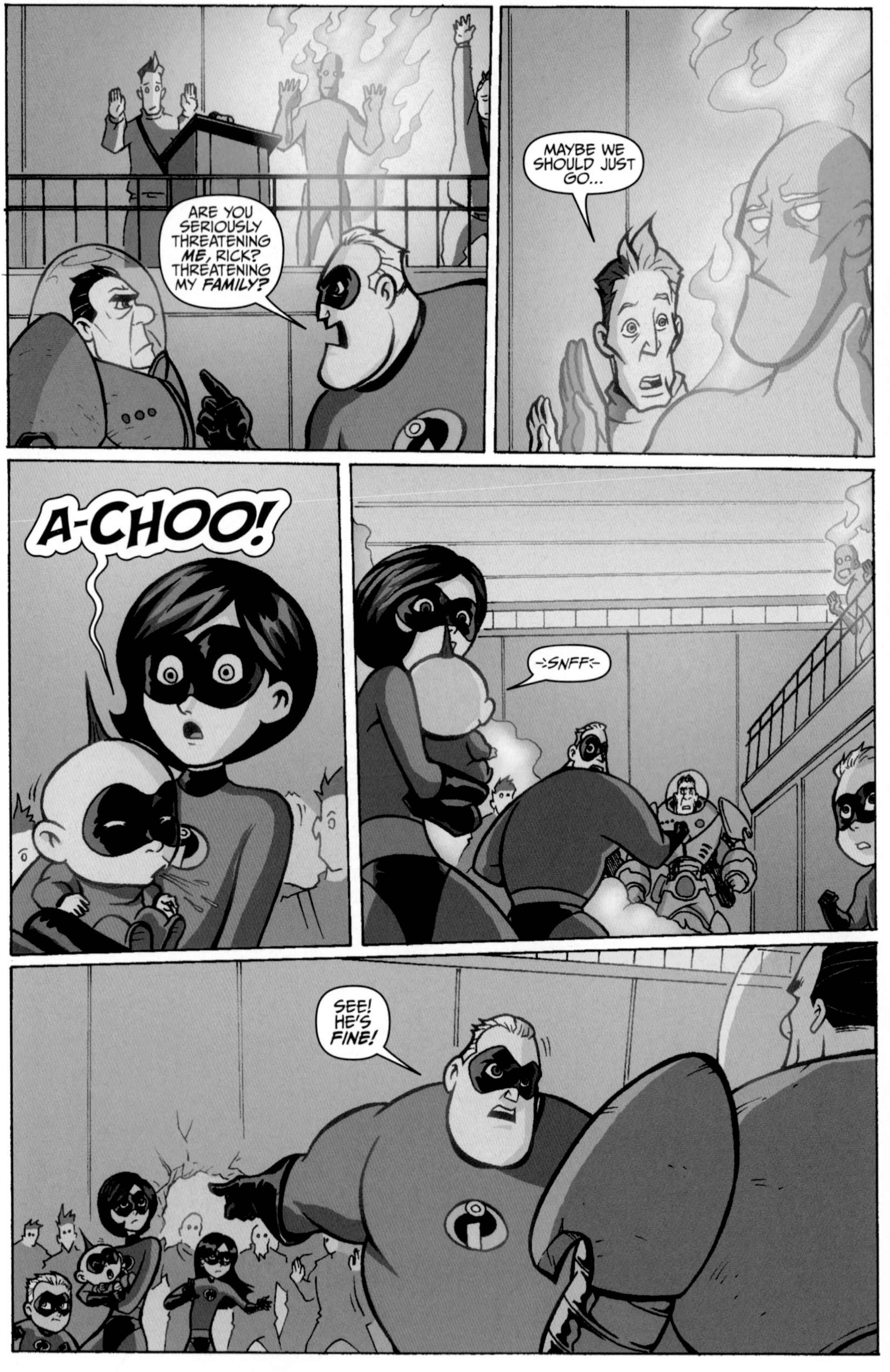

ARE YOU SERIOUSLY THREATENING *ME*, RICK? THREATENING MY *FAMILY*?
MAYBE WE SHOULD JUST GO...
A-CHOO!
SNFF
SEE! HE'S *FINE*!

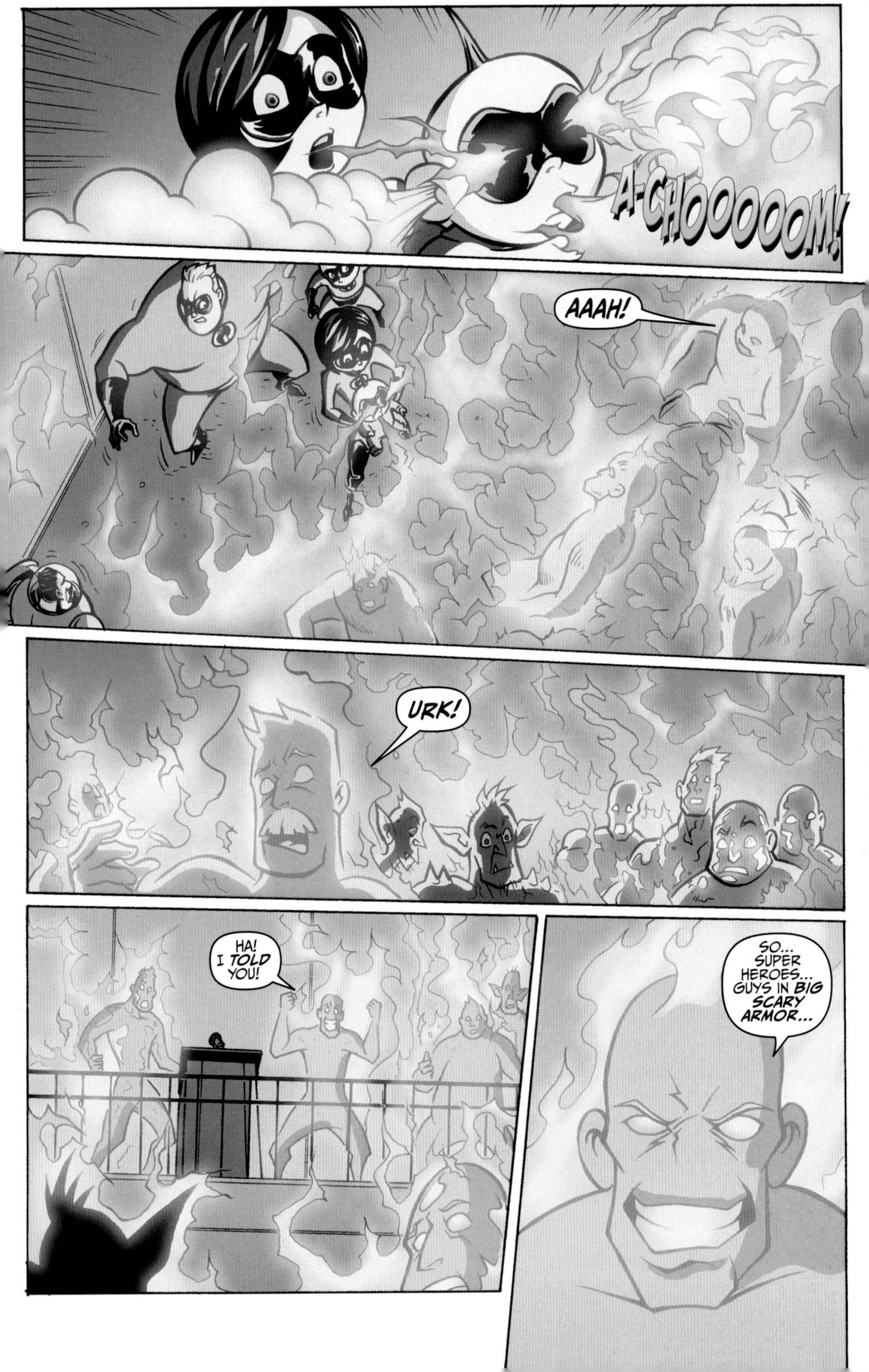
A-CHOOOOOM!
AAAH!
URK!
HA! I TOLD YOU!
SO... SUPER HEROES... GUYS IN BIG SCARY ARMOR...

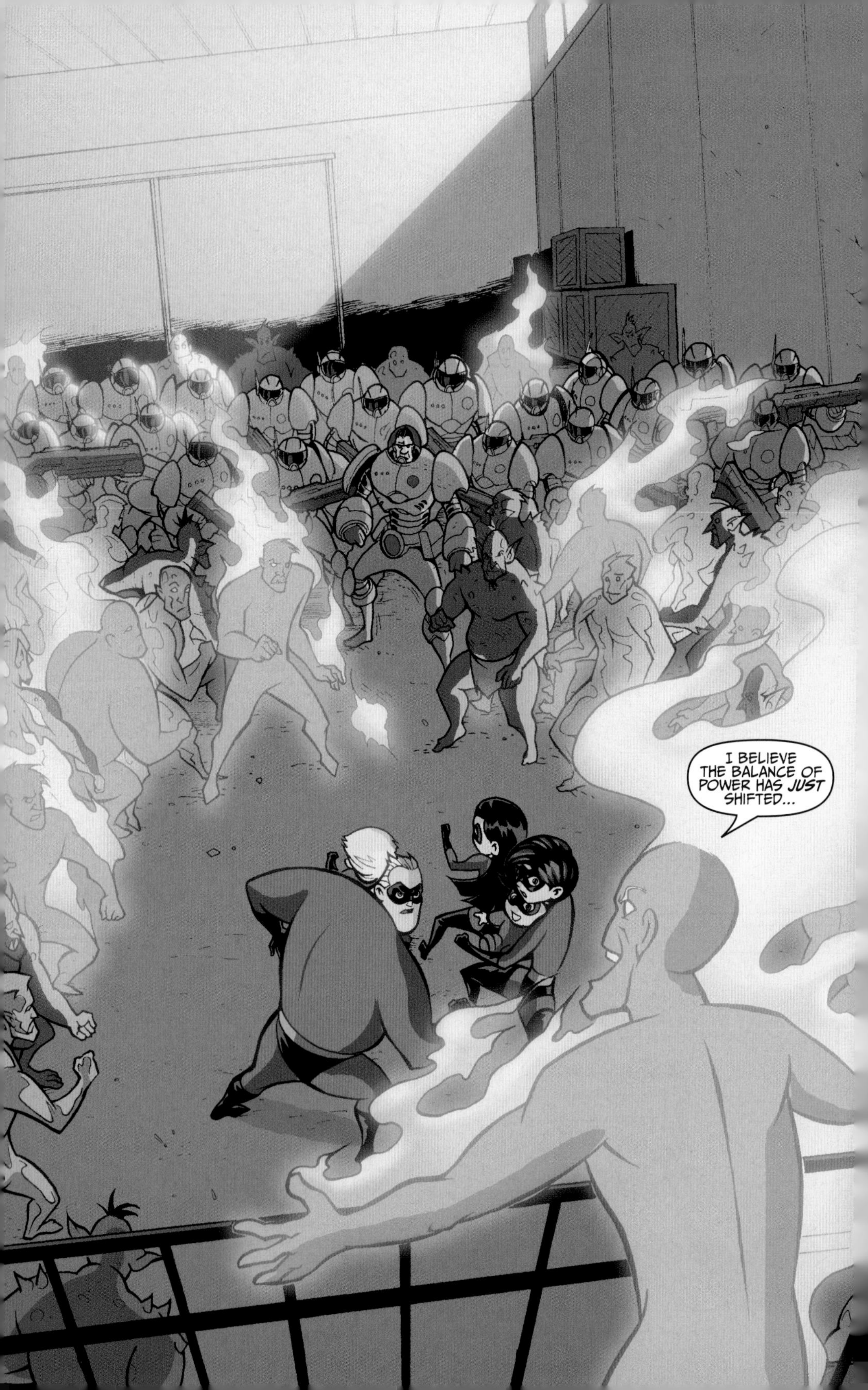
I BELIEVE THE BALANCE OF POWER HAS *JUST* SHIFTED...

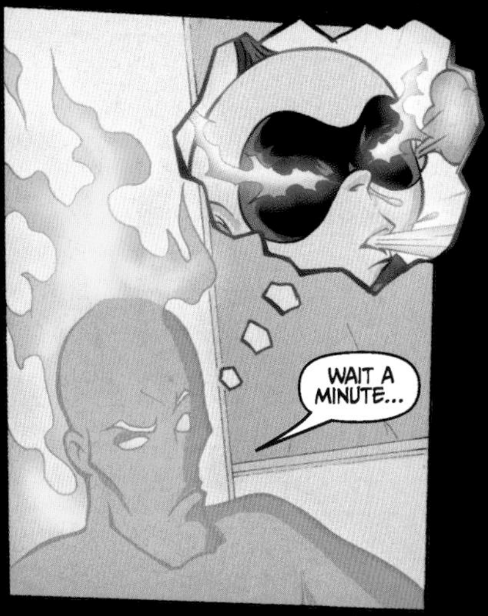
WAIT A MINUTE...

CHAPTER TWO

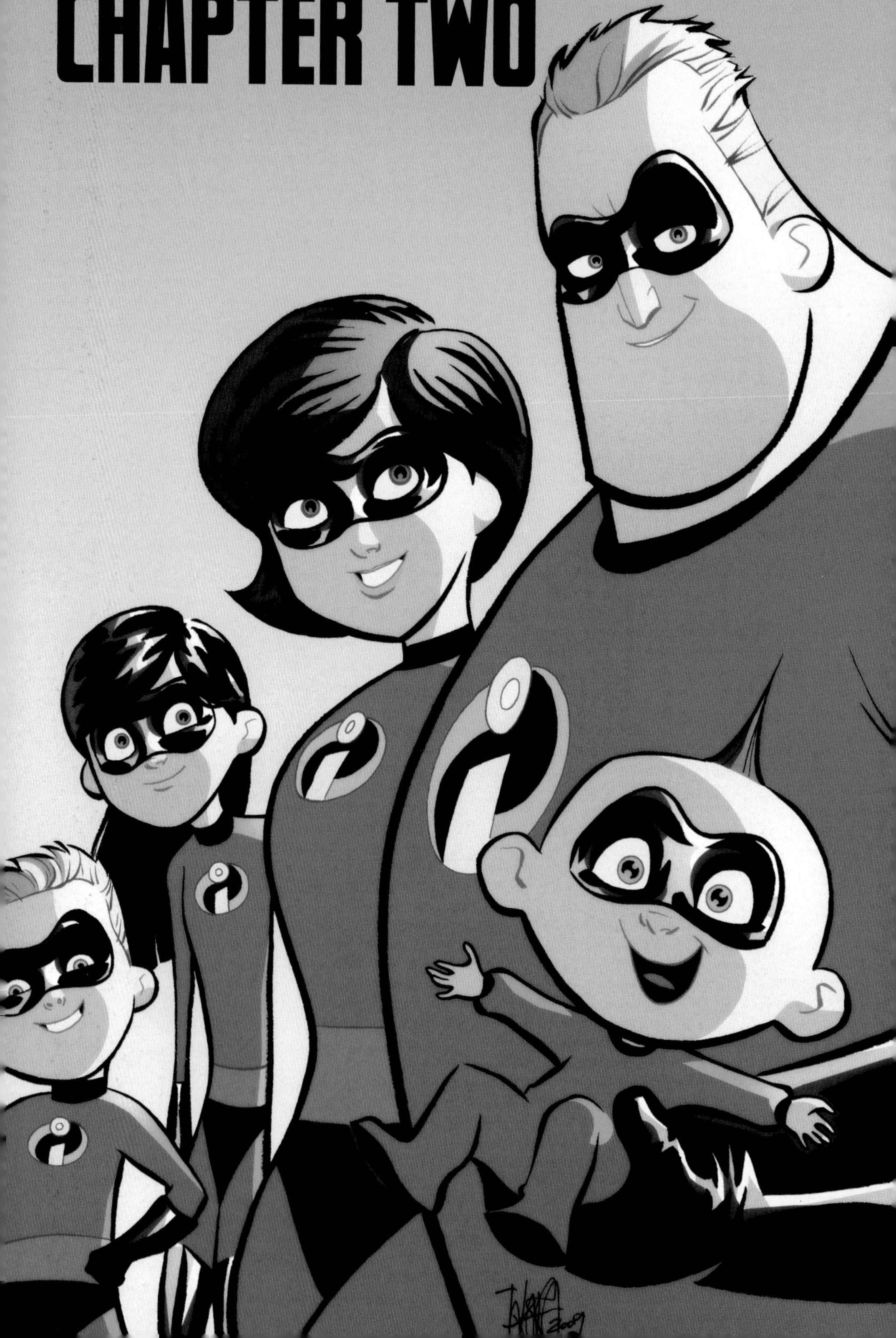

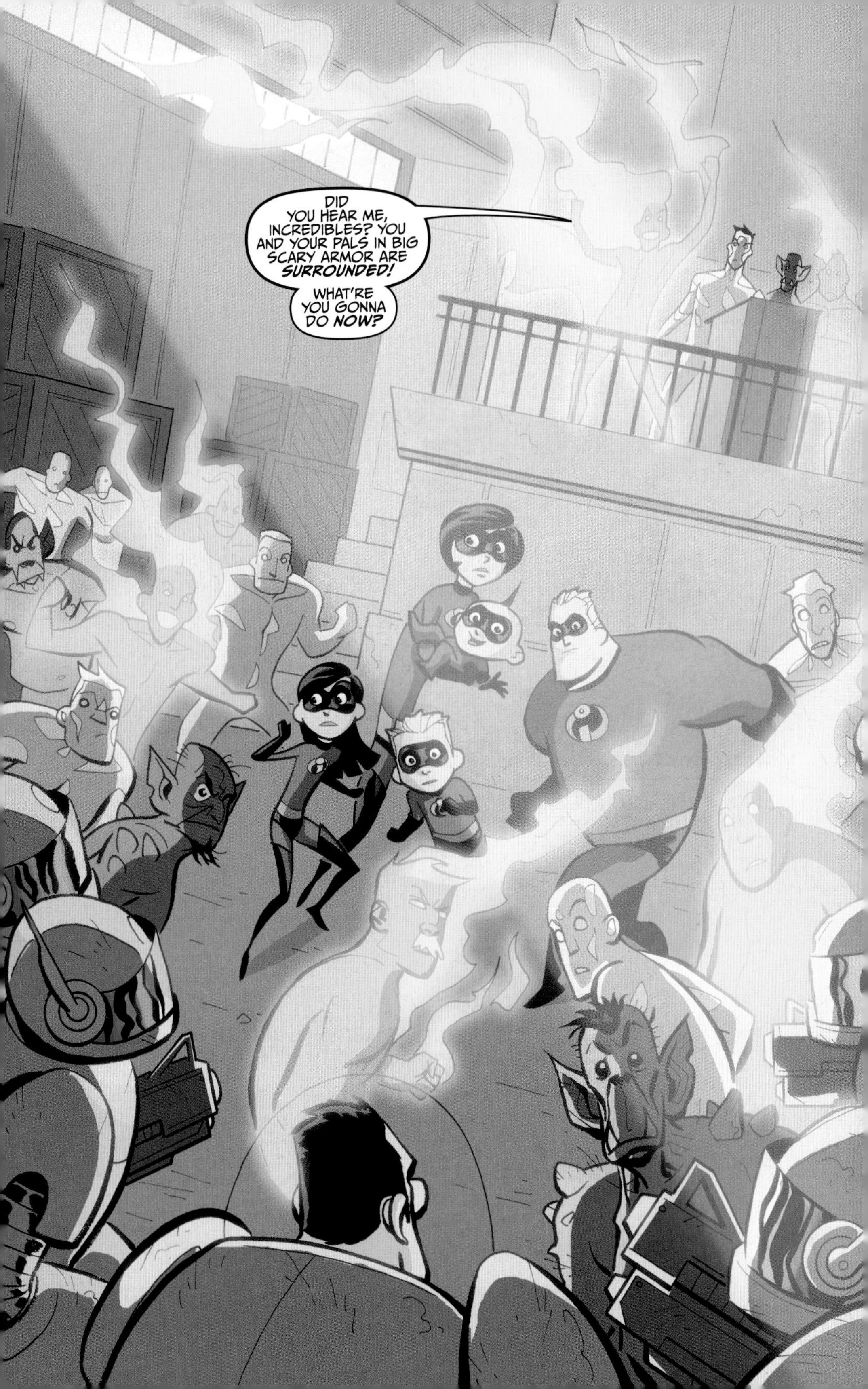
DID YOU HEAR ME, INCREDIBLES? YOU AND YOUR PALS IN BIG SCARY ARMOR ARE **SURROUNDED!**
WHAT'RE YOU GONNA DO **NOW?**

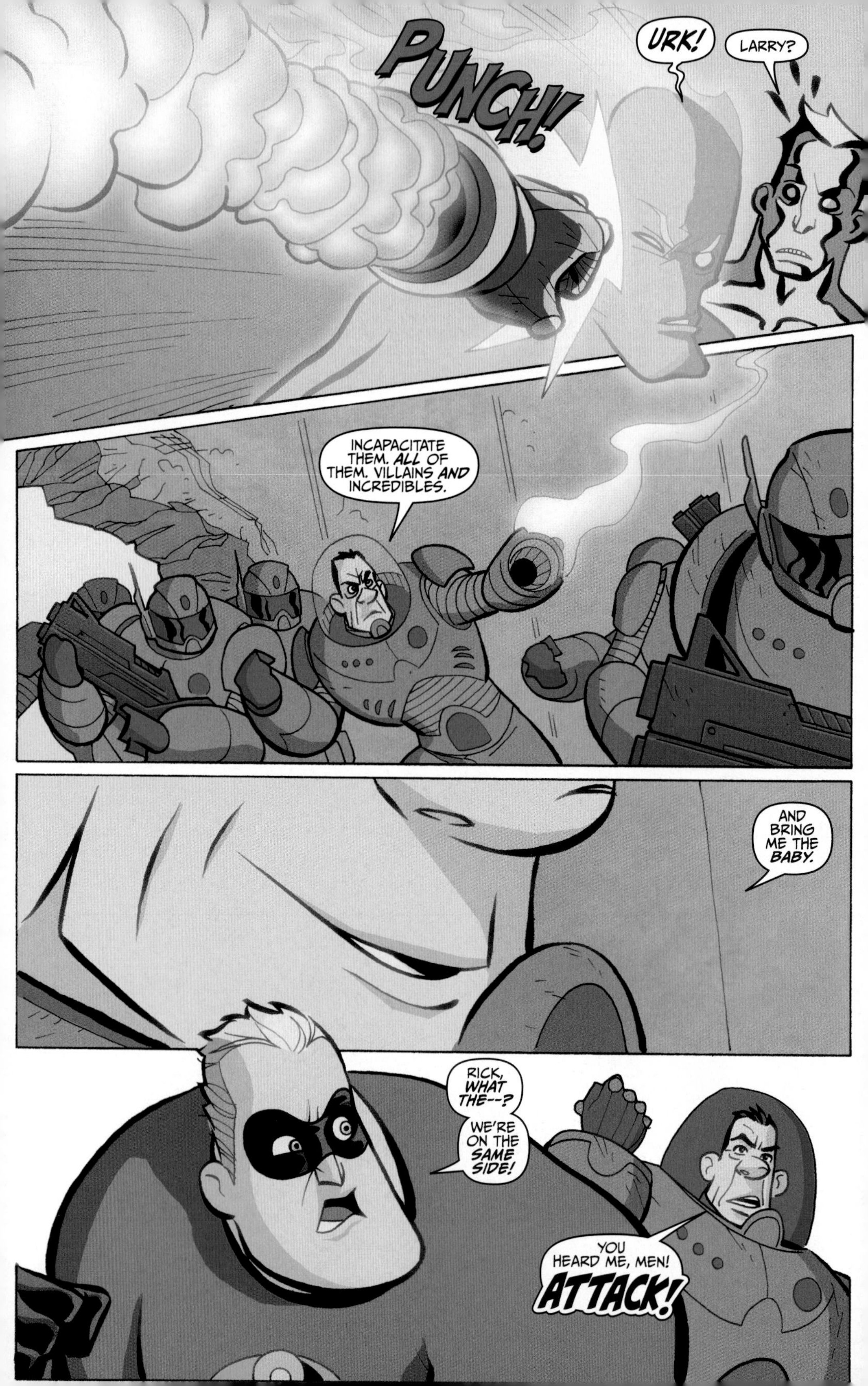
PUNCH!
URK!
LARRY?
INCAPACITATE THEM. ALL OF THEM. VILLAINS AND INCREDIBLES.
AND BRING ME THE BABY.
RICK, WHAT THE--?
WE'RE ON THE SAME SIDE!
YOU HEARD ME, MEN! ATTACK!

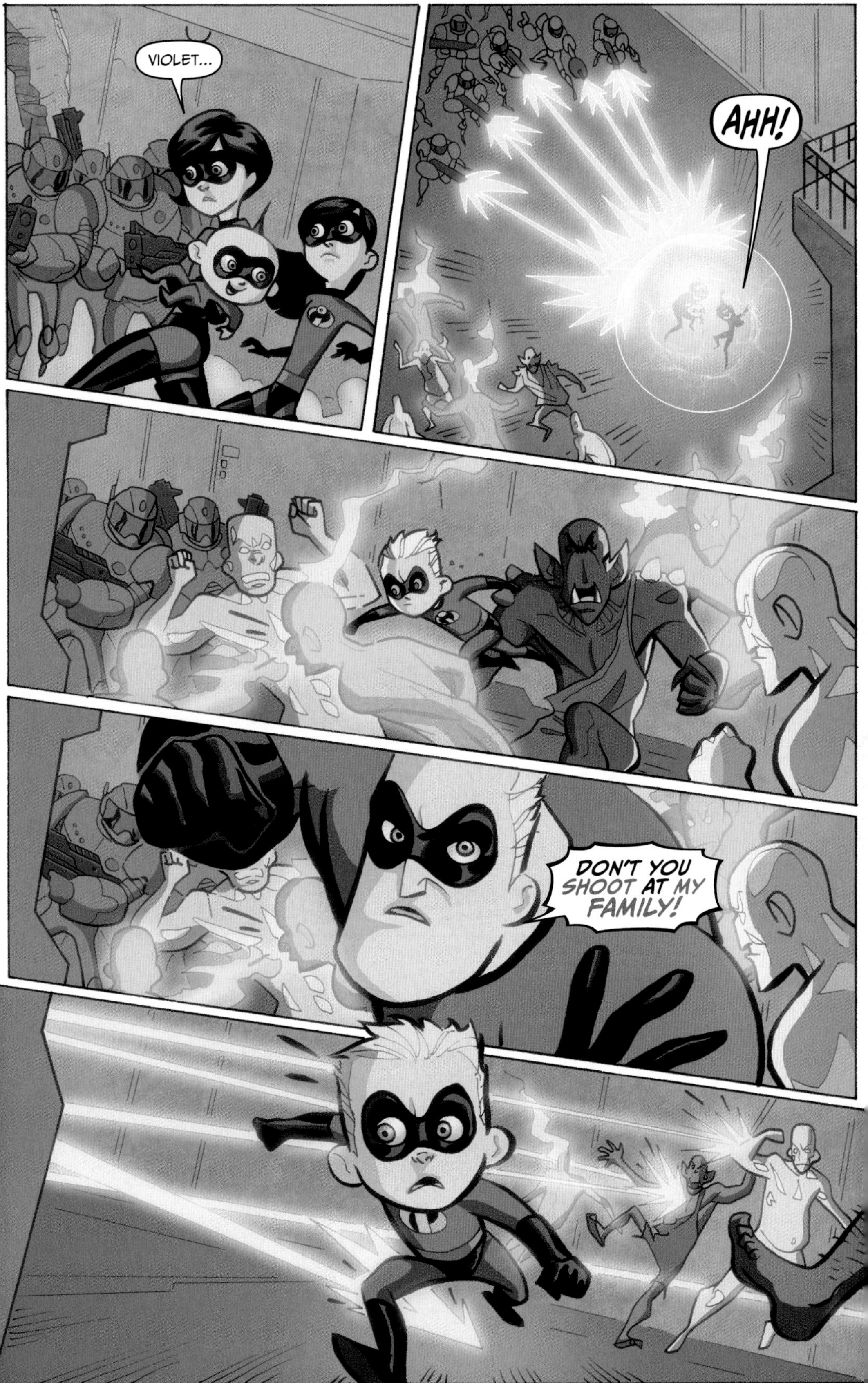
VIOLET...
AHH!
DON'T YOU SHOOT AT MY FAMILY!

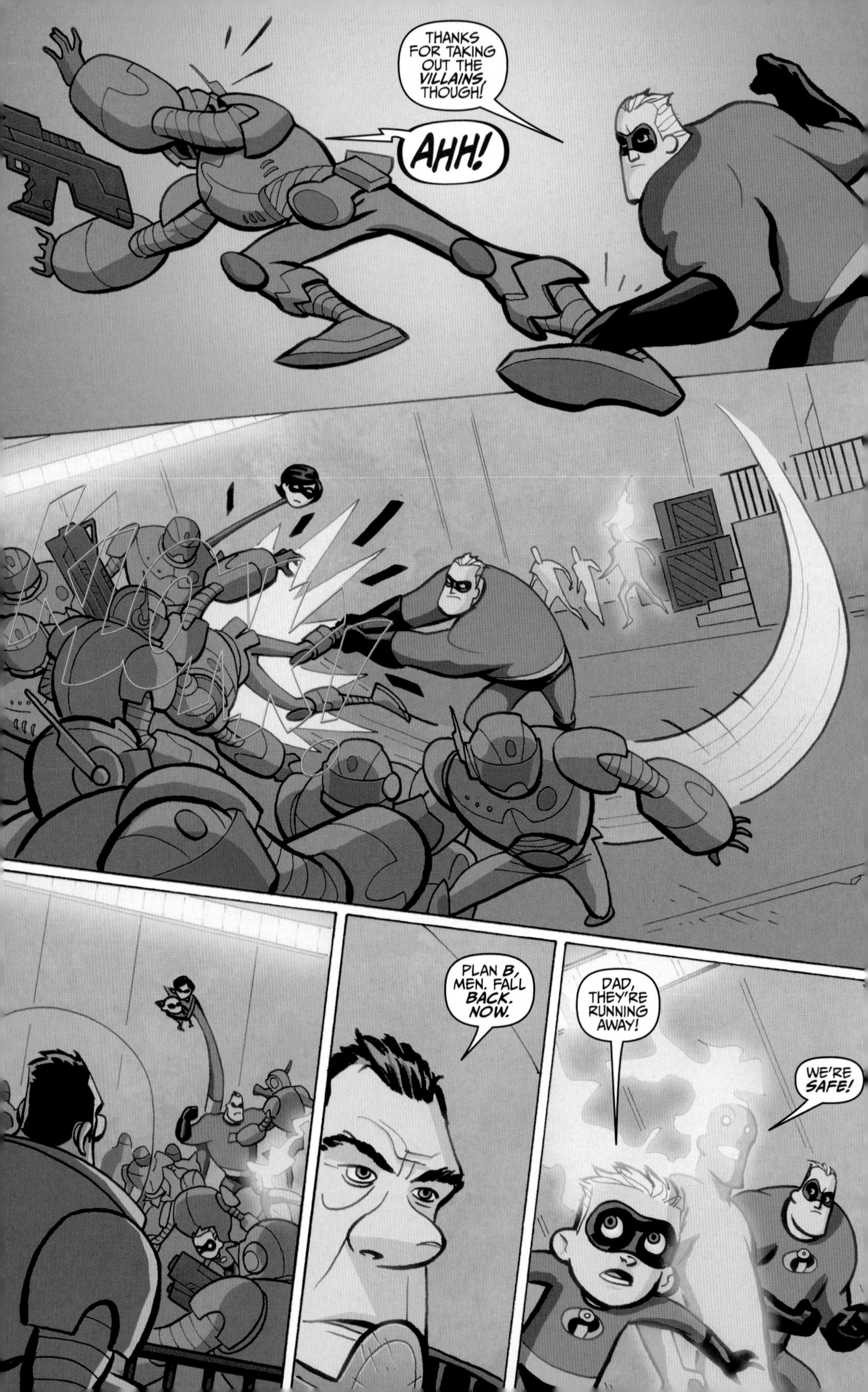
THANKS FOR TAKING OUT THE VILLAINS, THOUGH!
AHH!
PLAN B, MEN. FALL BACK. NOW.
DAD, THEY'RE RUNNING AWAY!
WE'RE SAFE!

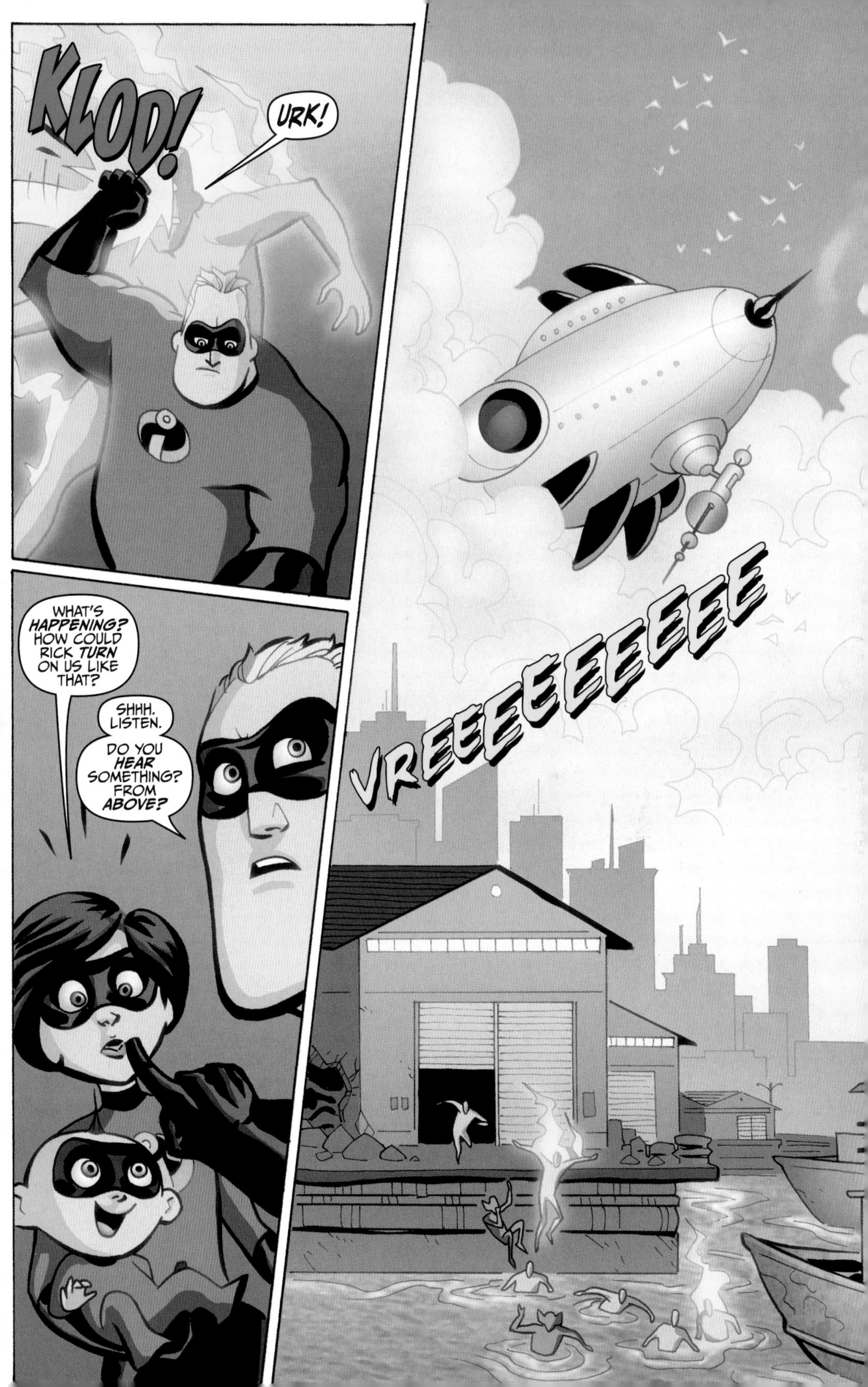
KLOD!
URK!
WHAT'S HAPPENING? HOW COULD RICK TURN ON US LIKE THAT?
SHHH. LISTEN.
DO YOU HEAR SOMETHING? FROM ABOVE?
VREEEEEEEEEEE

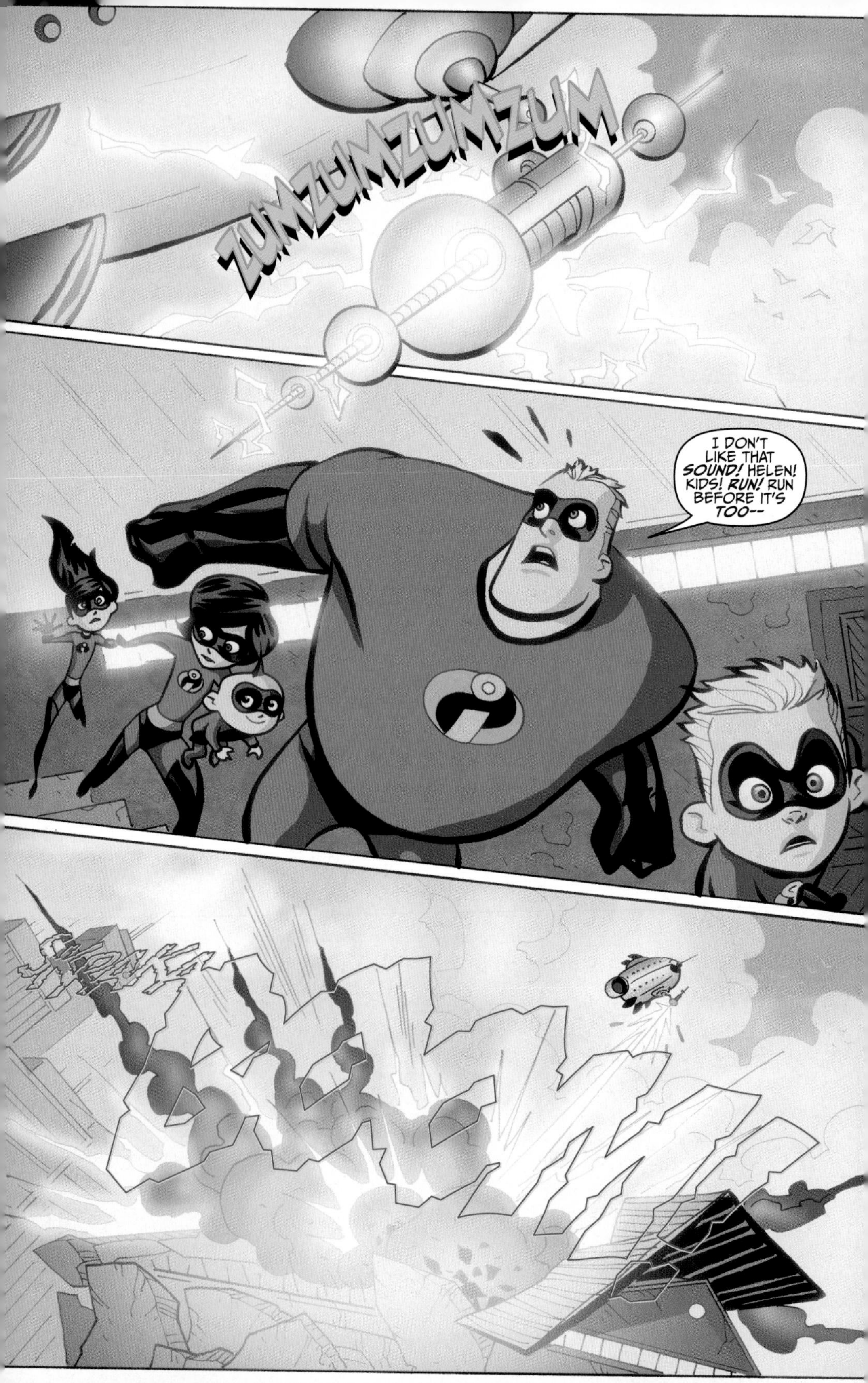
ZUMZUMZUMZUM
I DON'T LIKE THAT SOUND! HELEN! KIDS! RUN! RUN BEFORE IT'S TOO--

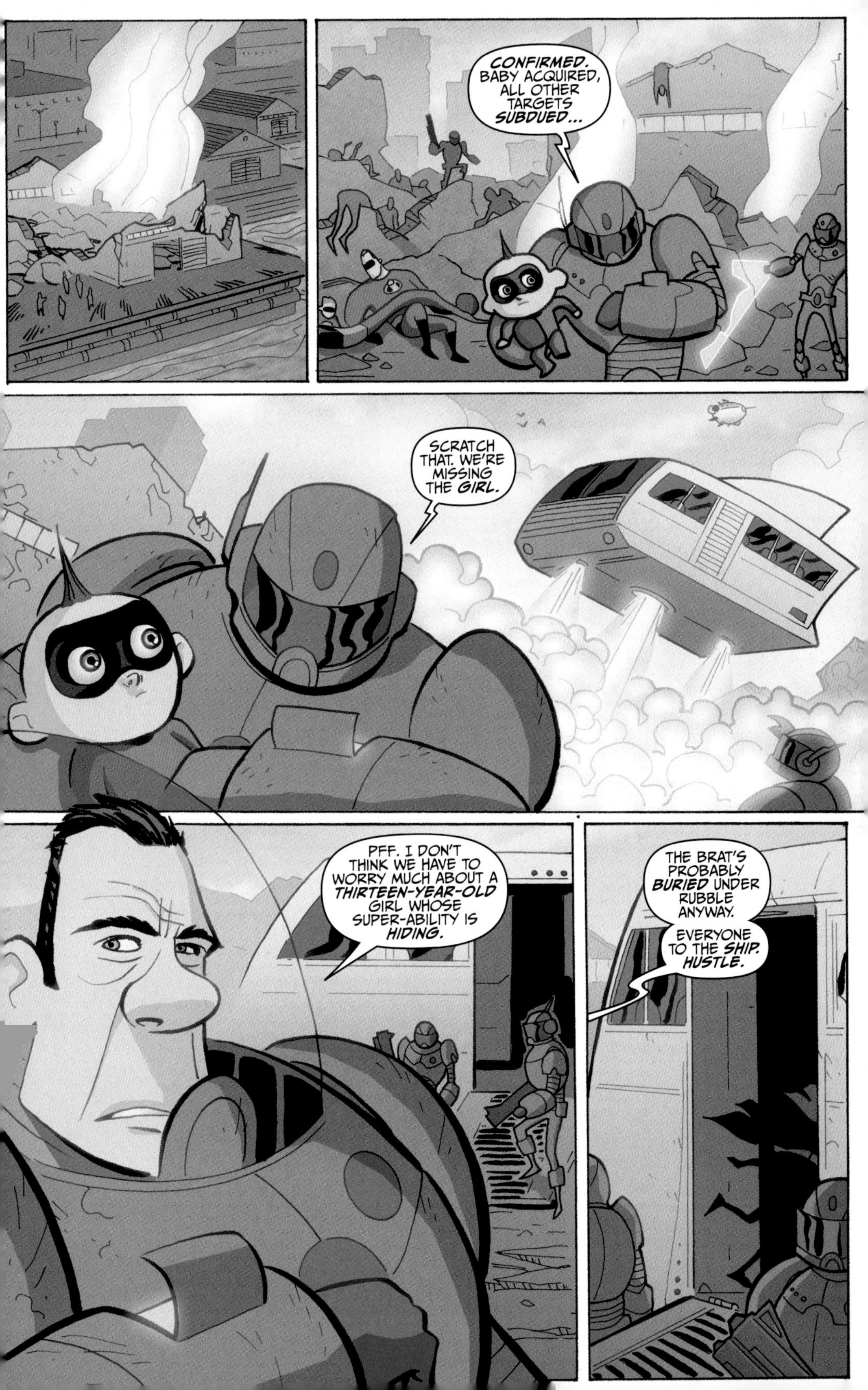
CONFIRMED. BABY ACQUIRED, ALL OTHER TARGETS SUBDUED...
SCRATCH THAT. WE'RE MISSING THE GIRL.
PFF. I DON'T THINK WE HAVE TO WORRY MUCH ABOUT A THIRTEEN-YEAR-OLD GIRL WHOSE SUPER-ABILITY IS HIDING.
THE BRAT'S PROBABLY BURIED UNDER RUBBLE ANYWAY.
EVERYONE TO THE SHIP. HUSTLE.

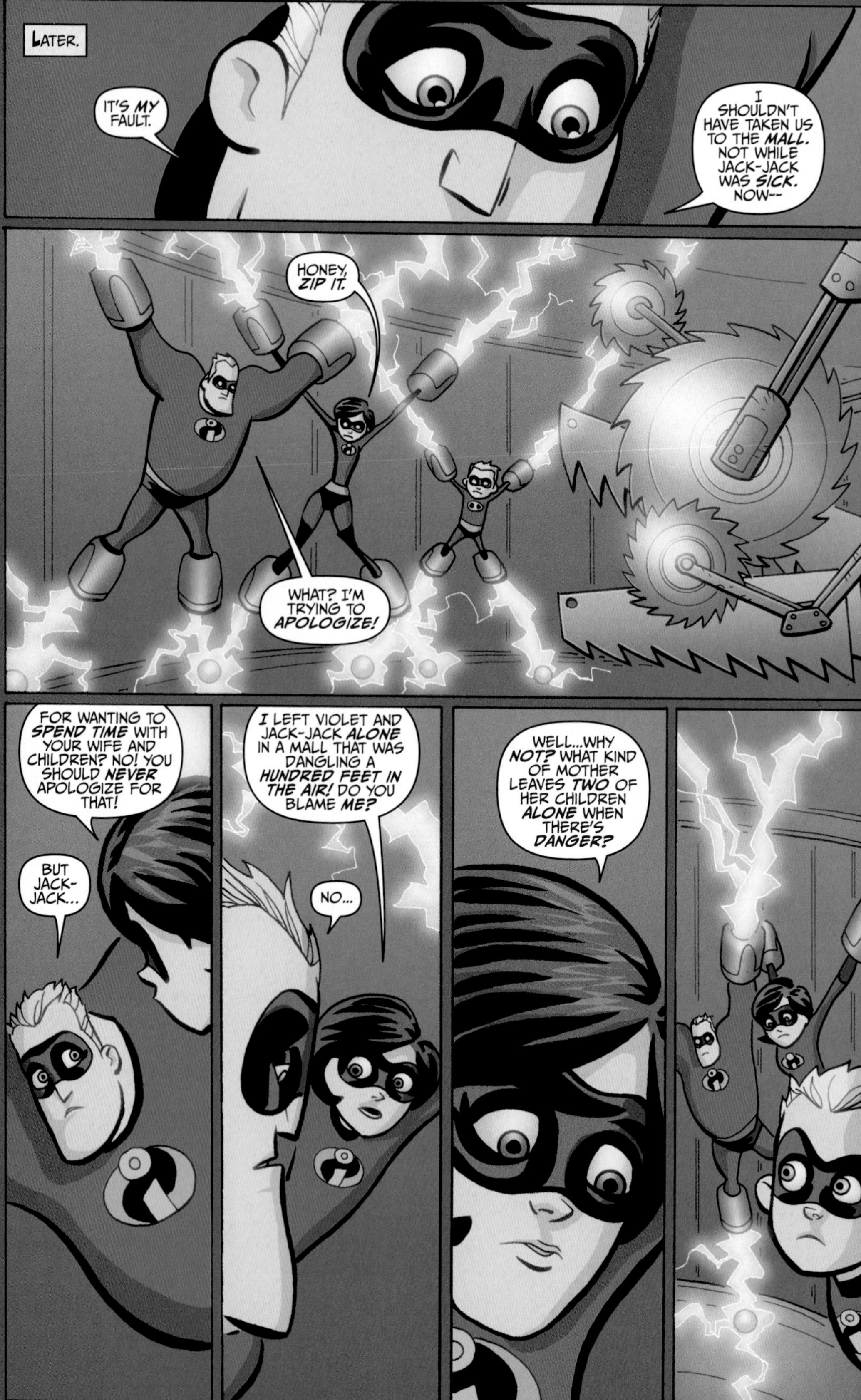
LATER.
IT'S MY FAULT.
I SHOULDN'T HAVE TAKEN US TO THE MALL. NOT WHILE JACK-JACK WAS SICK. NOW--
HONEY, ZIP IT.
WHAT? I'M TRYING TO APOLOGIZE!
FOR WANTING TO SPEND TIME WITH YOUR WIFE AND CHILDREN? NO! YOU SHOULD NEVER APOLOGIZE FOR THAT!
BUT JACK-JACK...
I LEFT VIOLET AND JACK-JACK ALONE IN A MALL THAT WAS DANGLING A HUNDRED FEET IN THE AIR! DO YOU BLAME ME?
NO...
WELL...WHY NOT? WHAT KIND OF MOTHER LEAVES TWO OF HER CHILDREN ALONE WHEN THERE'S DANGER?

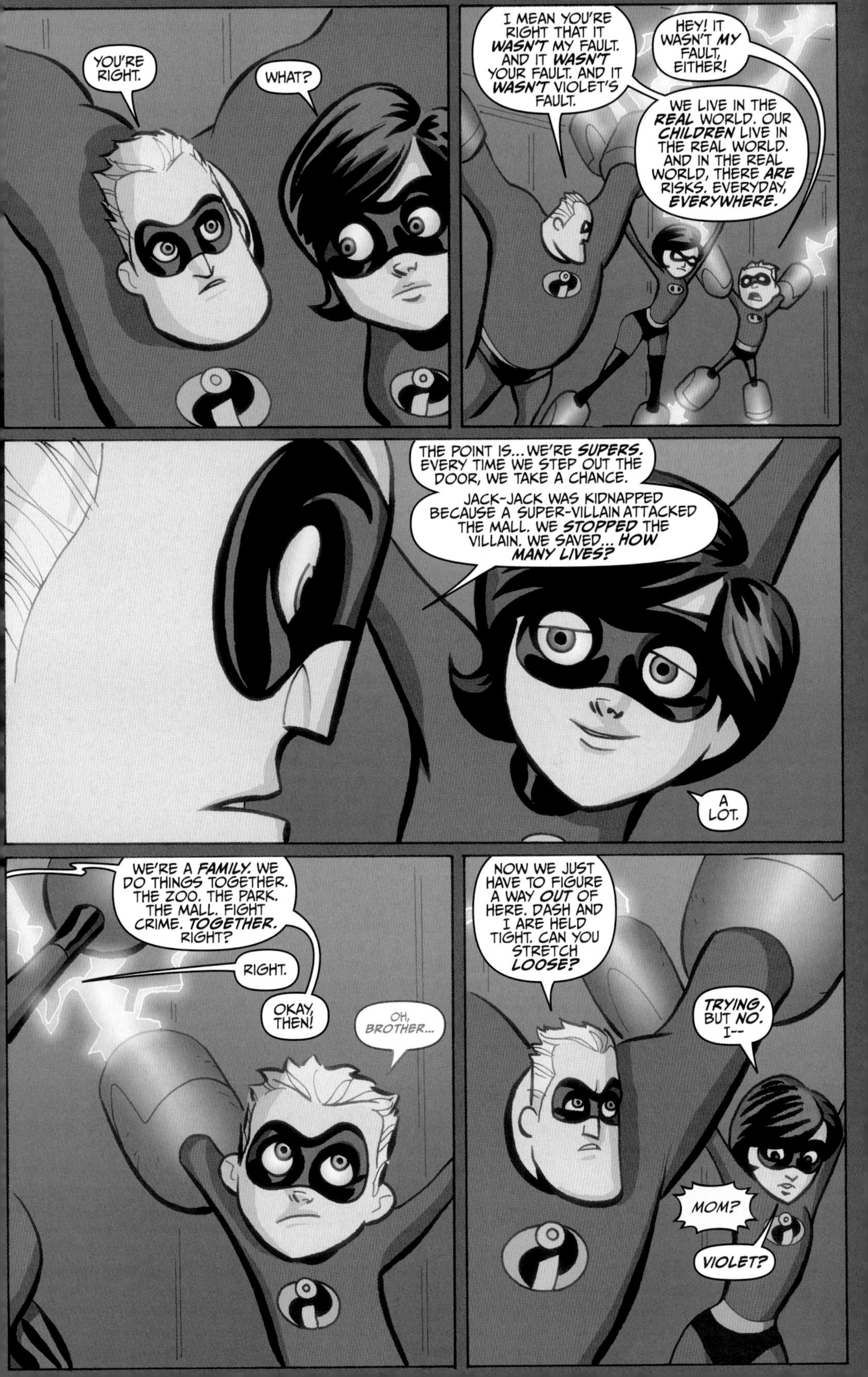
YOU'RE RIGHT.
WHAT?
I MEAN YOU'RE RIGHT THAT IT WASN'T MY FAULT. AND IT WASN'T YOUR FAULT. AND IT WASN'T VIOLET'S FAULT.
HEY! IT WASN'T MY FAULT, EITHER!
WE LIVE IN THE REAL WORLD. OUR CHILDREN LIVE IN THE REAL WORLD. AND IN THE REAL WORLD, THERE ARE RISKS. EVERYDAY, EVERYWHERE.
THE POINT IS... WE'RE SUPERS. EVERY TIME WE STEP OUT THE DOOR, WE TAKE A CHANCE.
JACK-JACK WAS KIDNAPPED BECAUSE A SUPER-VILLAIN ATTACKED THE MALL. WE STOPPED THE VILLAIN. WE SAVED... HOW MANY LIVES?
A LOT.
WE'RE A FAMILY. WE DO THINGS TOGETHER. THE ZOO. THE PARK. THE MALL. FIGHT CRIME. TOGETHER. RIGHT?
RIGHT.
OKAY, THEN!
OH, BROTHER...
NOW WE JUST HAVE TO FIGURE A WAY OUT OF HERE. DASH AND I ARE HELD TIGHT. CAN YOU STRETCH LOOSE?
TRYING, BUT NO. I--
MOM?
VIOLET?

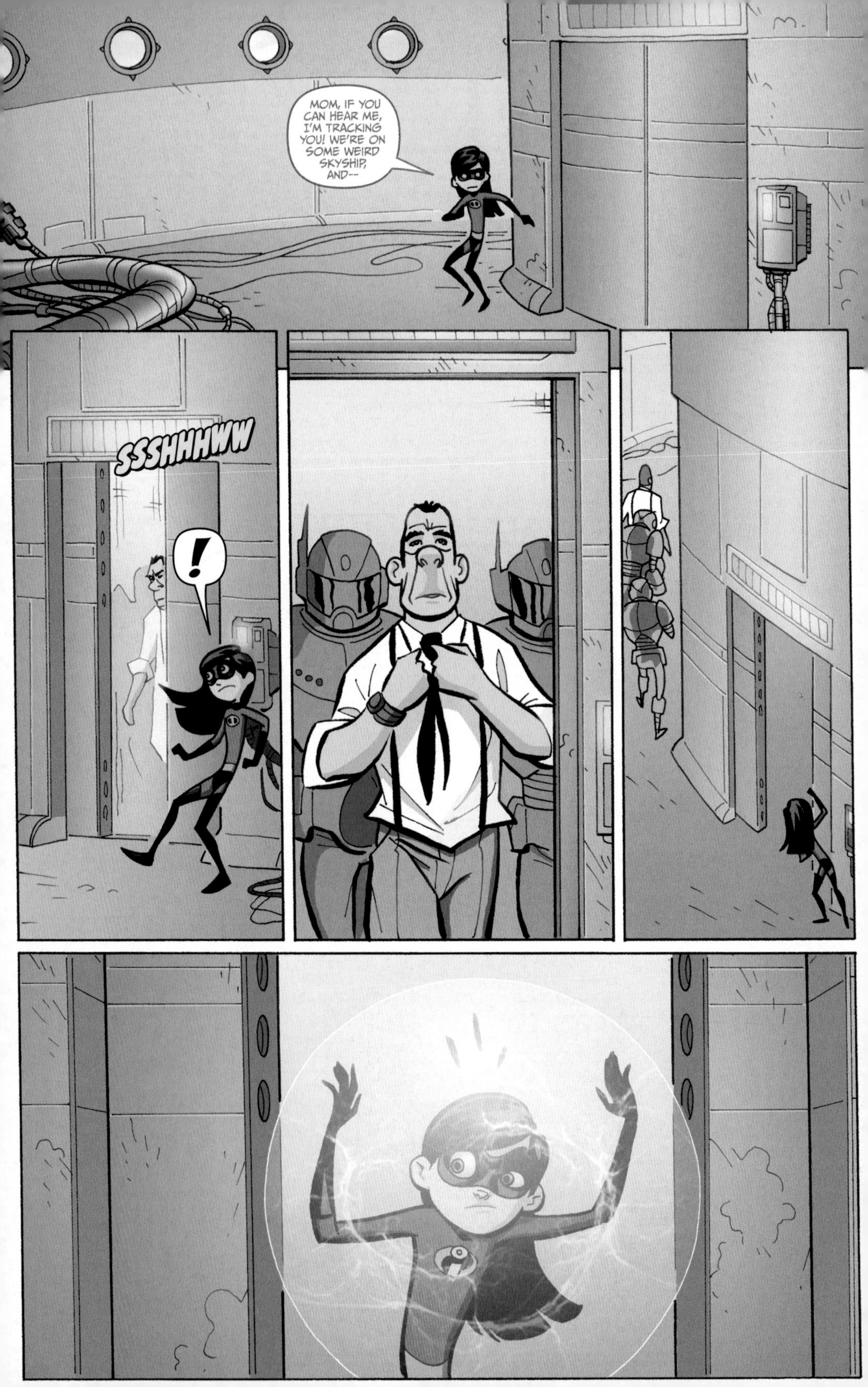
MOM, IF YOU CAN HEAR ME, I'M TRACKING YOU! WE'RE ON SOME WEIRD SKYSHIP, AND--
SSSHHHWW
!

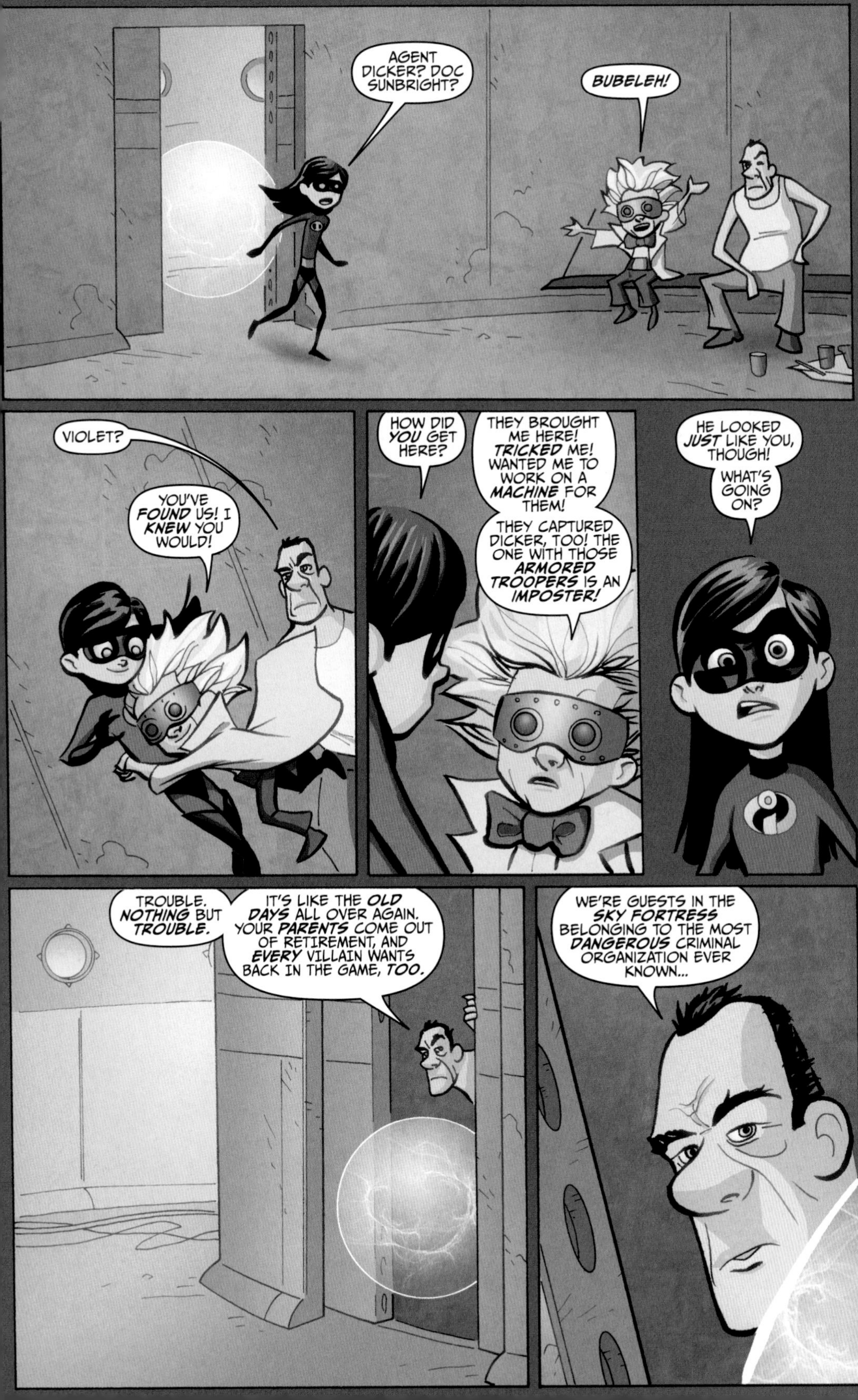
AGENT DICKER? DOC SUNBRIGHT?
BUBELEH!
VIOLET?
YOU'VE FOUND US! I KNEW YOU WOULD!
HOW DID YOU GET HERE?
THEY BROUGHT ME HERE! TRICKED ME! WANTED ME TO WORK ON A MACHINE FOR THEM!
THEY CAPTURED DICKER, TOO! THE ONE WITH THOSE ARMORED TROOPERS IS AN IMPOSTER!
HE LOOKED JUST LIKE YOU, THOUGH!
WHAT'S GOING ON?
TROUBLE. NOTHING BUT TROUBLE.
IT'S LIKE THE OLD DAYS ALL OVER AGAIN. YOUR PARENTS COME OUT OF RETIREMENT, AND EVERY VILLAIN WANTS BACK IN THE GAME, TOO.
WE'RE GUESTS IN THE SKY FORTRESS BELONGING TO THE MOST DANGEROUS CRIMINAL ORGANIZATION EVER KNOWN...

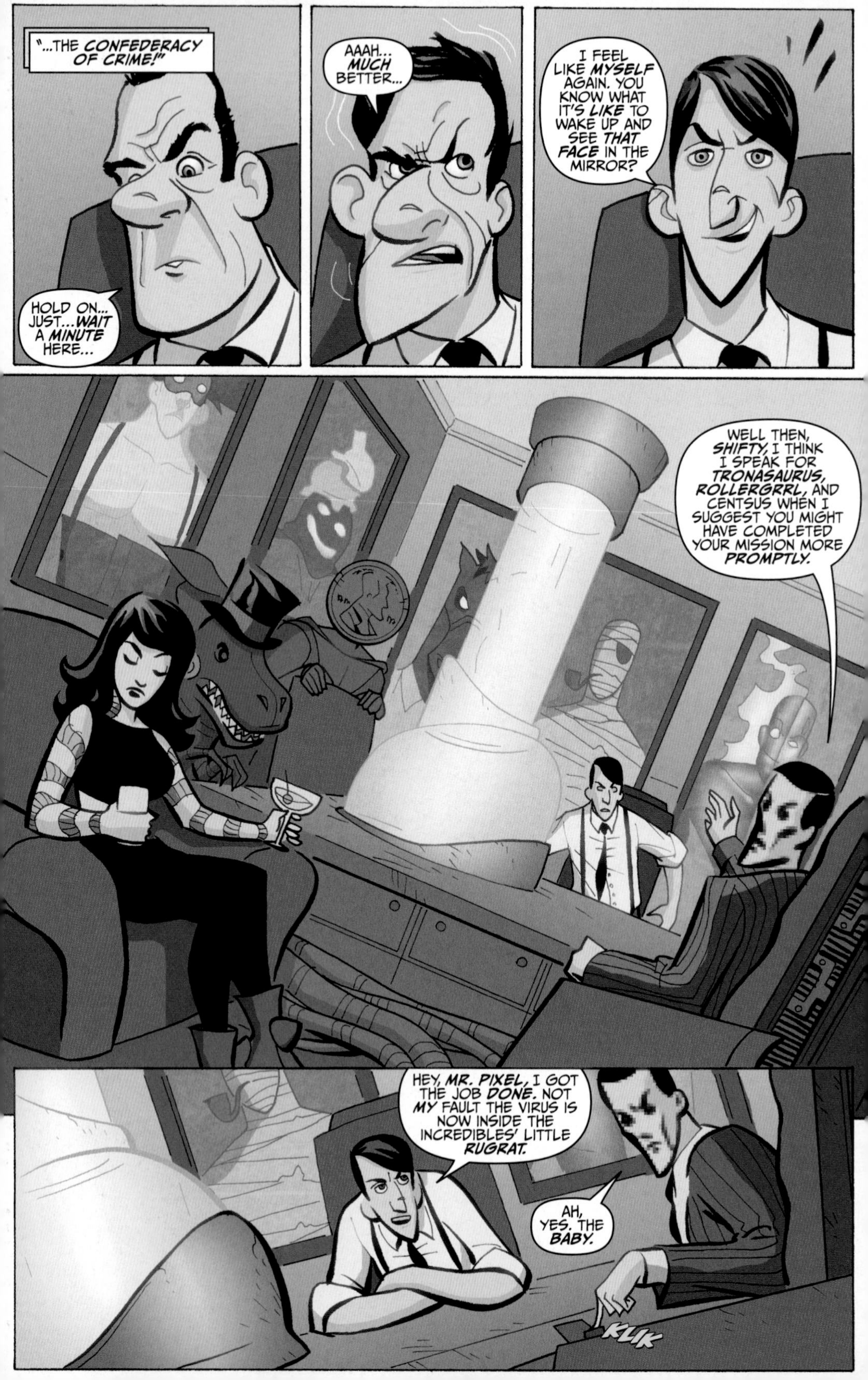
"...THE CONFEDERACY OF CRIME!"
HOLD ON... JUST...WAIT A MINUTE HERE...
AAAH... MUCH BETTER...
I FEEL LIKE MYSELF AGAIN. YOU KNOW WHAT IT'S LIKE TO WAKE UP AND SEE THAT FACE IN THE MIRROR?
WELL THEN, SHIFTY, I THINK I SPEAK FOR TRONASAURUS, ROLLERGRRL, AND CENTSUS WHEN I SUGGEST YOU MIGHT HAVE COMPLETED YOUR MISSION MORE PROMPTLY.
HEY, MR. PIXEL, I GOT THE JOB DONE. NOT MY FAULT THE VIRUS IS NOW INSIDE THE INCREDIBLES' LITTLE RUGRAT.
AH, YES. THE BABY.
KLIK

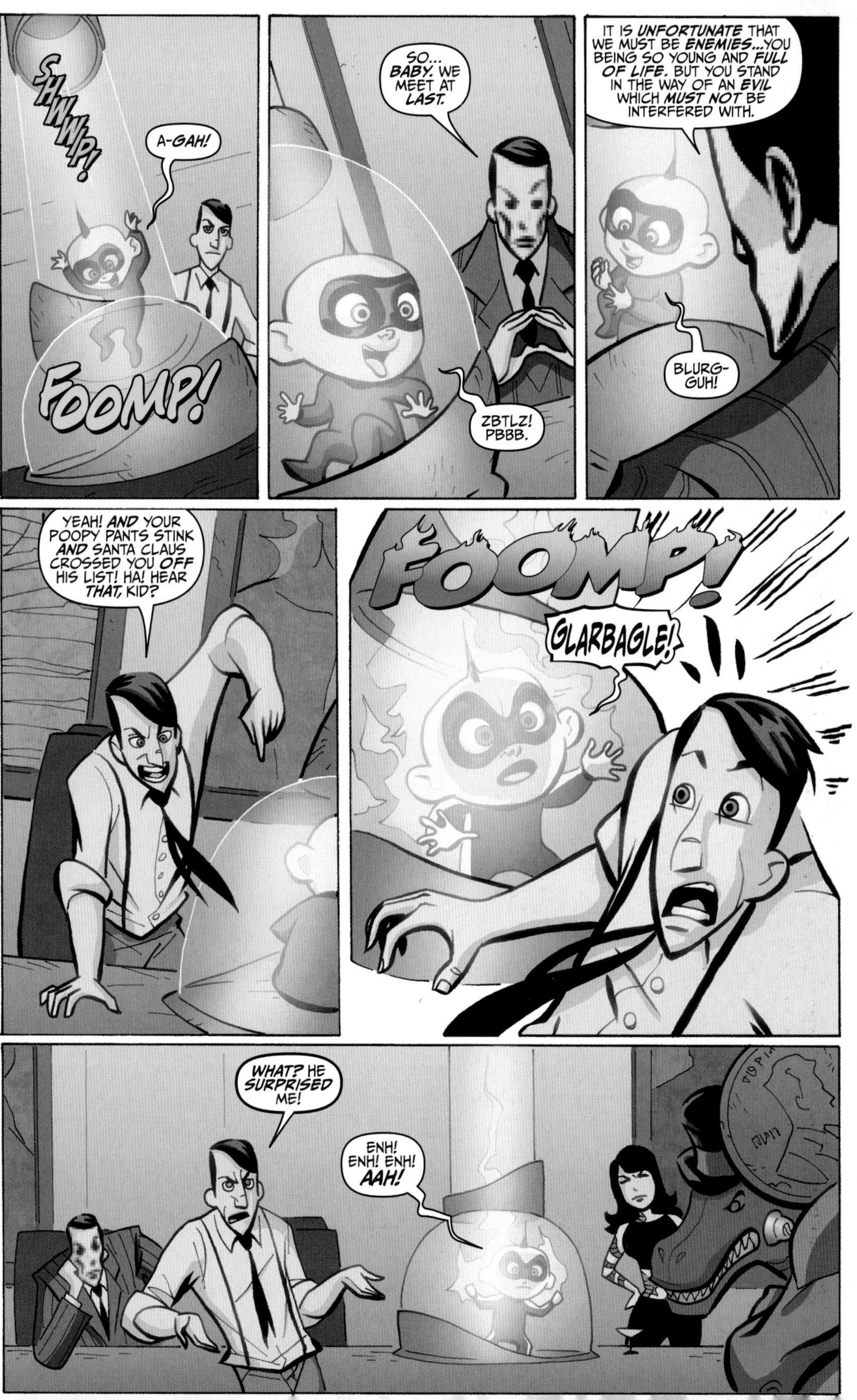
SHWWIP!
A-GAH!
FOOMP!
SO... BABY. WE MEET AT LAST.
ZBTLZ! PBBB.
IT IS UNFORTUNATE THAT WE MUST BE ENEMIES...YOU BEING SO YOUNG AND FULL OF LIFE. BUT YOU STAND IN THE WAY OF AN EVIL WHICH MUST NOT BE INTERFERED WITH.
BLURG-GUH!
YEAH! AND YOUR POOPY PANTS STINK AND SANTA CLAUS CROSSED YOU OFF HIS LIST! HA! HEAR THAT, KID?
FOOMP!
GLARBAGLE!
WHAT? HE SURPRISED ME!
ENH! ENH! ENH! AAH!

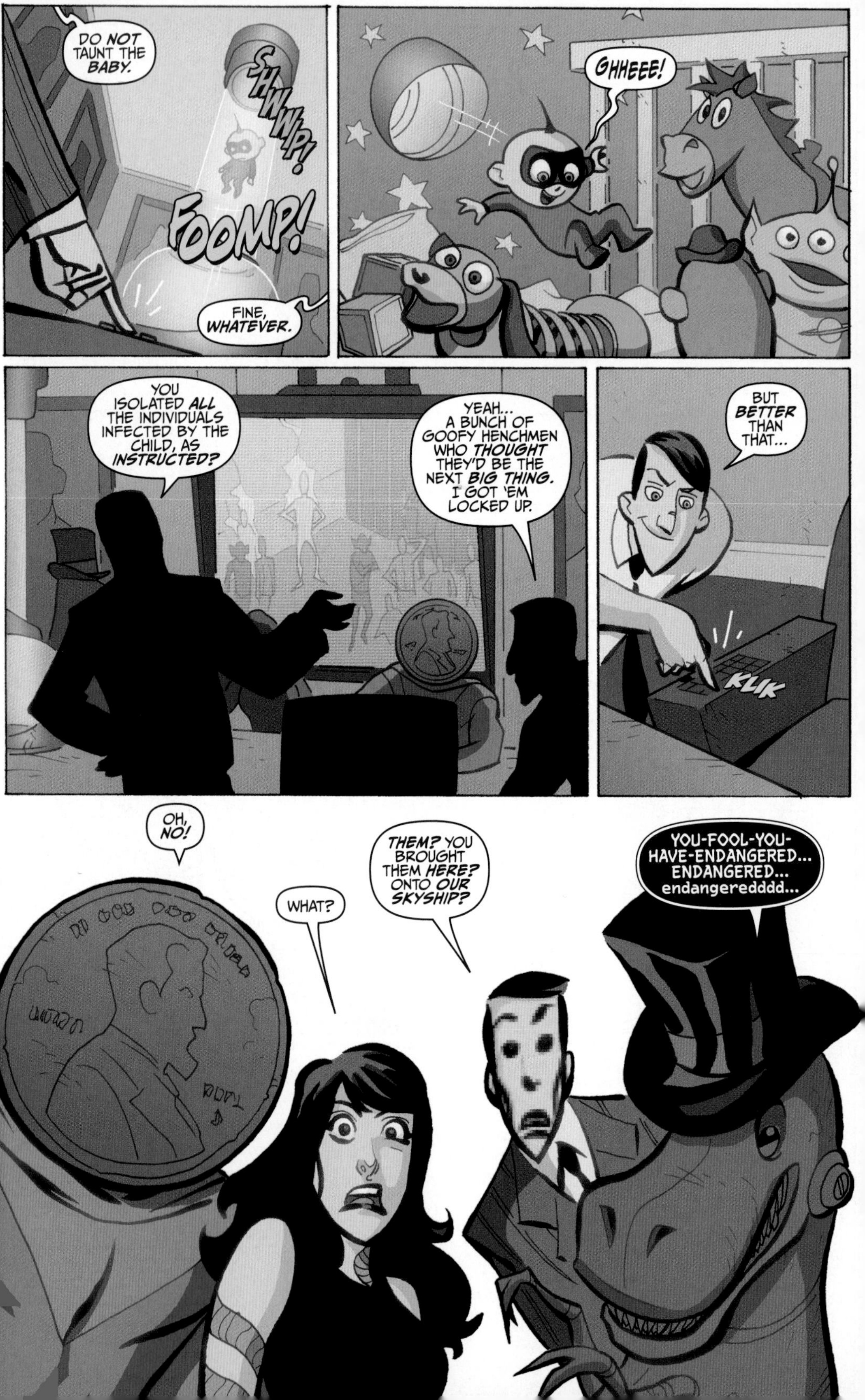
DO NOT TAUNT THE BABY.
SHWWIP!
FOOMP!
FINE, WHATEVER.
GHHEEE!
YOU ISOLATED ALL THE INDIVIDUALS INFECTED BY THE CHILD, AS INSTRUCTED?
YEAH... A BUNCH OF GOOFY HENCHMEN WHO THOUGHT THEY'D BE THE NEXT BIG THING. I GOT 'EM LOCKED UP.
BUT BETTER THAN THAT...
KLIK
OH, NO!
WHAT?
THEM? YOU BROUGHT THEM HERE? ONTO OUR SKYSHIP?
YOU-FOOL-YOU-HAVE-ENDANGERED... ENDANGERED... endangeredddd...

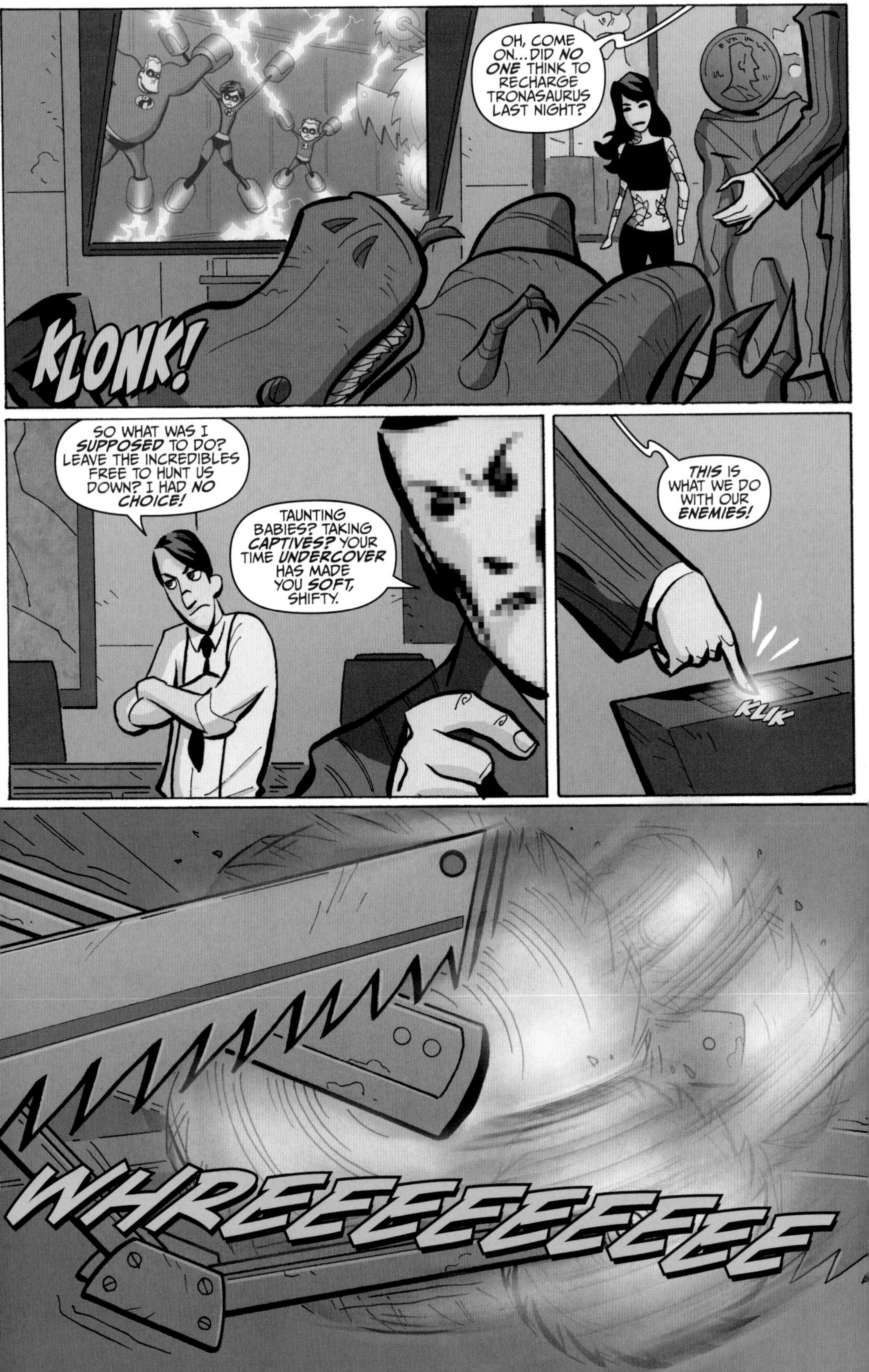
OH, COME ON...DID NO ONE THINK TO RECHARGE TRONASAURUS LAST NIGHT?
KLONK!
SO WHAT WAS I SUPPOSED TO DO? LEAVE THE INCREDIBLES FREE TO HUNT US DOWN? I HAD NO CHOICE!
TAUNTING BABIES? TAKING CAPTIVES? YOUR TIME UNDERCOVER HAS MADE YOU SOFT, SHIFTY.
THIS IS WHAT WE DO WITH OUR ENEMIES!
KLIK
WHREEEEEEEEEE

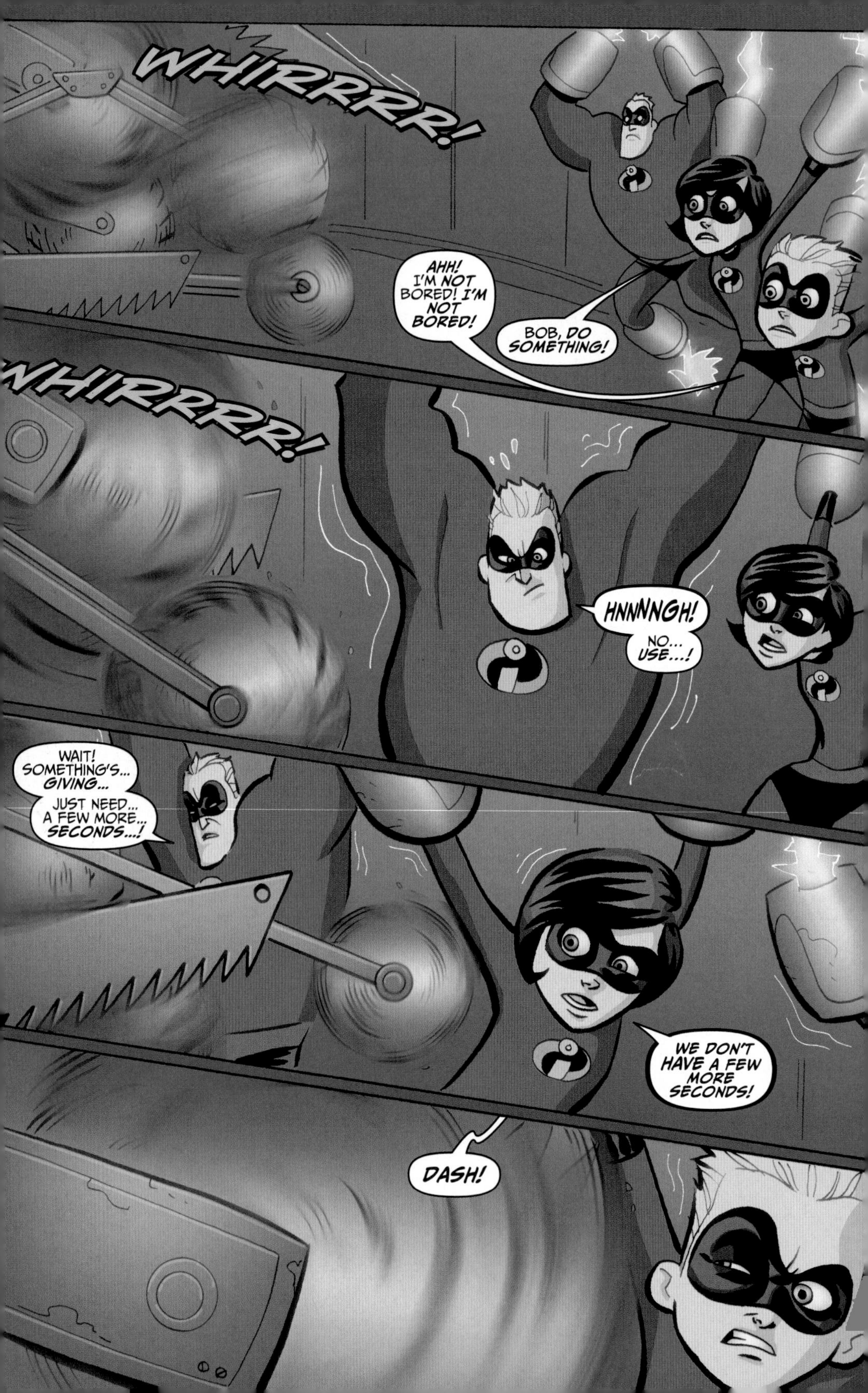
WHIRRRR!
AHH! I'M NOT BORED! I'M NOT BORED!
BOB, DO SOMETHING!
WHIRRRR!
HNNNNGH!
NO... USE...!
WAIT! SOMETHING'S... GIVING... JUST NEED... A FEW MORE... SECONDS...!
WE DON'T HAVE A FEW MORE SECONDS!
DASH!

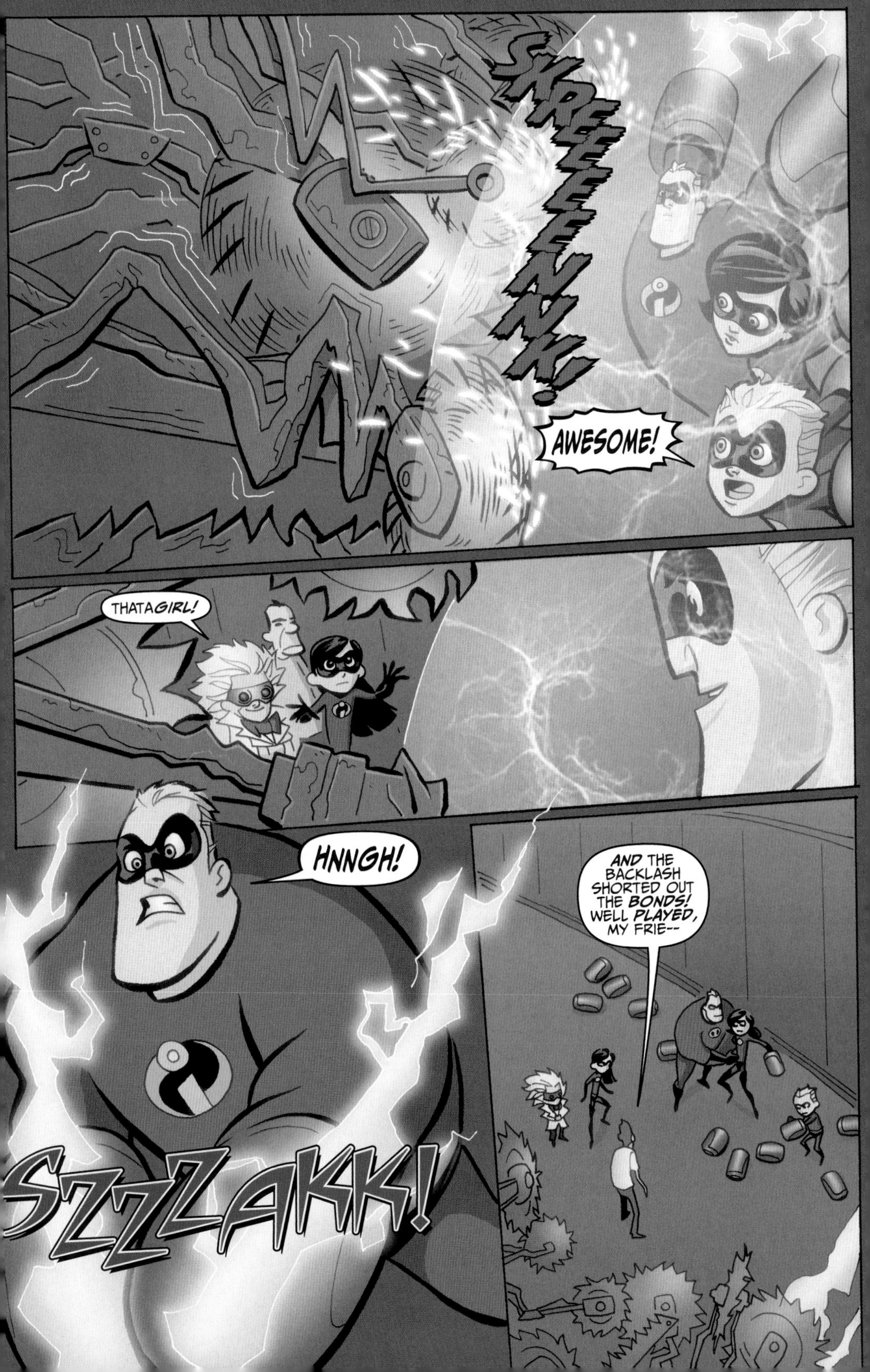

SKREEEENNK!
AWESOME!
THATA GIRL!
HNNGH!
SZZZAKK!
AND THE BACKLASH SHORTED OUT THE BONDS! WELL PLAYED, MY FRIE--

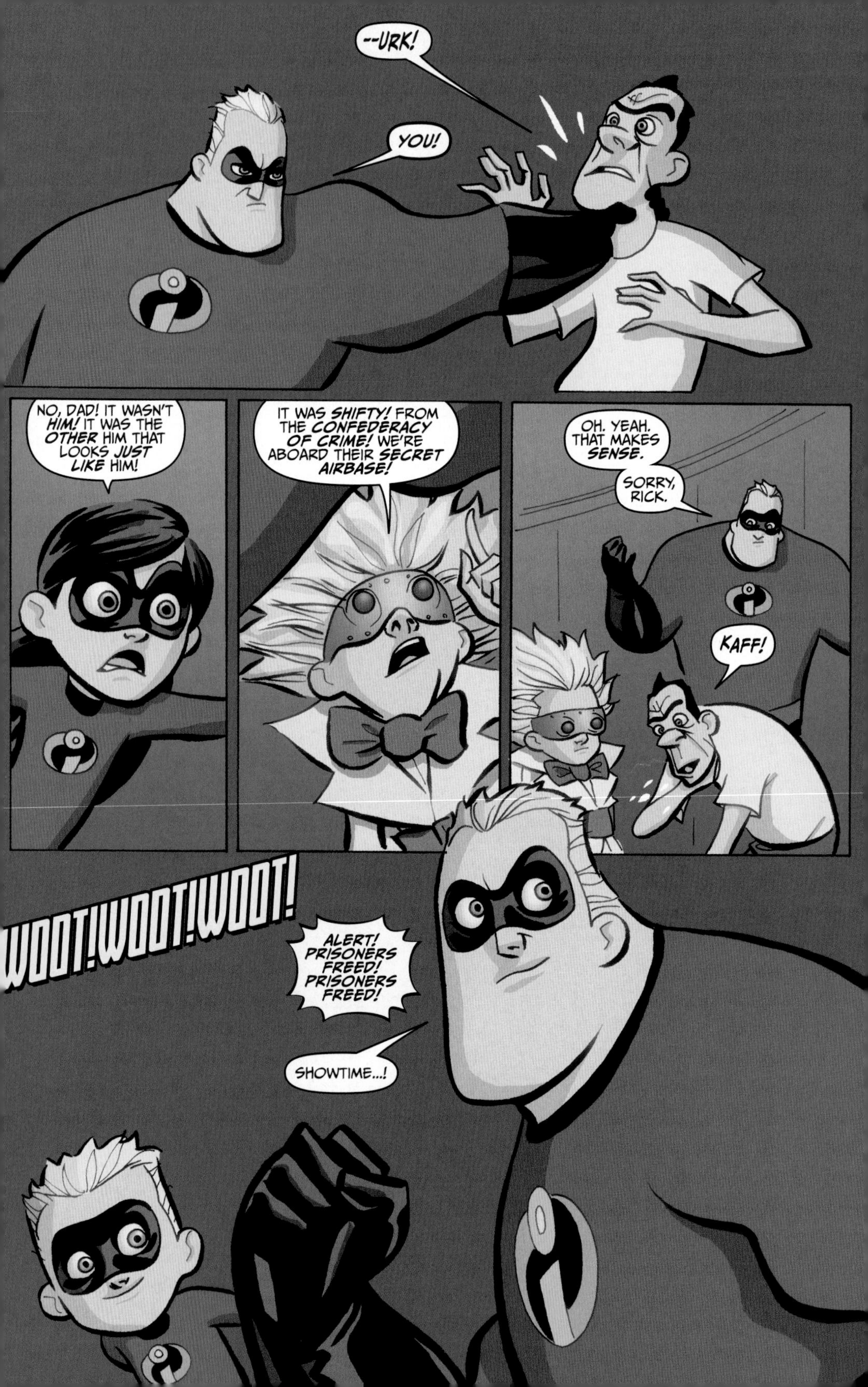
--URK!
YOU!
NO, DAD! IT WASN'T HIM! IT WAS THE OTHER HIM THAT LOOKS JUST LIKE HIM!
IT WAS SHIFTY! FROM THE CONFEDERACY OF CRIME! WE'RE ABOARD THEIR SECRET AIRBASE!
OH. YEAH. THAT MAKES SENSE.
SORRY, RICK.
KAFF!
WOOT!WOOT!WOOT!
ALERT! PRISONERS FREED! PRISONERS FREED!
SHOWTIME...!

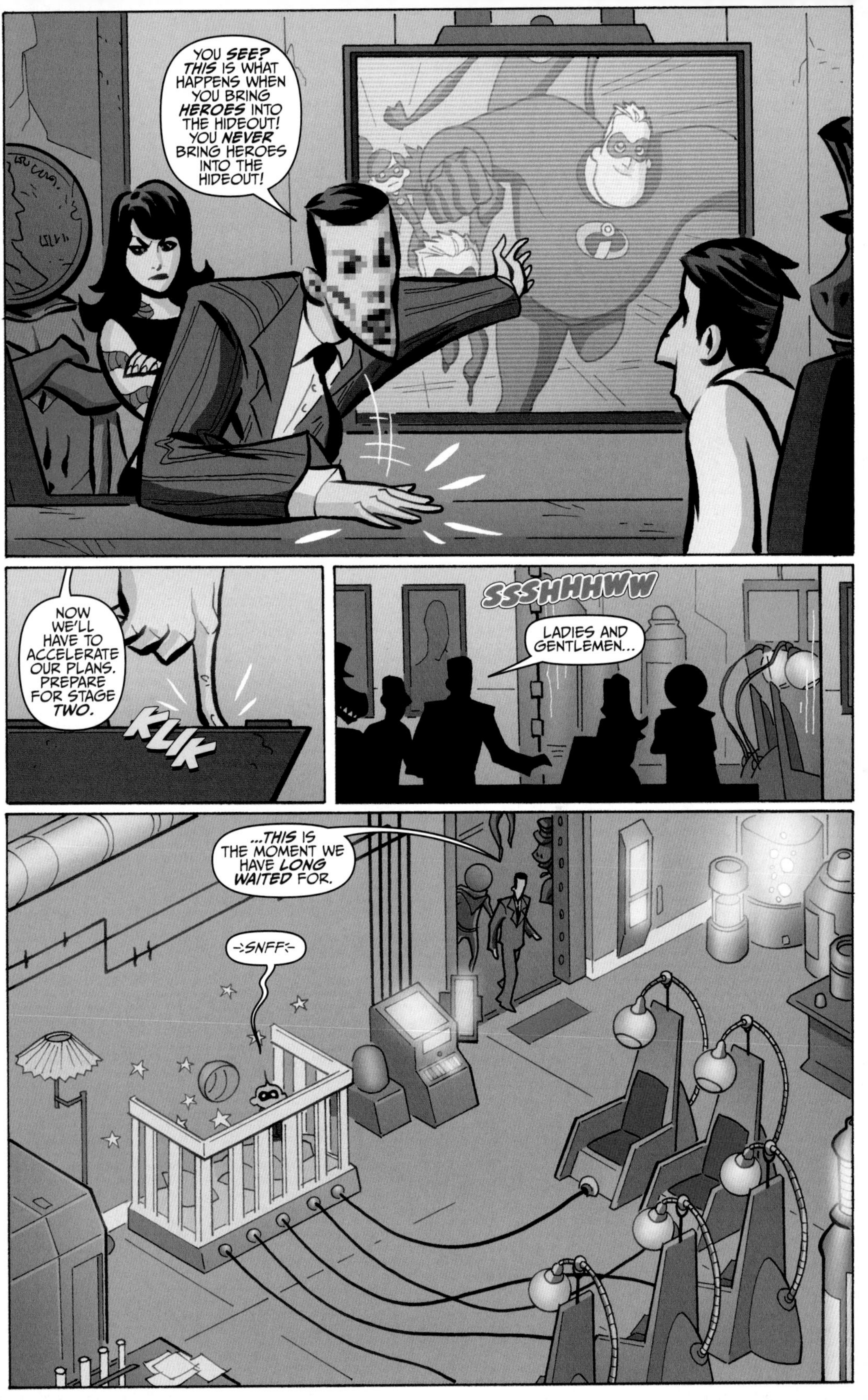

YOU SEE? THIS IS WHAT HAPPENS WHEN YOU BRING HEROES INTO THE HIDEOUT! YOU NEVER BRING HEROES INTO THE HIDEOUT!
NOW WE'LL HAVE TO ACCELERATE OUR PLANS. PREPARE FOR STAGE TWO.
KLIK
SSSHHHWW
LADIES AND GENTLEMEN...
...THIS IS THE MOMENT WE HAVE LONG WAITED FOR.
-SNFF-

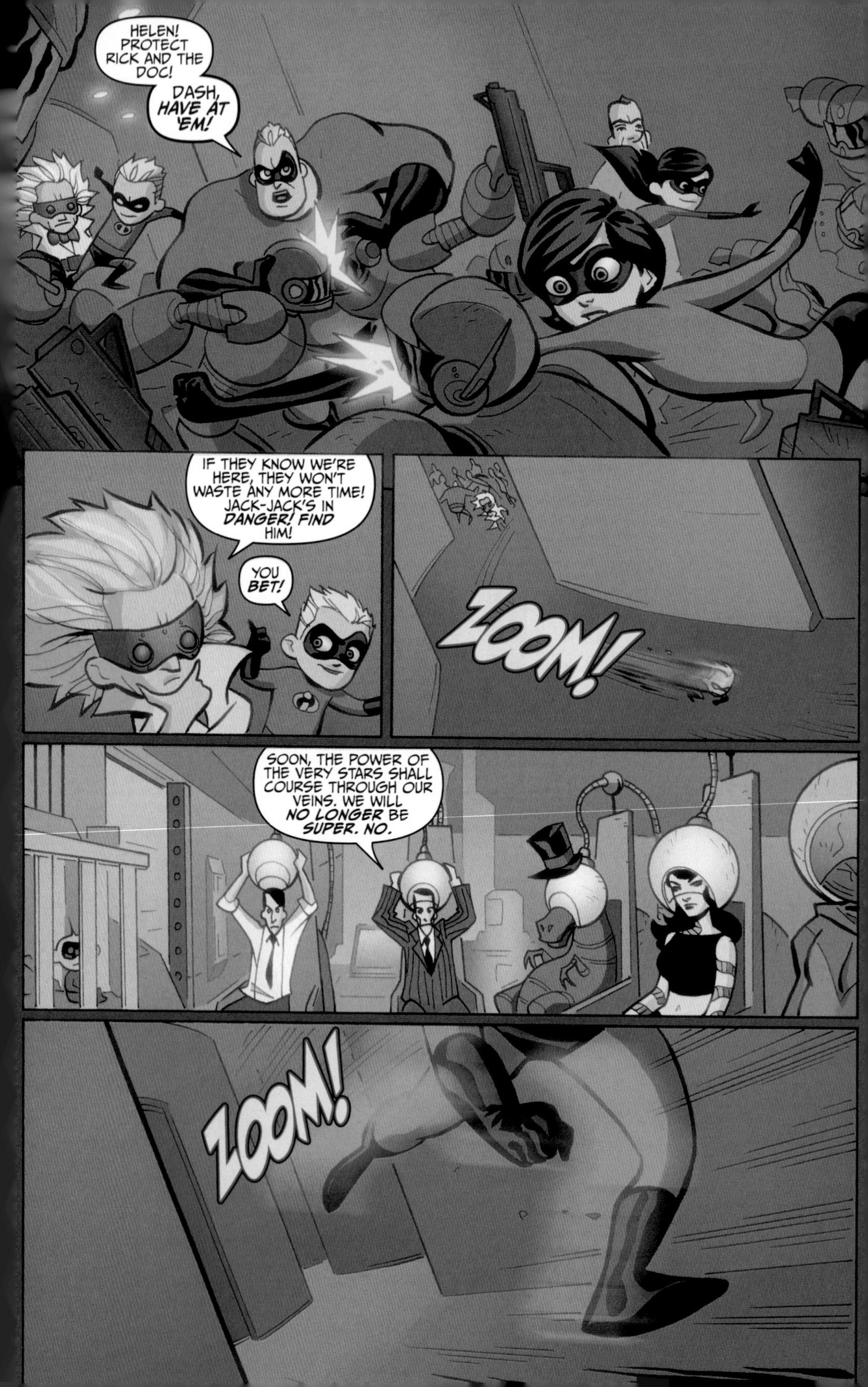
HELEN! PROTECT RICK AND THE DOC!
DASH, HAVE AT 'EM!
IF THEY KNOW WE'RE HERE, THEY WON'T WASTE ANY MORE TIME! JACK-JACK'S IN DANGER! FIND HIM!
YOU BET!
ZOOM!
SOON, THE POWER OF THE VERY STARS SHALL COURSE THROUGH OUR VEINS. WE WILL NO LONGER BE SUPER. NO.
ZOOM!

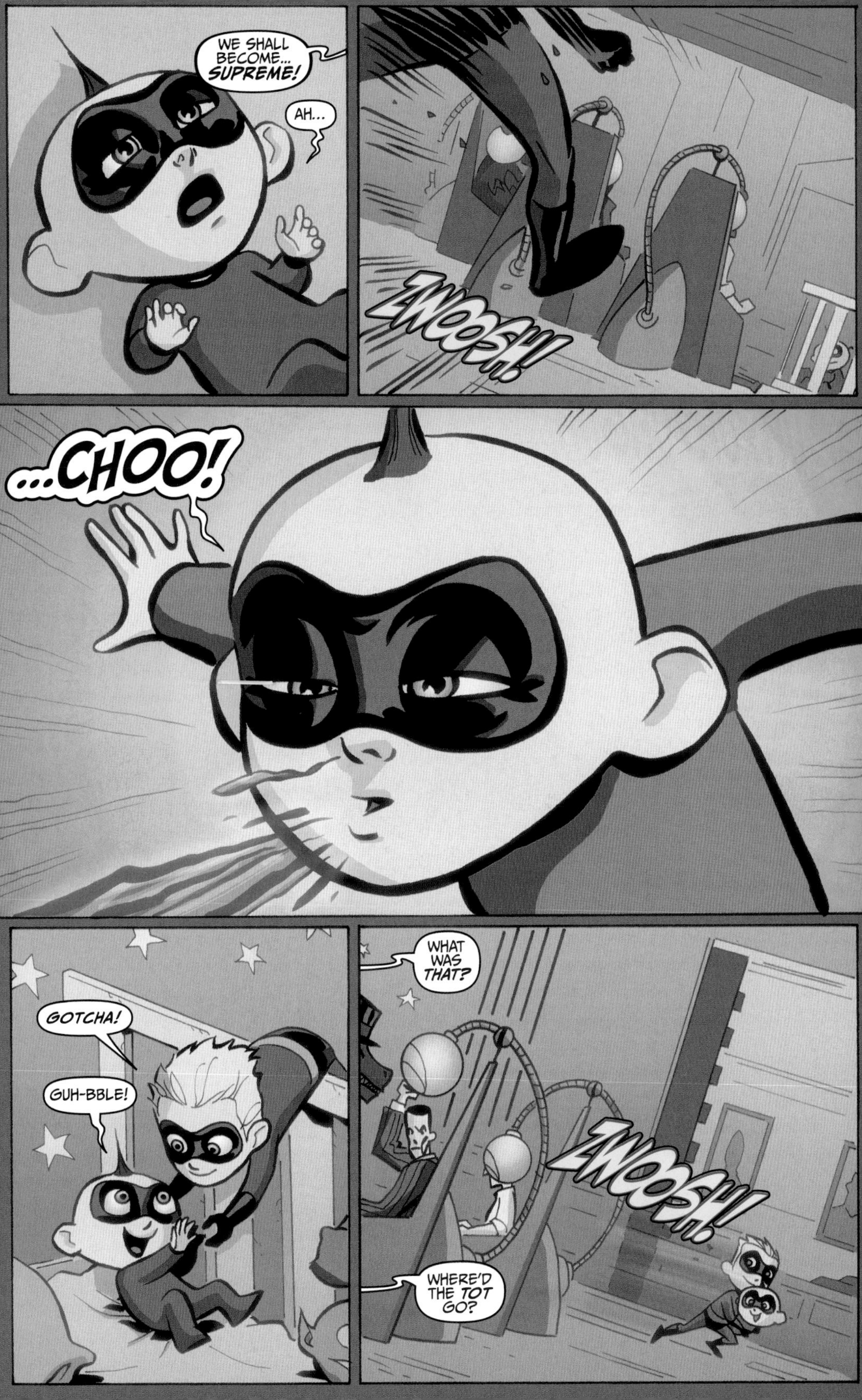
WE SHALL BECOME... SUPREME!
AH...
ZWOOSH!!
...CHOO!
GOTCHA!
GUH-BBLE!
WHAT WAS THAT?
ZWOOSH!!
WHERE'D THE TOT GO?

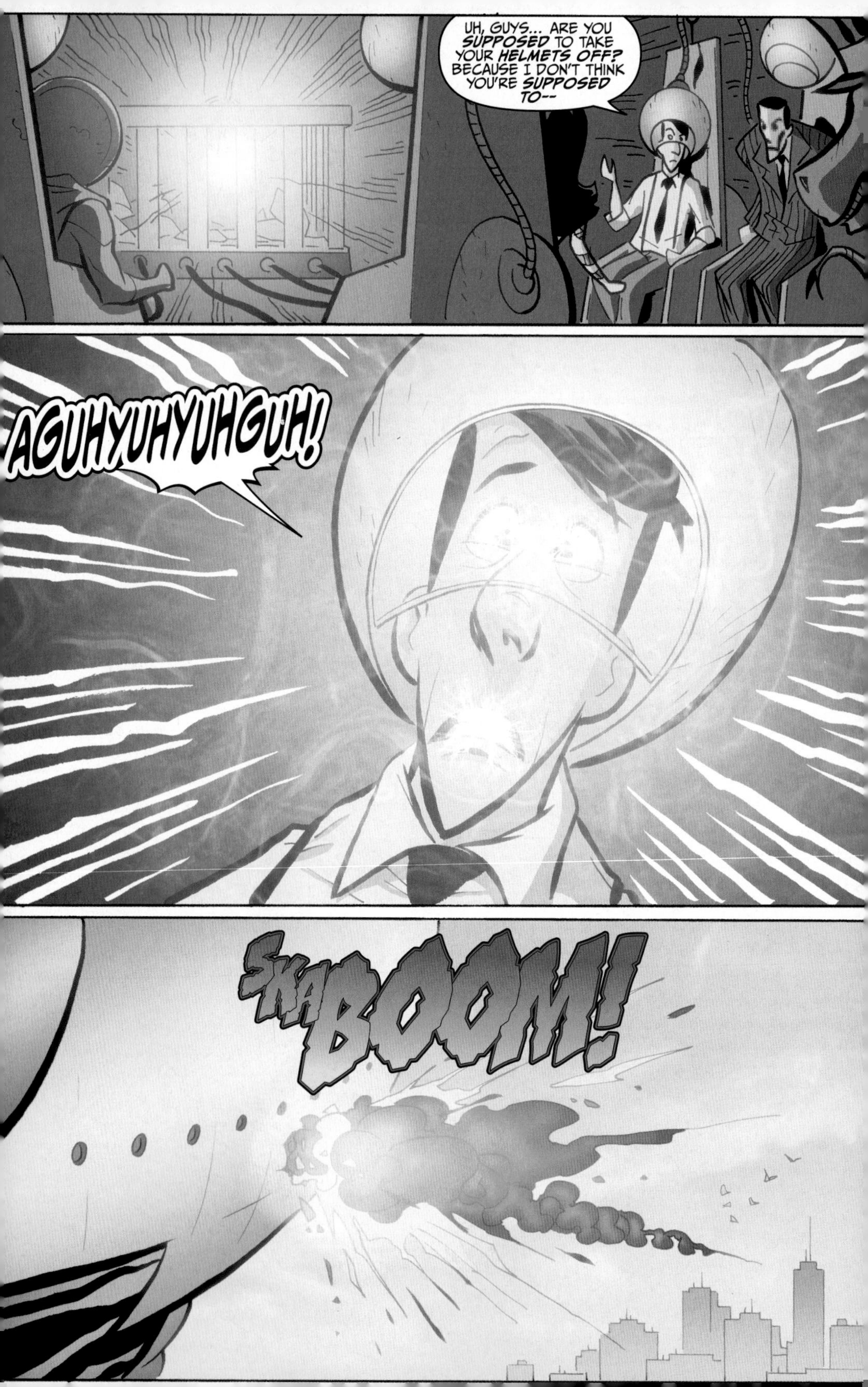
UH, GUYS... ARE YOU SUPPOSED TO TAKE YOUR HELMETS OFF? BECAUSE I DON'T THINK YOU'RE SUPPOSED TO--
AGUHYUHYUHGUH!
SKA BOOM!

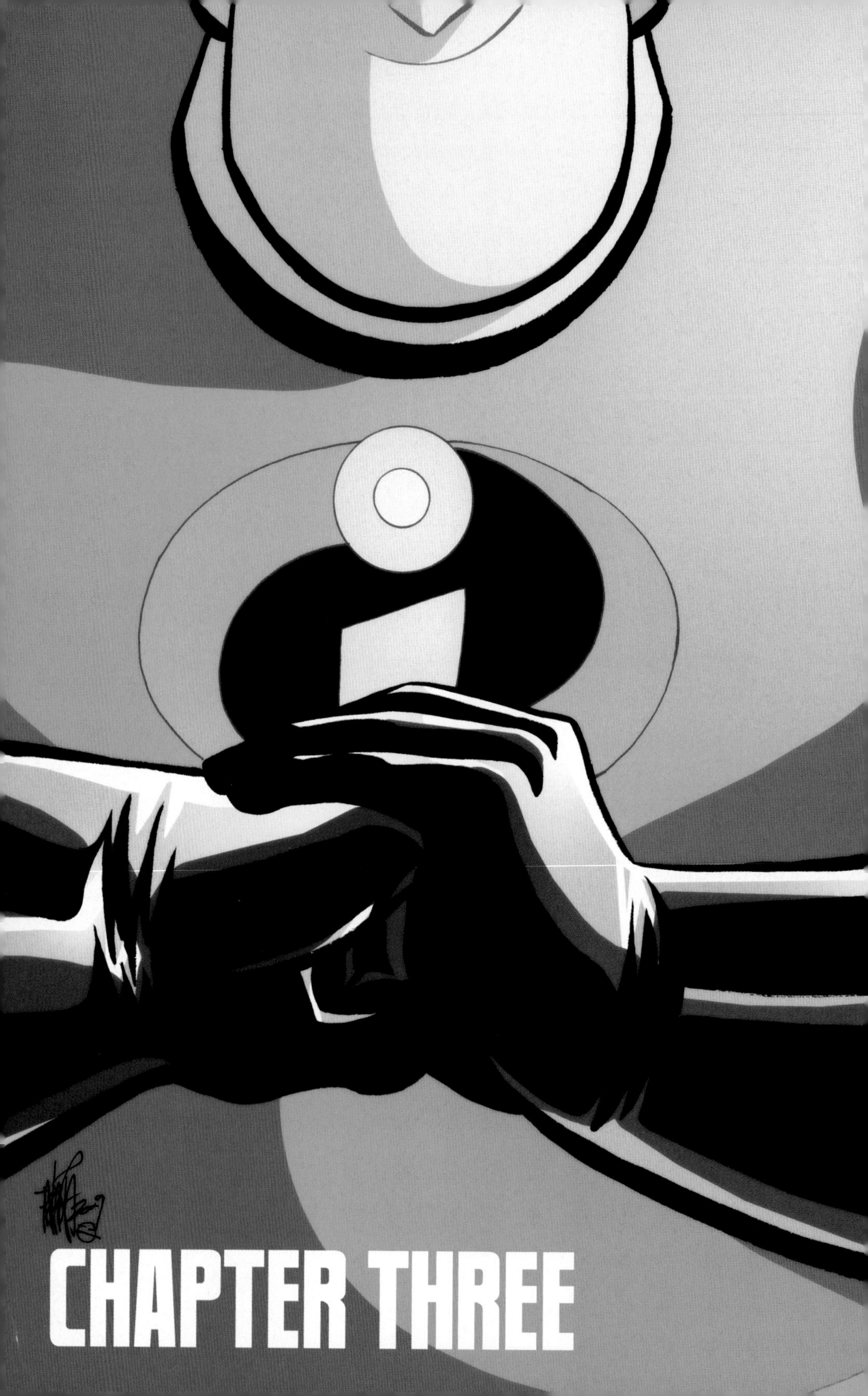

CHAPTER THREE

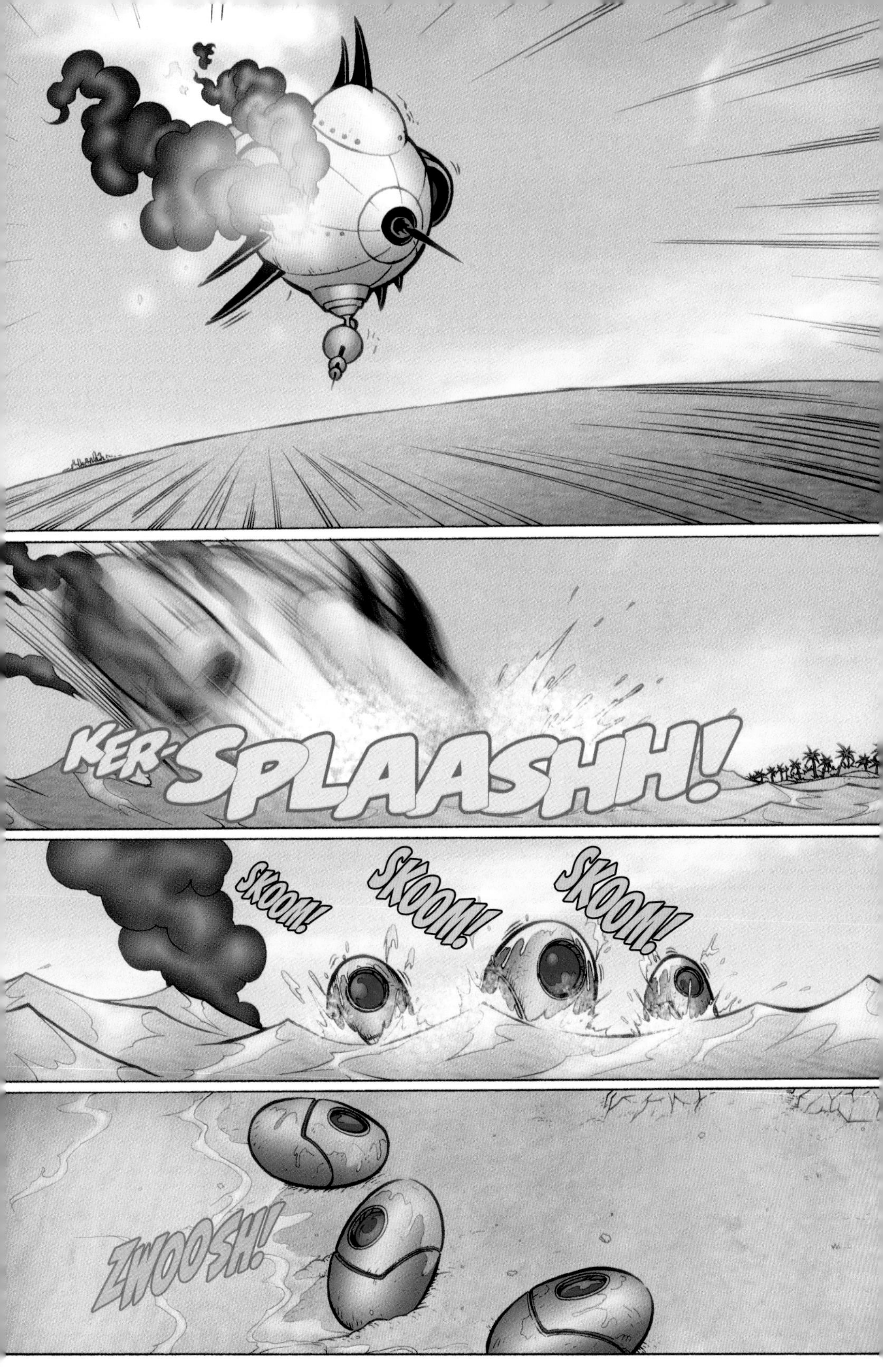
KER-SPLAASHH!
SKOOM!
SKOOM!
SKOOM!
ZWOOSH!

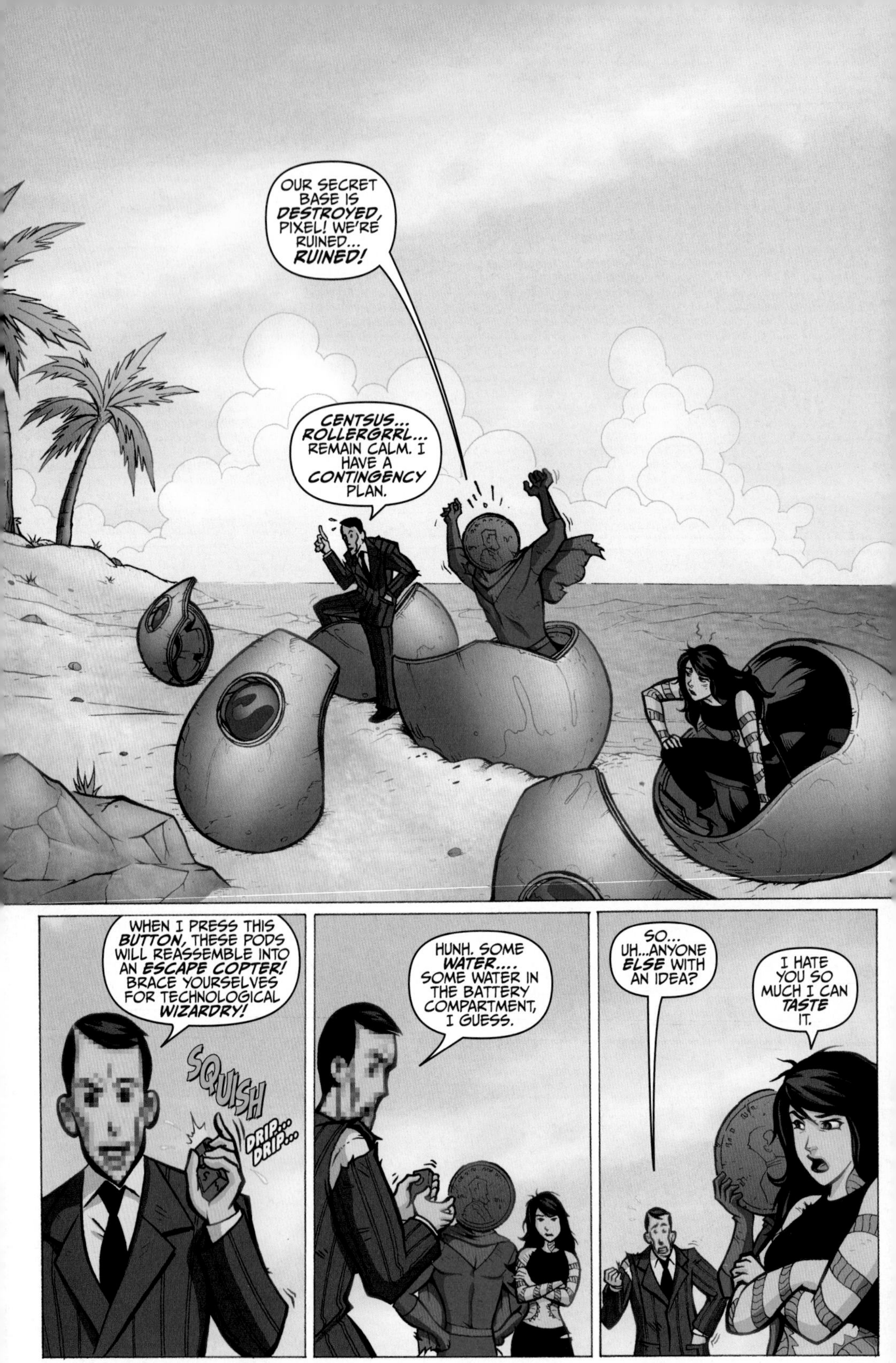
OUR SECRET BASE IS DESTROYED, PIXEL! WE'RE RUINED... RUINED!
CENTSUS... ROLLERGRRL... REMAIN CALM. I HAVE A CONTINGENCY PLAN.
WHEN I PRESS THIS BUTTON, THESE PODS WILL REASSEMBLE INTO AN ESCAPE COPTER! BRACE YOURSELVES FOR TECHNOLOGICAL WIZARDRY!
SQUISH
DRIP... DRIP...
HUNH. SOME WATER.... SOME WATER IN THE BATTERY COMPARTMENT, I GUESS.
SO... UH...ANYONE ELSE WITH AN IDEA?
I HATE YOU SO MUCH I CAN TASTE IT.

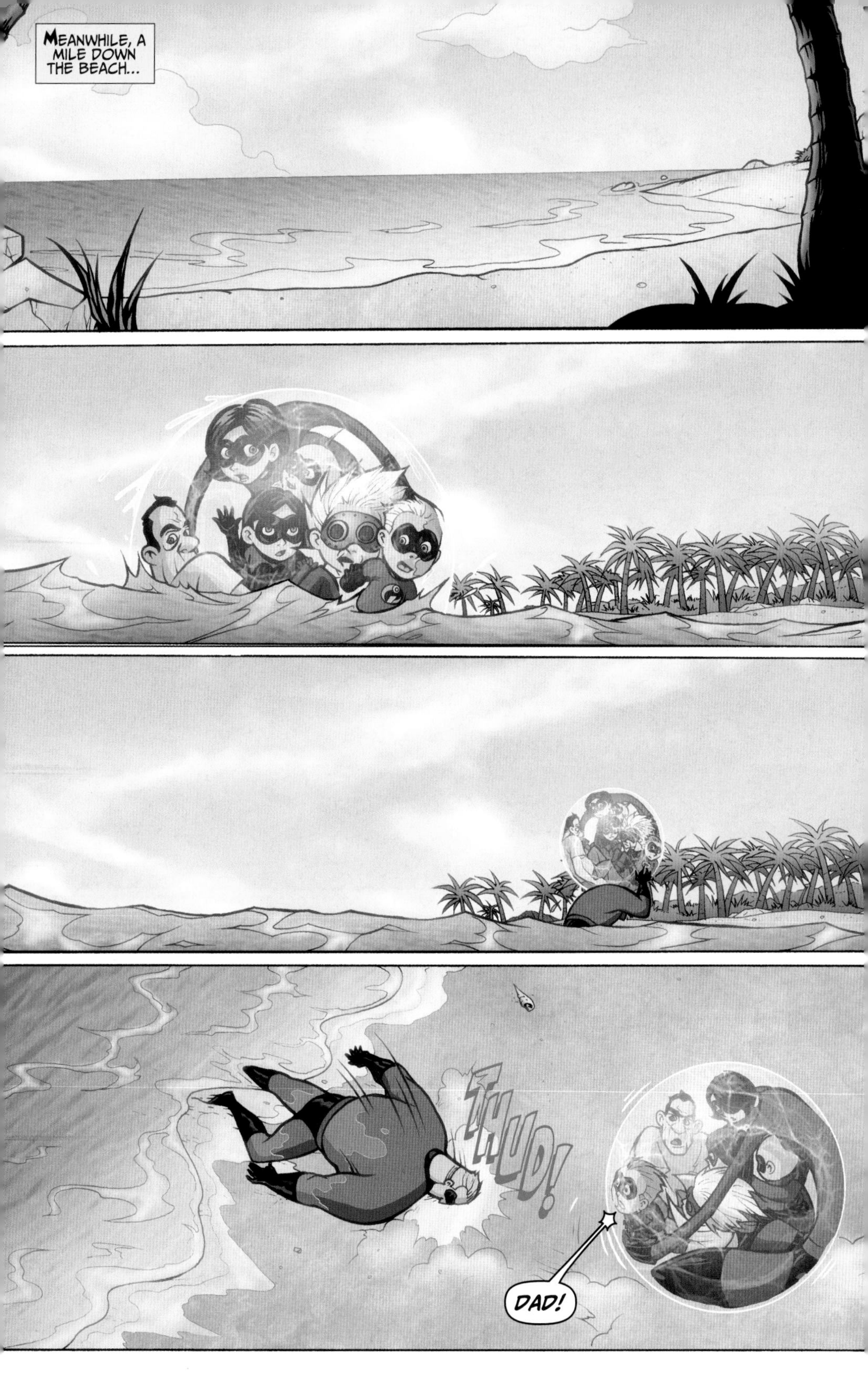
MEANWHILE, A MILE DOWN THE BEACH...
THUD!
DAD!

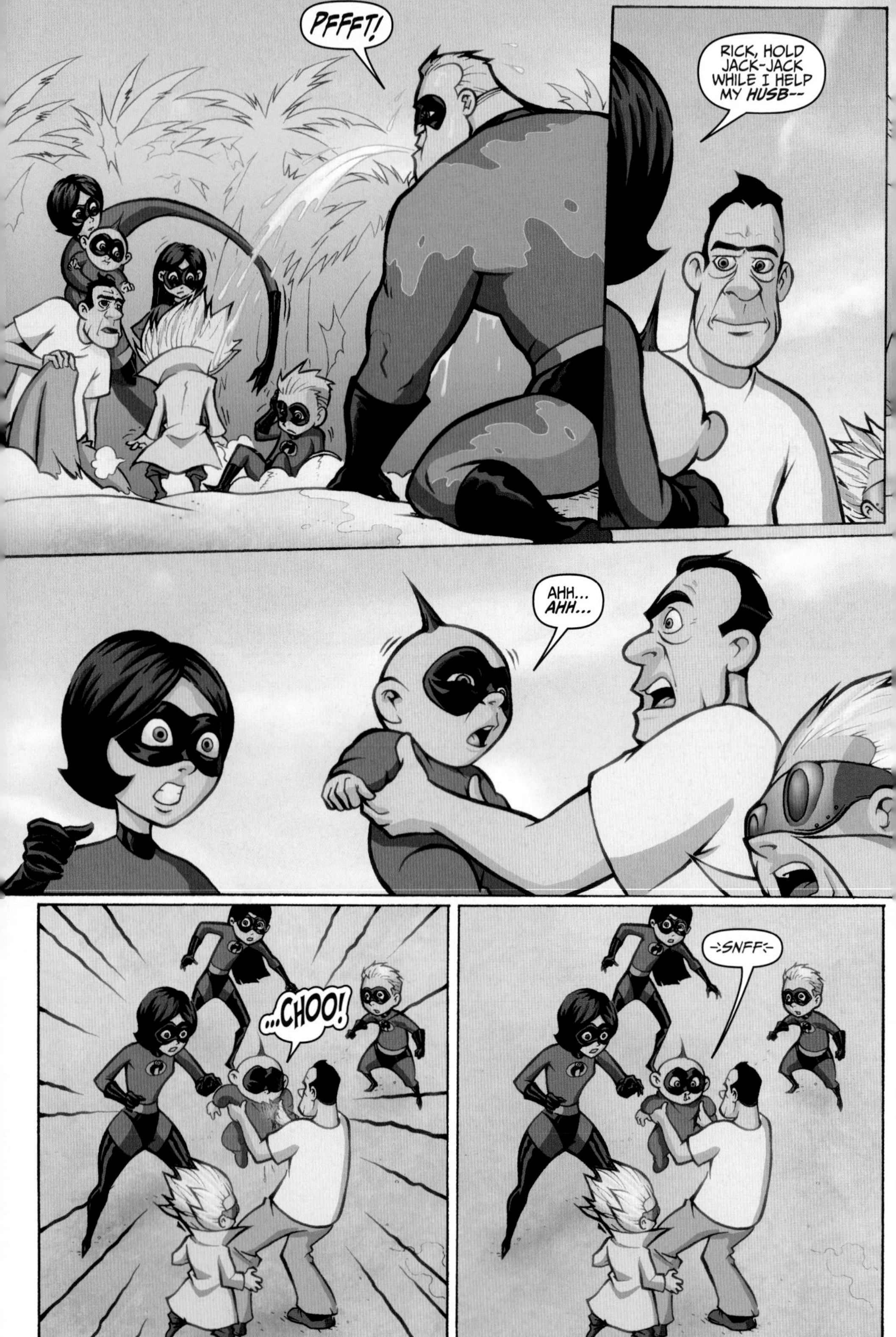
PFFFT!
RICK, HOLD JACK-JACK WHILE I HELP MY HUSB--
AHH... AHH...
...CHOO!
SNFF

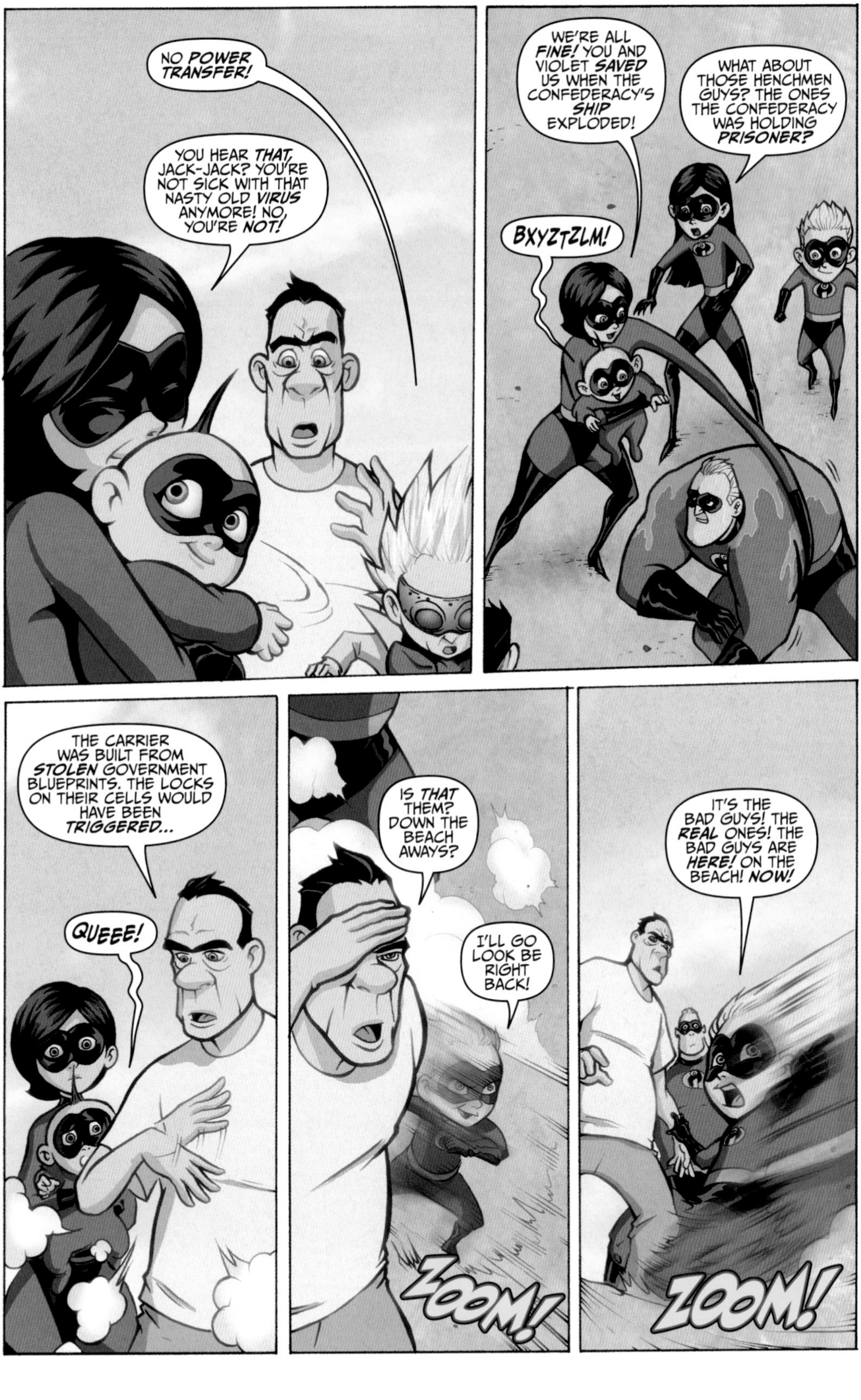
NO POWER TRANSFER!
YOU HEAR THAT, JACK-JACK? YOU'RE NOT SICK WITH THAT NASTY OLD VIRUS ANYMORE! NO, YOU'RE NOT!
WE'RE ALL FINE! YOU AND VIOLET SAVED US WHEN THE CONFEDERACY'S SHIP EXPLODED!
BXYZTZLM!
WHAT ABOUT THOSE HENCHMEN GUYS? THE ONES THE CONFEDERACY WAS HOLDING PRISONER?
THE CARRIER WAS BUILT FROM STOLEN GOVERNMENT BLUEPRINTS. THE LOCKS ON THEIR CELLS WOULD HAVE BEEN TRIGGERED...
QUEEE!
IS THAT THEM? DOWN THE BEACH AWAYS?
I'LL GO LOOK BE RIGHT BACK!
ZOOM!
IT'S THE BAD GUYS! THE REAL ONES! THE BAD GUYS ARE HERE! ON THE BEACH! NOW!
ZOOM!

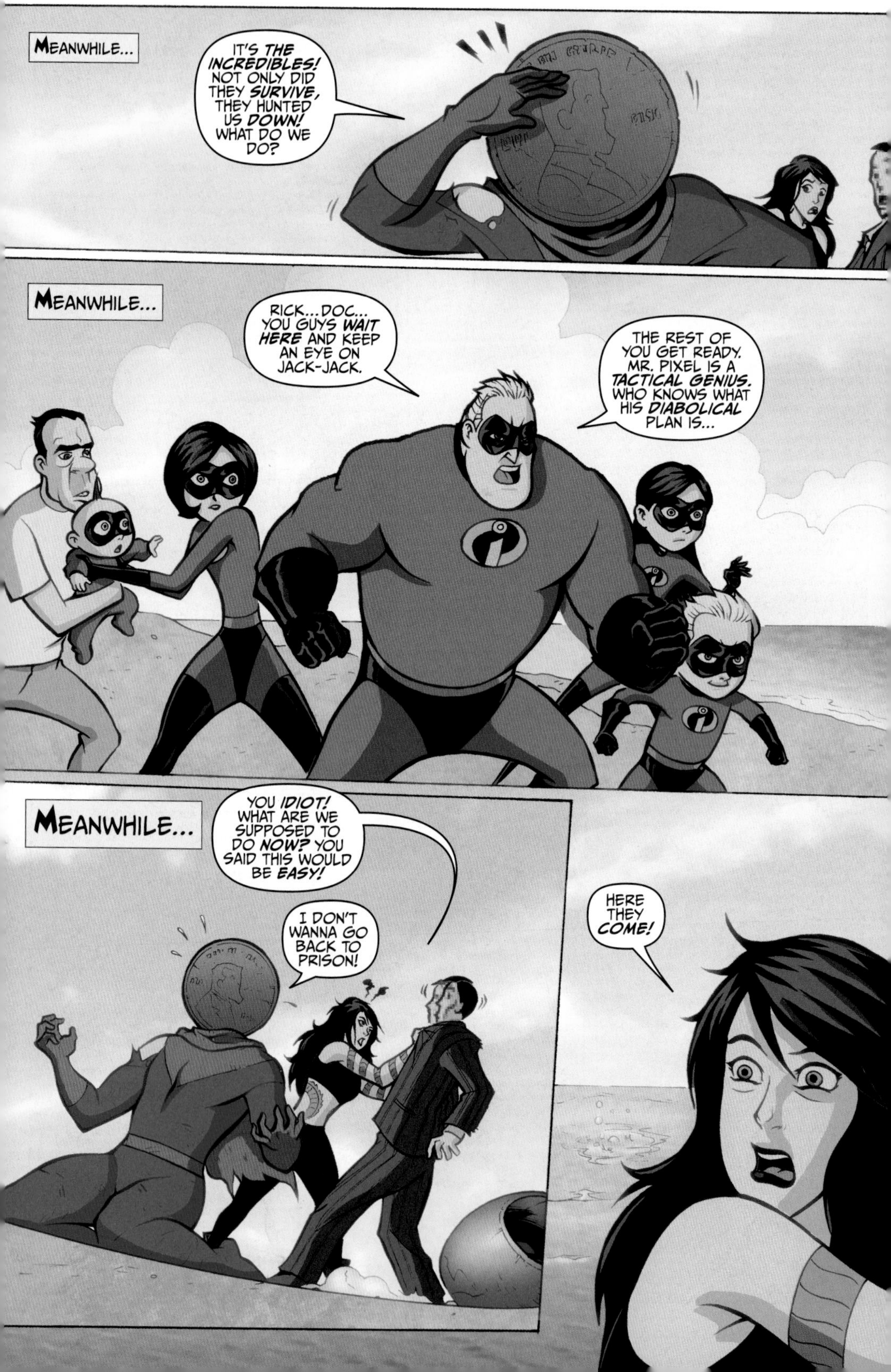
MEANWHILE...
IT'S THE INCREDIBLES! NOT ONLY DID THEY SURVIVE, THEY HUNTED US DOWN! WHAT DO WE DO?
MEANWHILE...
RICK...DOC... YOU GUYS WAIT HERE AND KEEP AN EYE ON JACK-JACK.
THE REST OF YOU GET READY. MR. PIXEL IS A TACTICAL GENIUS. WHO KNOWS WHAT HIS DIABOLICAL PLAN IS...
MEANWHILE...
YOU IDIOT! WHAT ARE WE SUPPOSED TO DO NOW? YOU SAID THIS WOULD BE EASY!
I DON'T WANNA GO BACK TO PRISON!
HERE THEY COME!

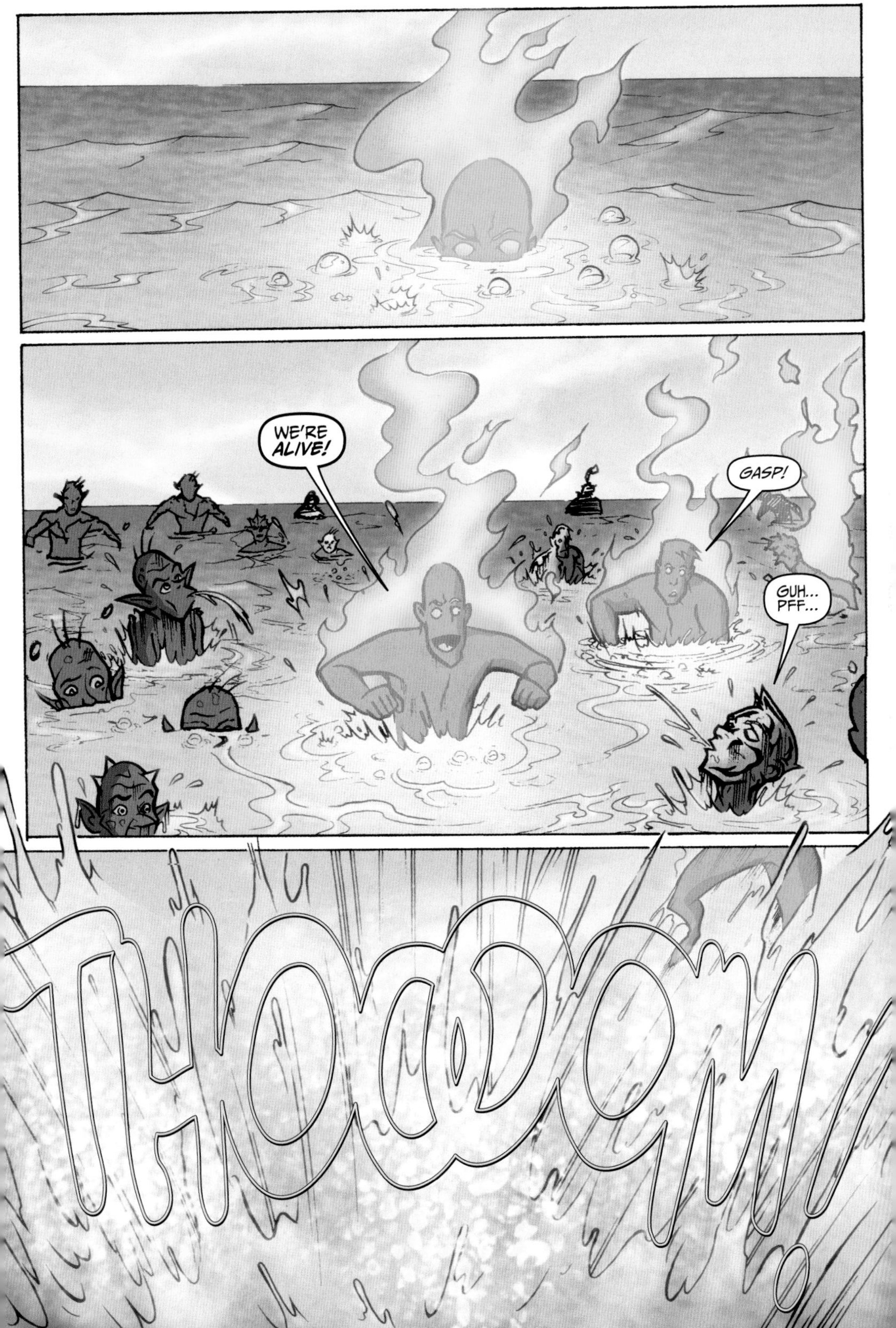
WE'RE ALIVE!
GASP!
GUH... PFF...
THOOOM!

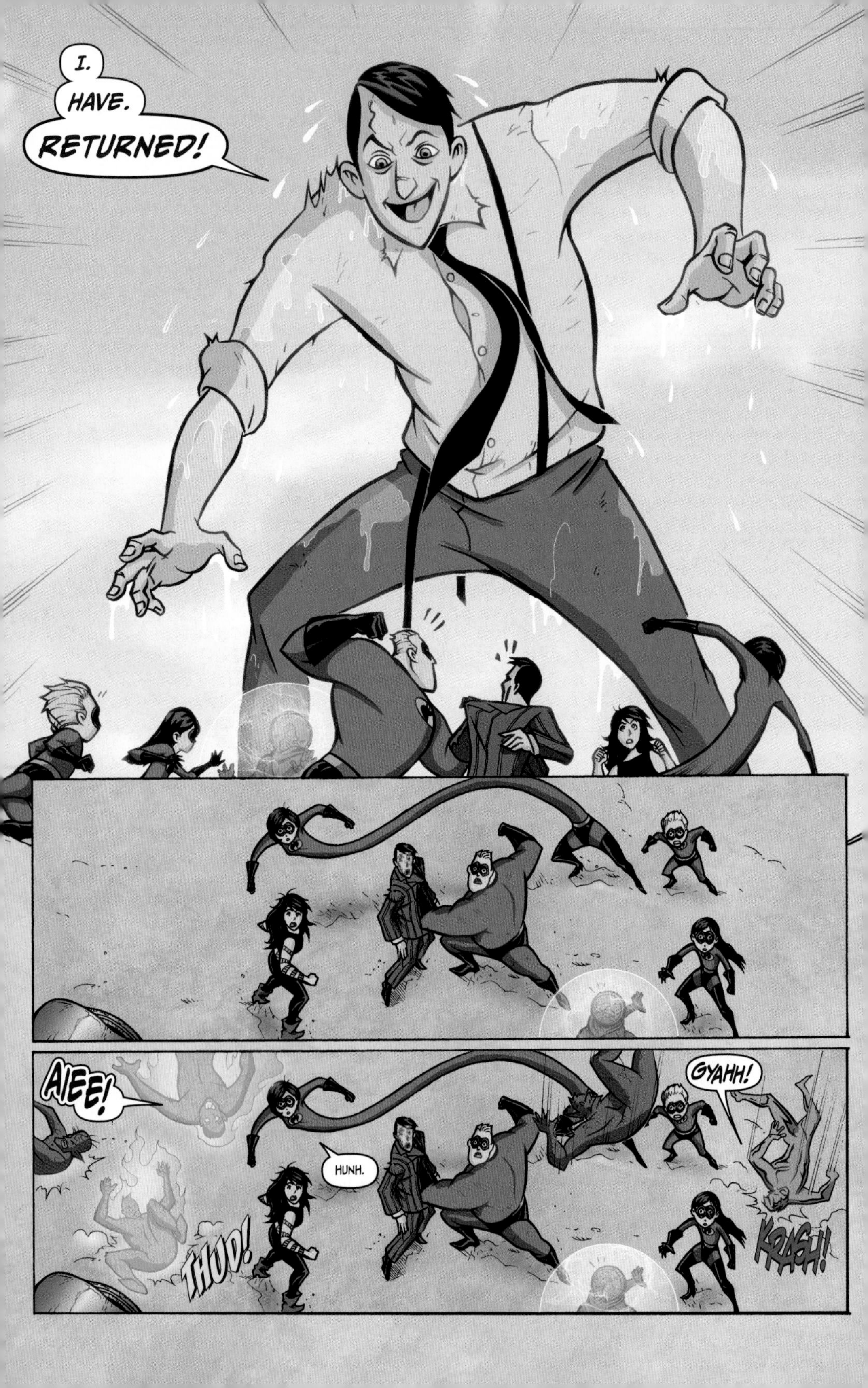
I.
HAVE.
RETURNED!
AIEE!
GYAHH!
HUNH.
THUD!
KRASH!

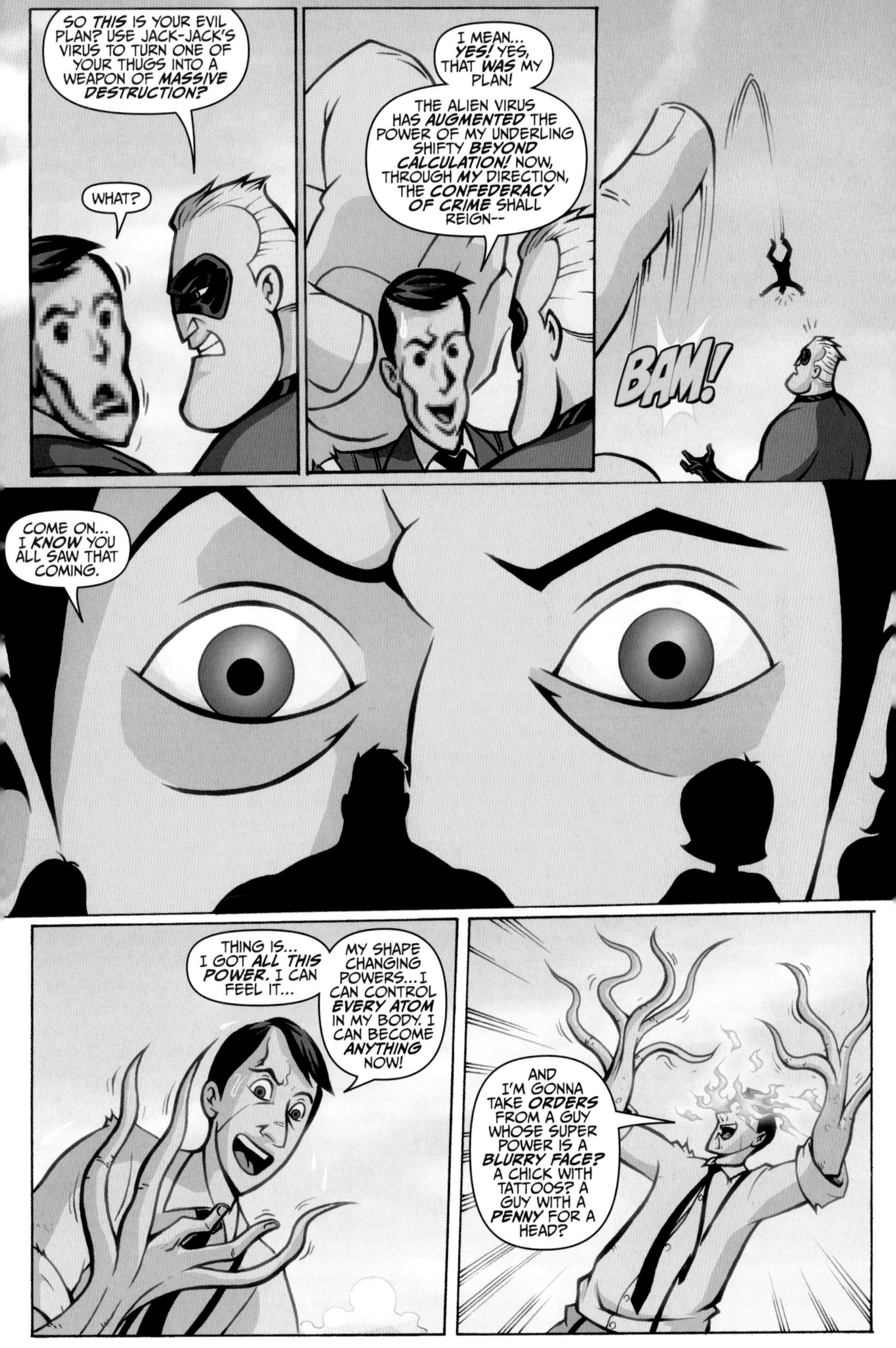

SO THIS IS YOUR EVIL PLAN? USE JACK-JACK'S VIRUS TO TURN ONE OF YOUR THUGS INTO A WEAPON OF MASSIVE DESTRUCTION?
WHAT?
I MEAN... YES! YES, THAT WAS MY PLAN!
THE ALIEN VIRUS HAS AUGMENTED THE POWER OF MY UNDERLING SHIFTY BEYOND CALCULATION! NOW, THROUGH MY DIRECTION, THE CONFEDERACY OF CRIME SHALL REIGN--
BAM!
COME ON... I KNOW YOU ALL SAW THAT COMING.
THING IS... I GOT ALL THIS POWER. I CAN FEEL IT...
MY SHAPE CHANGING POWERS...I CAN CONTROL EVERY ATOM IN MY BODY. I CAN BECOME ANYTHING NOW!
AND I'M GONNA TAKE ORDERS FROM A GUY WHOSE SUPER POWER IS A BLURRY FACE? A CHICK WITH TATTOOS? A GUY WITH A PENNY FOR A HEAD?

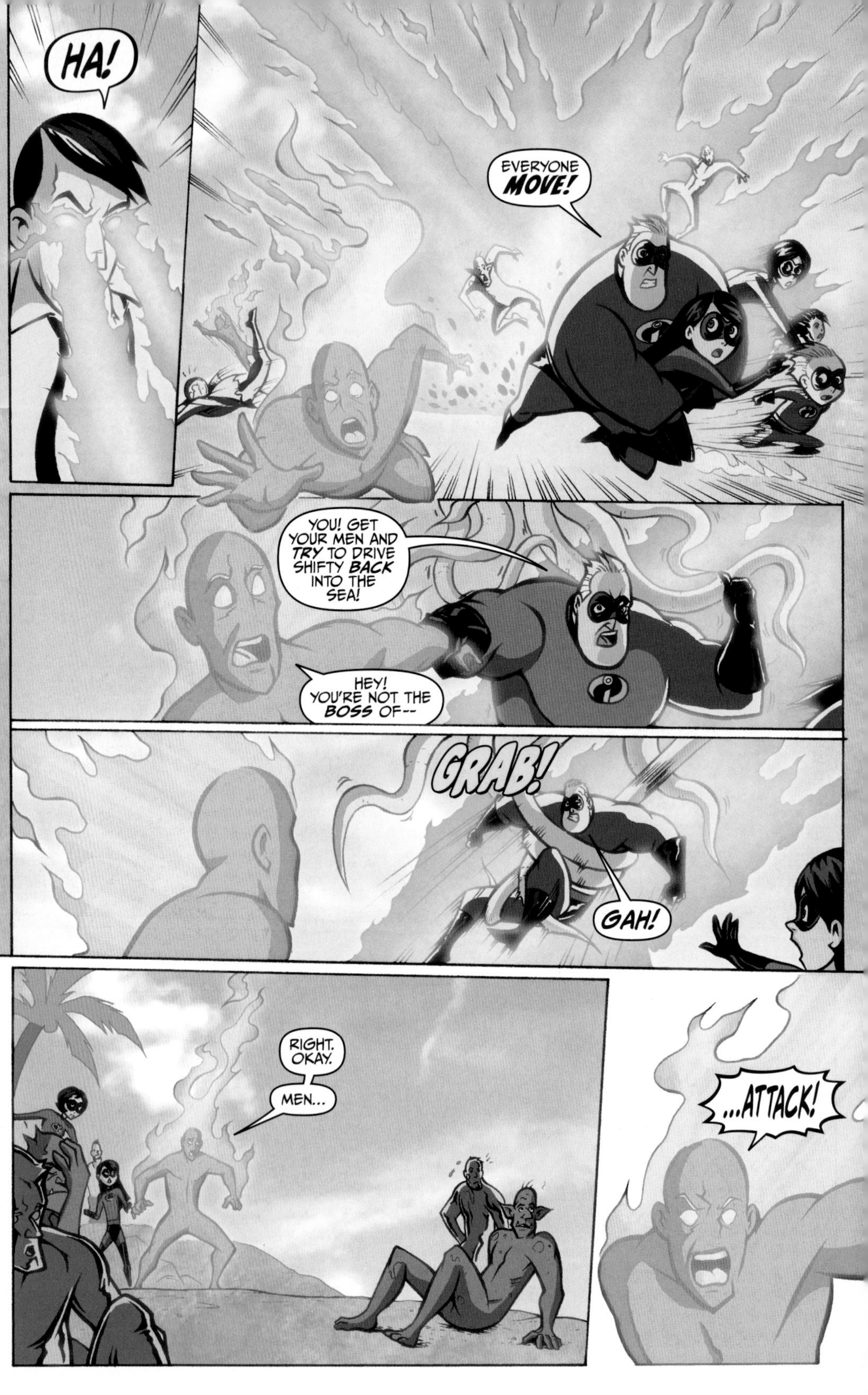
HA!
EVERYONE MOVE!
YOU! GET YOUR MEN AND TRY TO DRIVE SHIFTY BACK INTO THE SEA!
HEY! YOU'RE NOT THE BOSS OF--
GRAB!
GAH!
RIGHT. OKAY.
MEN...
...ATTACK!

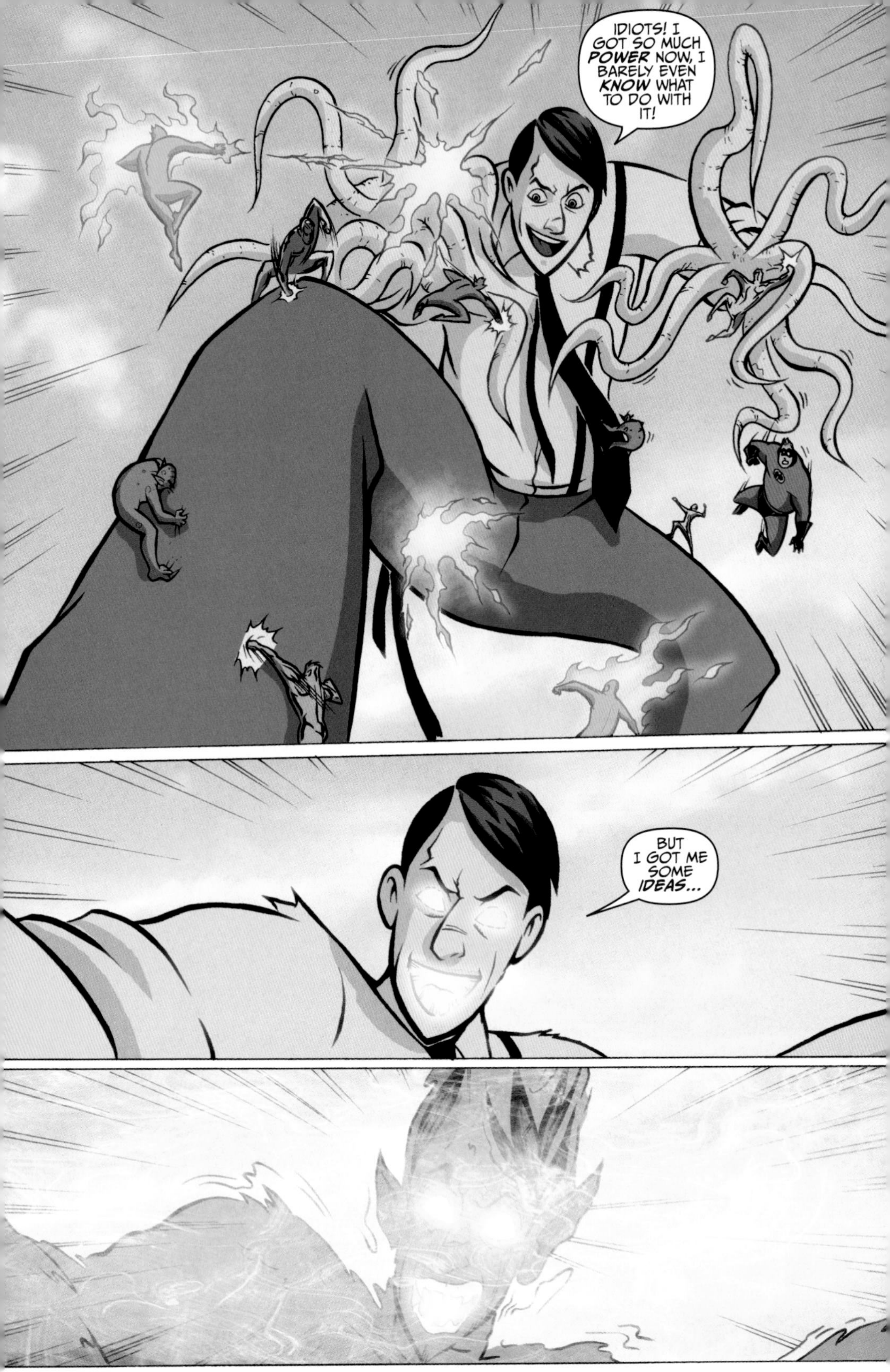
IDIOTS! I GOT SO MUCH POWER NOW, I BARELY EVEN KNOW WHAT TO DO WITH IT!
BUT I GOT ME SOME IDEAS...

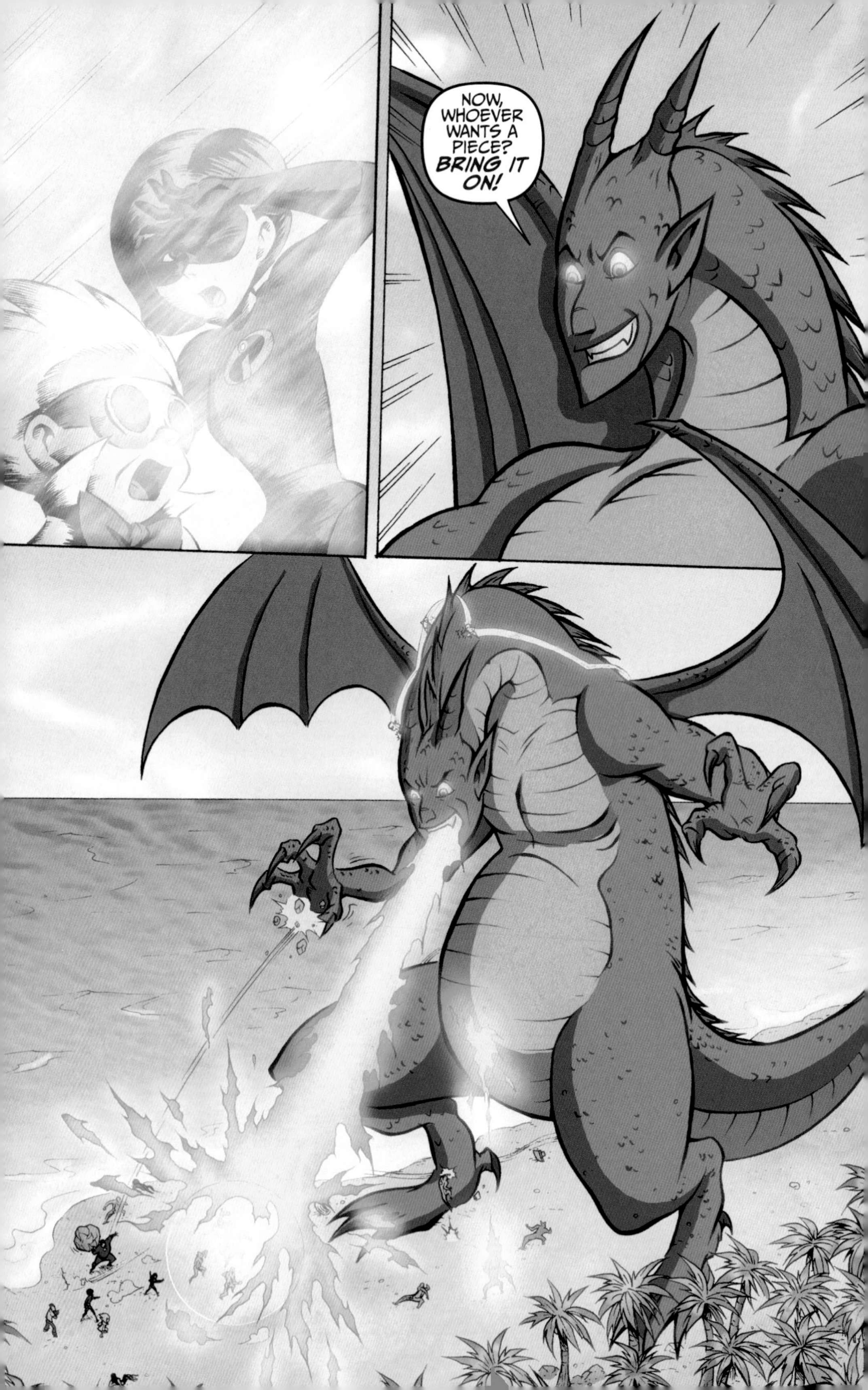
NOW, WHOEVER WANTS A PIECE? BRING IT ON!

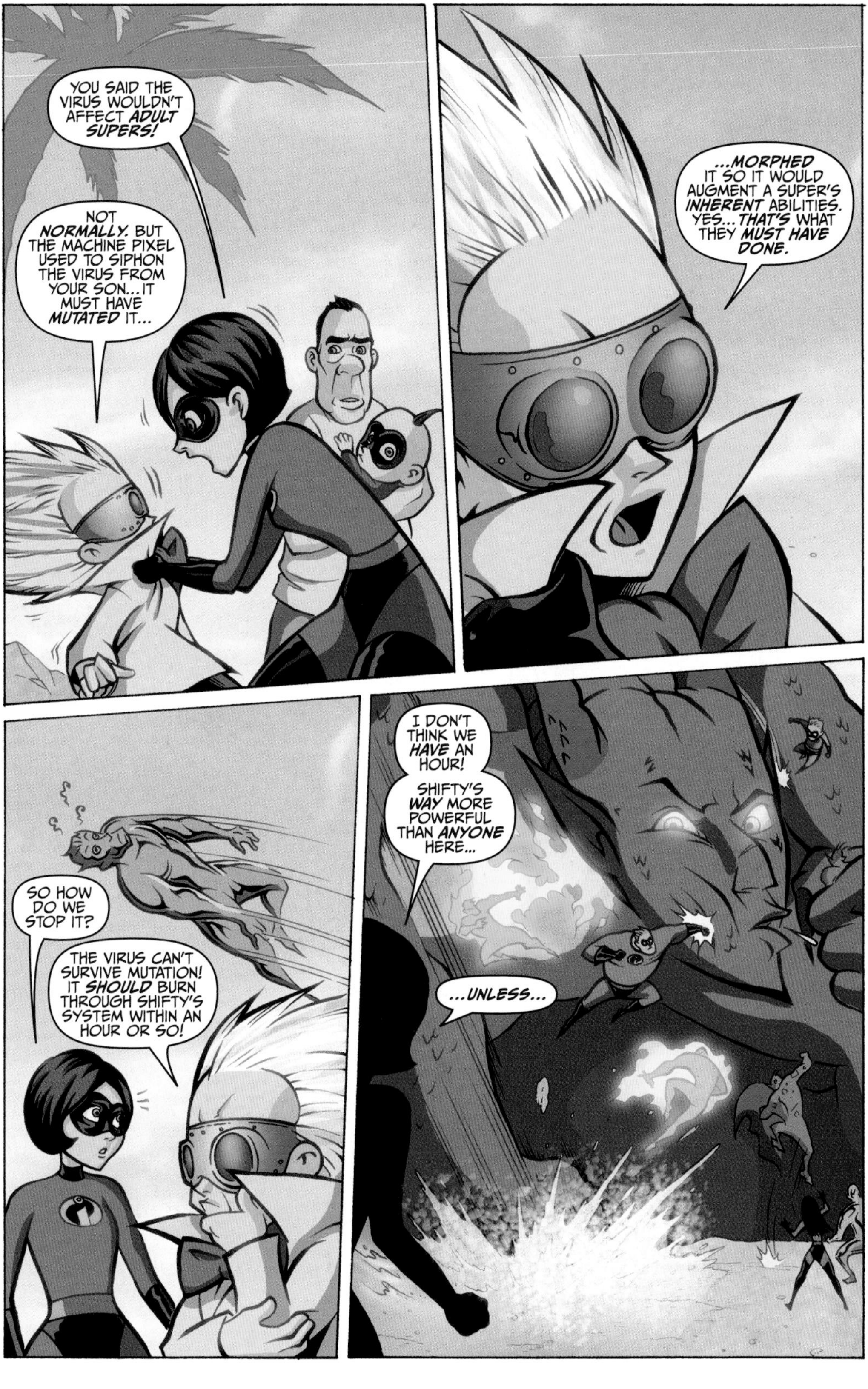
YOU SAID THE VIRUS WOULDN'T AFFECT ADULT SUPERS!
NOT NORMALLY. BUT THE MACHINE PIXEL USED TO SIPHON THE VIRUS FROM YOUR SON...IT MUST HAVE MUTATED IT...
...MORPHED IT SO IT WOULD AUGMENT A SUPER'S INHERENT ABILITIES. YES...THAT'S WHAT THEY MUST HAVE DONE.
SO HOW DO WE STOP IT?
THE VIRUS CAN'T SURVIVE MUTATION! IT SHOULD BURN THROUGH SHIFTY'S SYSTEM WITHIN AN HOUR OR SO!
I DON'T THINK WE HAVE AN HOUR!
SHIFTY'S WAY MORE POWERFUL THAN ANYONE HERE...
...UNLESS...

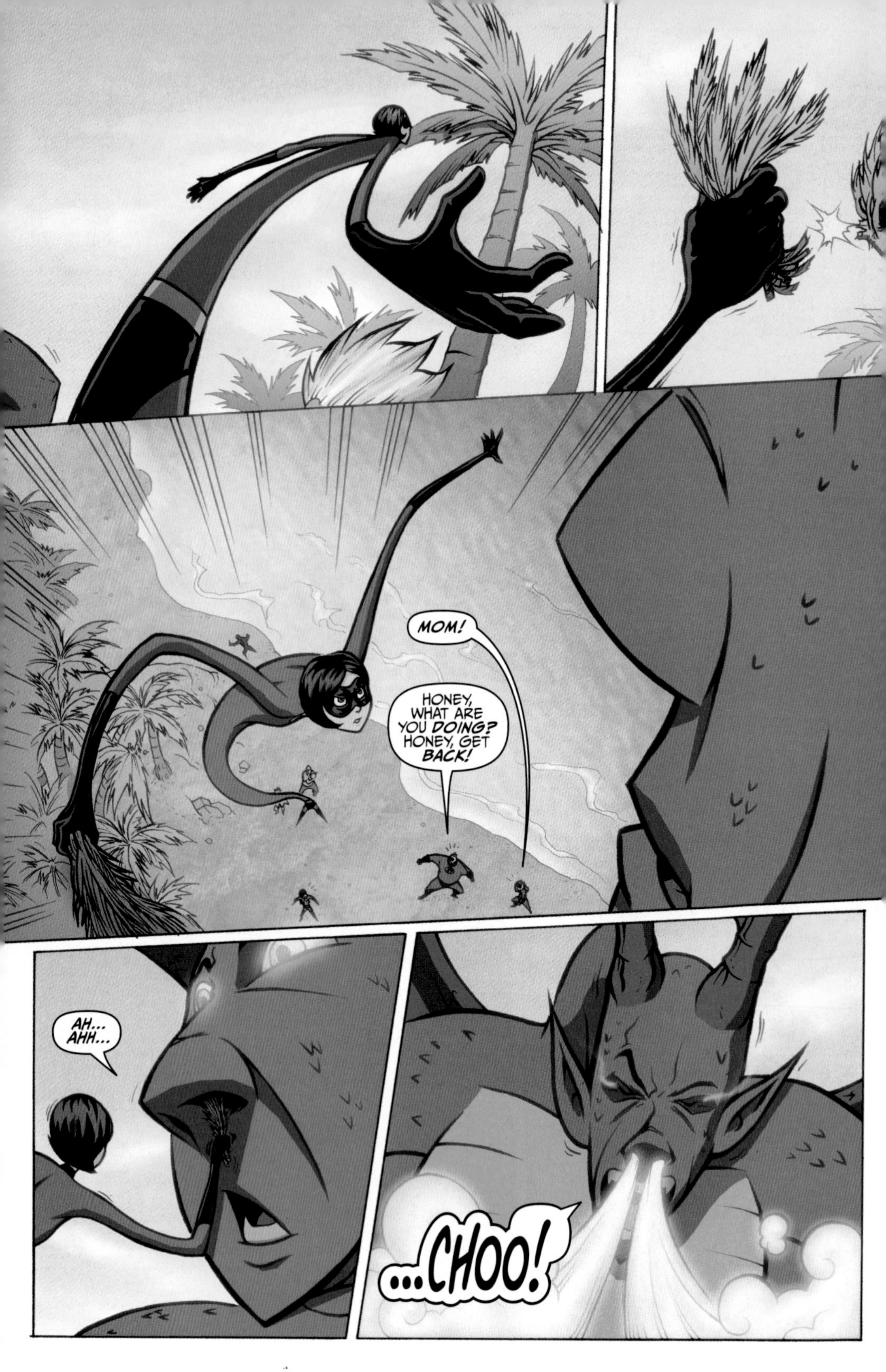
MOM!
HONEY, WHAT ARE YOU DOING? HONEY, GET BACK!
AH... AHH...
...CHOO!

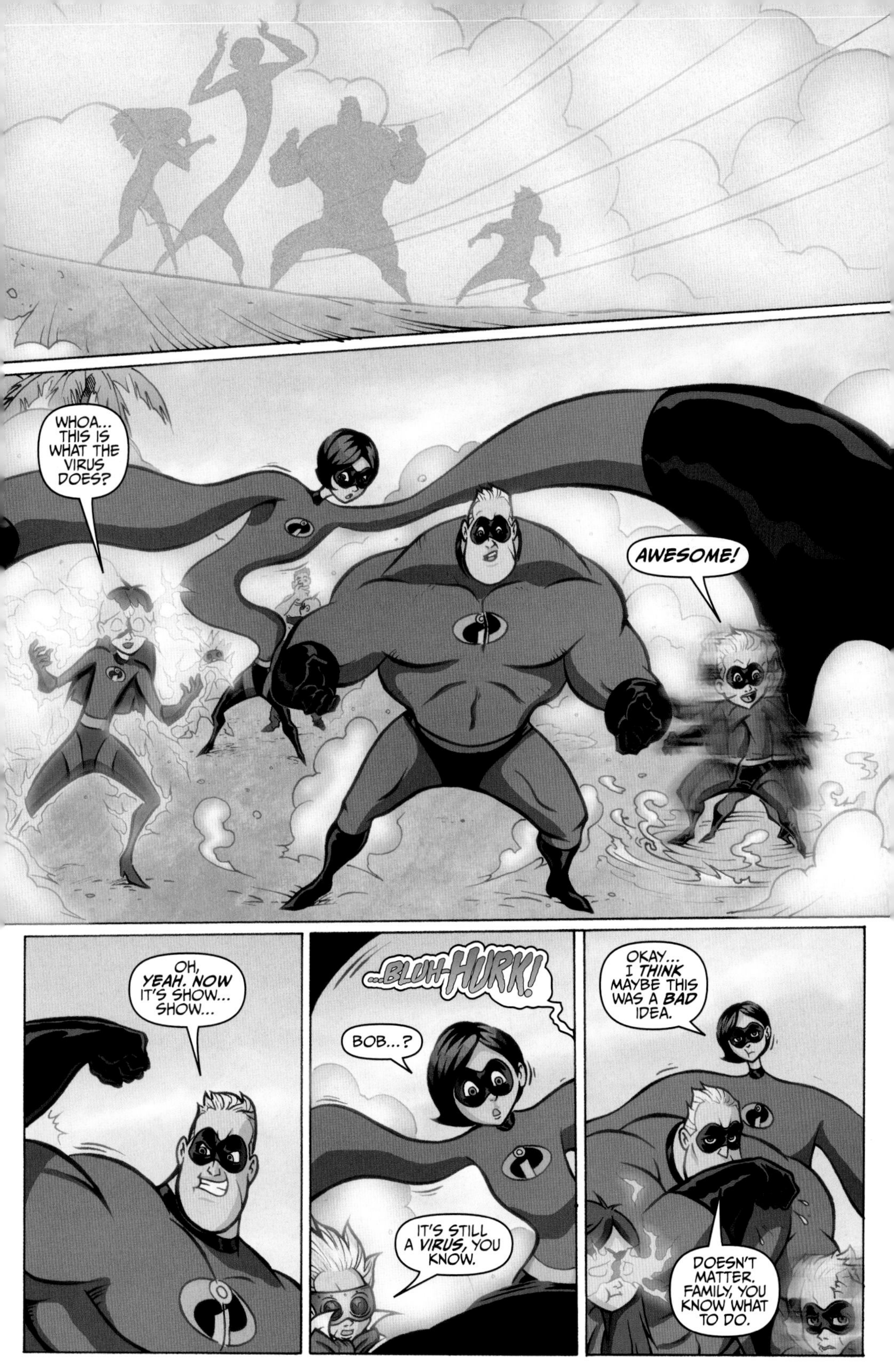
WHOA... THIS IS WHAT THE VIRUS DOES?
AWESOME!
OH, YEAH. NOW IT'S SHOW... SHOW...
...BLUH-HURK!
BOB...?
IT'S STILL A VIRUS, YOU KNOW.
OKAY... I THINK MAYBE THIS WAS A BAD IDEA.
DOESN'T MATTER. FAMILY, YOU KNOW WHAT TO DO.

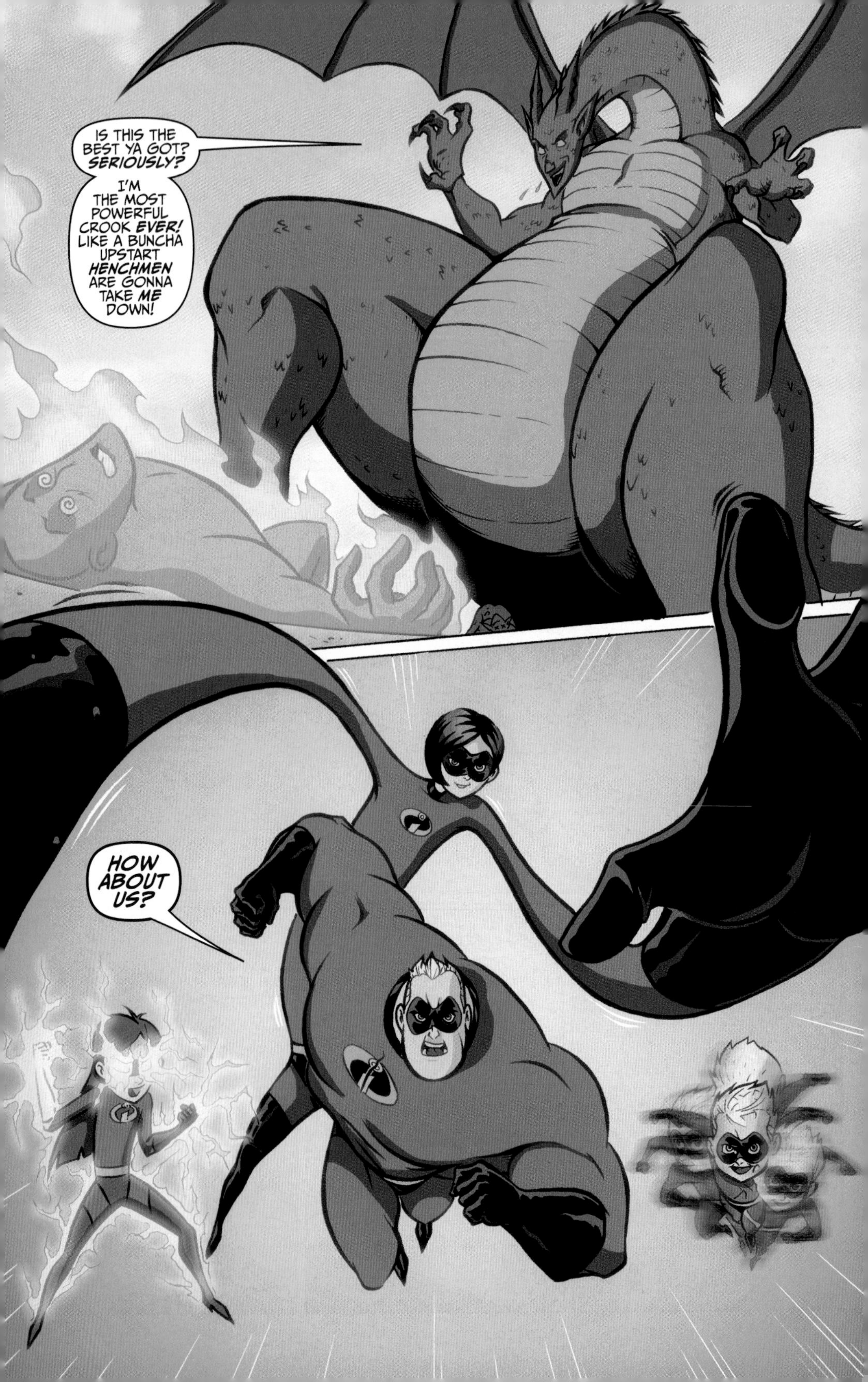
IS THIS THE BEST YA GOT? SERIOUSLY?
I'M THE MOST POWERFUL CROOK EVER! LIKE A BUNCHA UPSTART HENCHMEN ARE GONNA TAKE ME DOWN!
HOW ABOUT US?

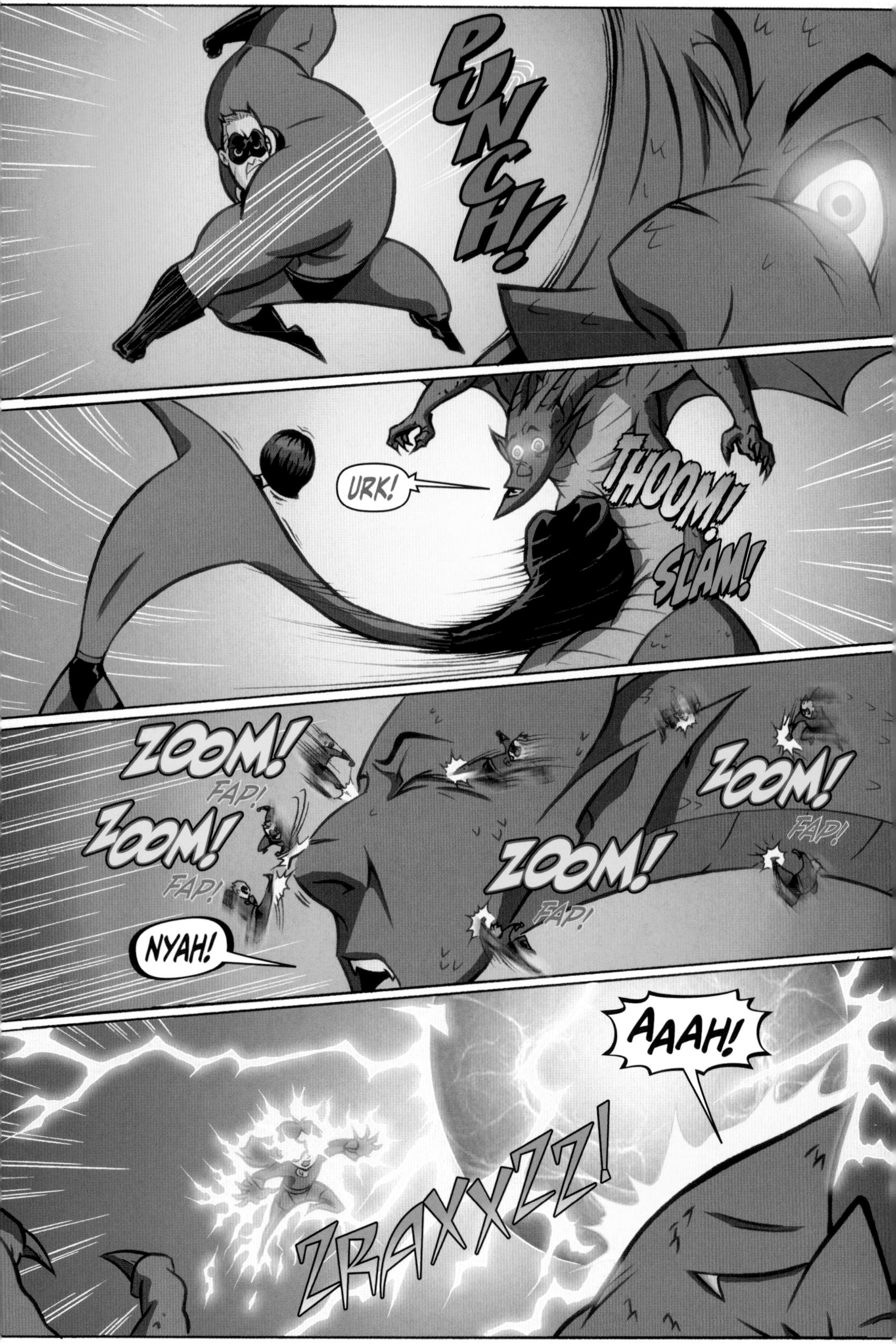
PUNCH!
URK!
THOOM!
SLAM!
ZOOM!
FAP!
ZOOM!
FAP!
NYAH!
ZOOM!
FAP!
ZOOM!
FAP!
AAAH!
ZRAXXZZ!

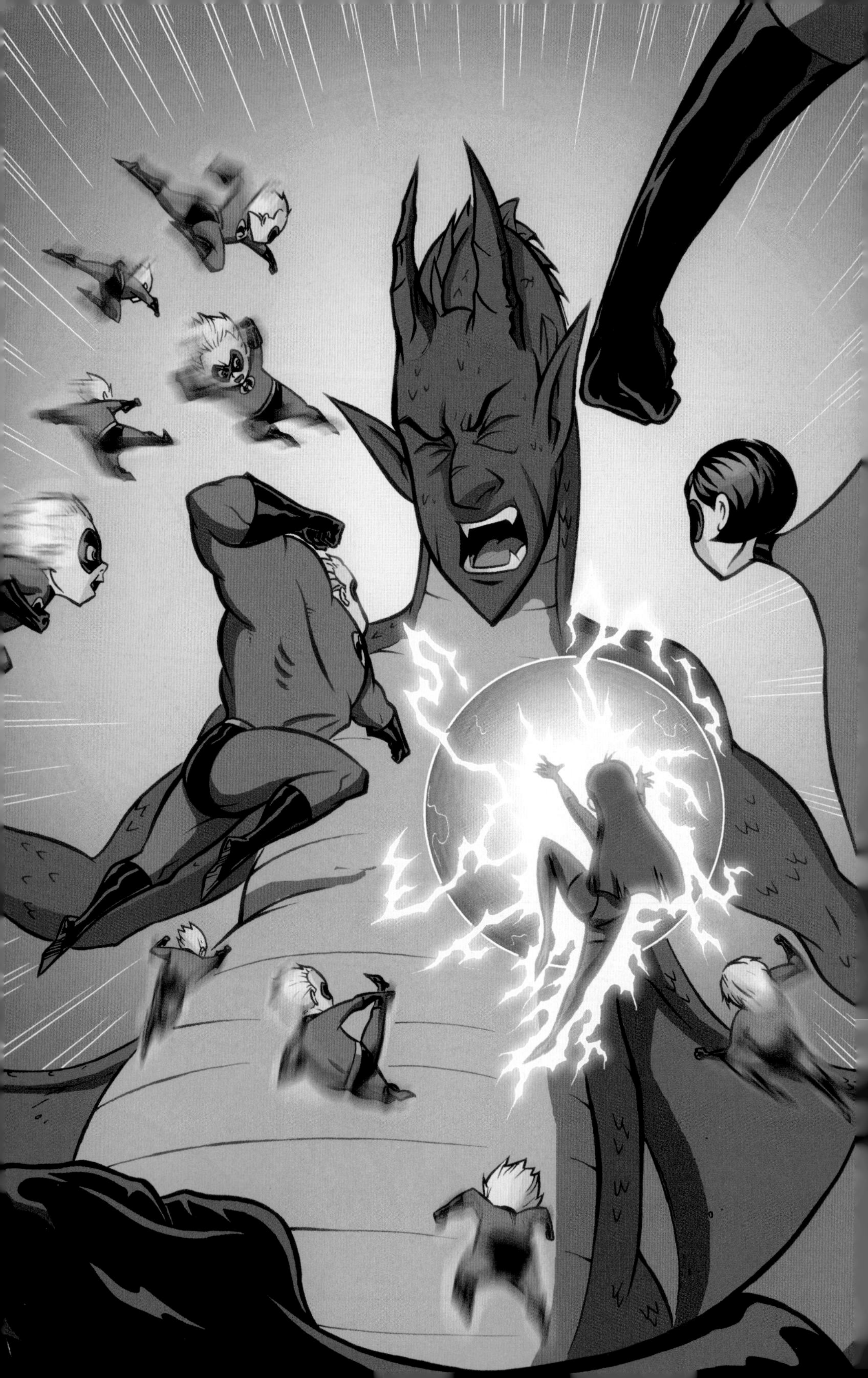

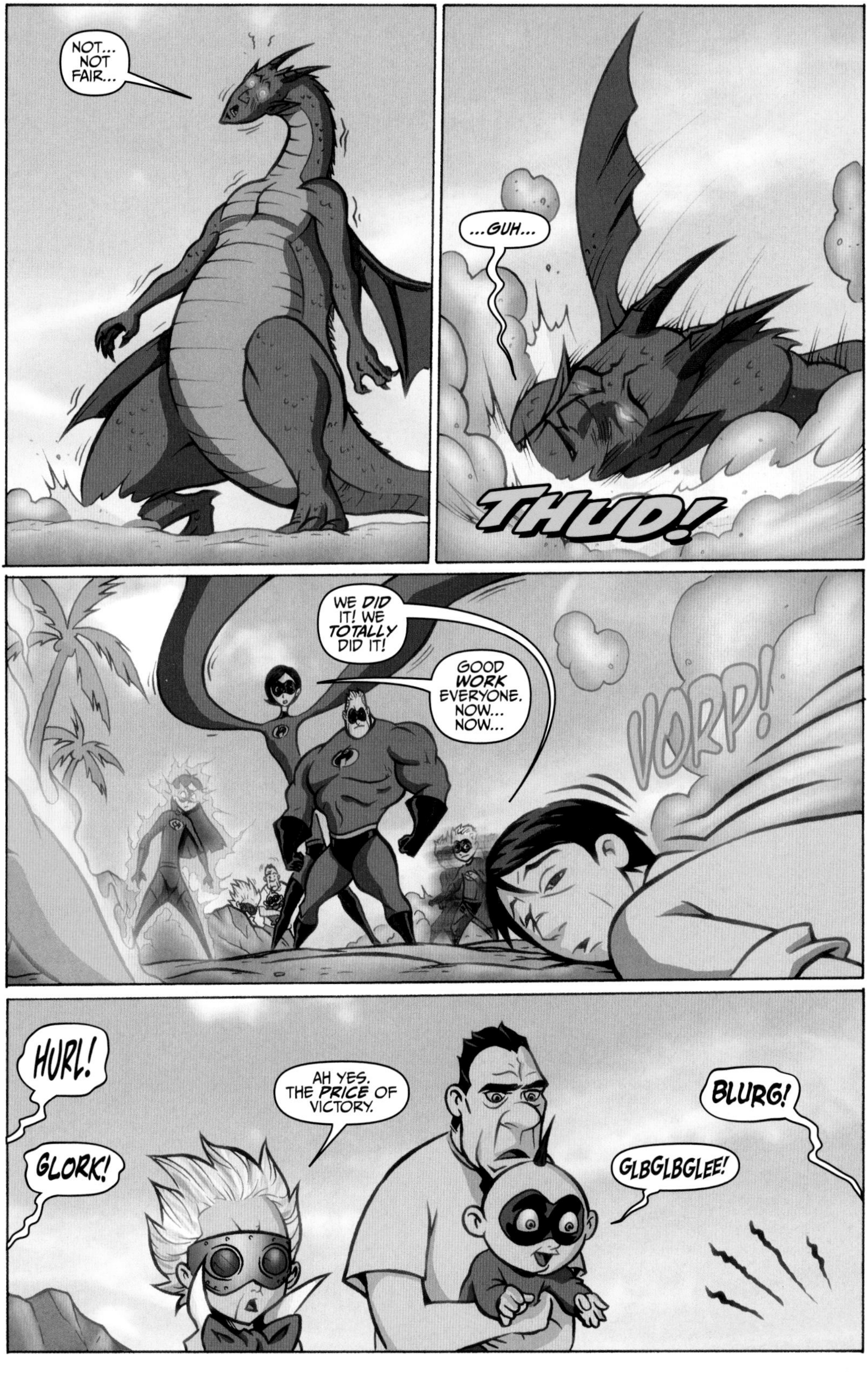
NOT... NOT FAIR...
...GUH...
THUD!
WE DID IT! WE TOTALLY DID IT!
GOOD WORK EVERYONE. NOW... NOW...
VORP!
HURL!
GLORK!
AH YES. THE PRICE OF VICTORY.
BLURG!
GLBGLBGLEE!

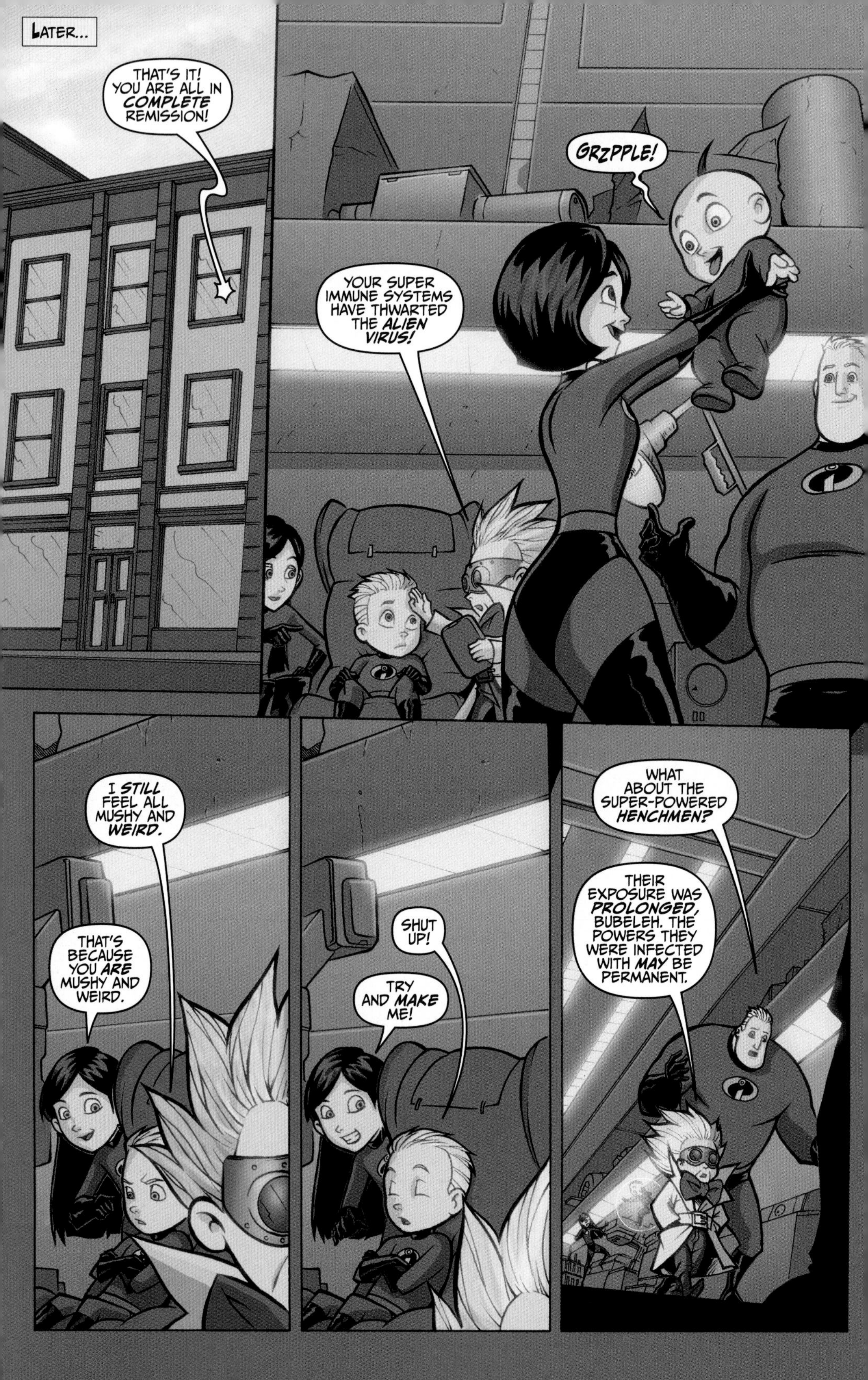
LATER...
THAT'S IT! YOU ARE ALL IN COMPLETE REMISSION!
GRZPPLE!
YOUR SUPER IMMUNE SYSTEMS HAVE THWARTED THE ALIEN VIRUS!
I STILL FEEL ALL MUSHY AND WEIRD.
THAT'S BECAUSE YOU ARE MUSHY AND WEIRD.
SHUT UP!
TRY AND MAKE ME!
WHAT ABOUT THE SUPER-POWERED HENCHMEN?
THEIR EXPOSURE WAS PROLONGED, BUBELEH. THE POWERS THEY WERE INFECTED WITH MAY BE PERMANENT.

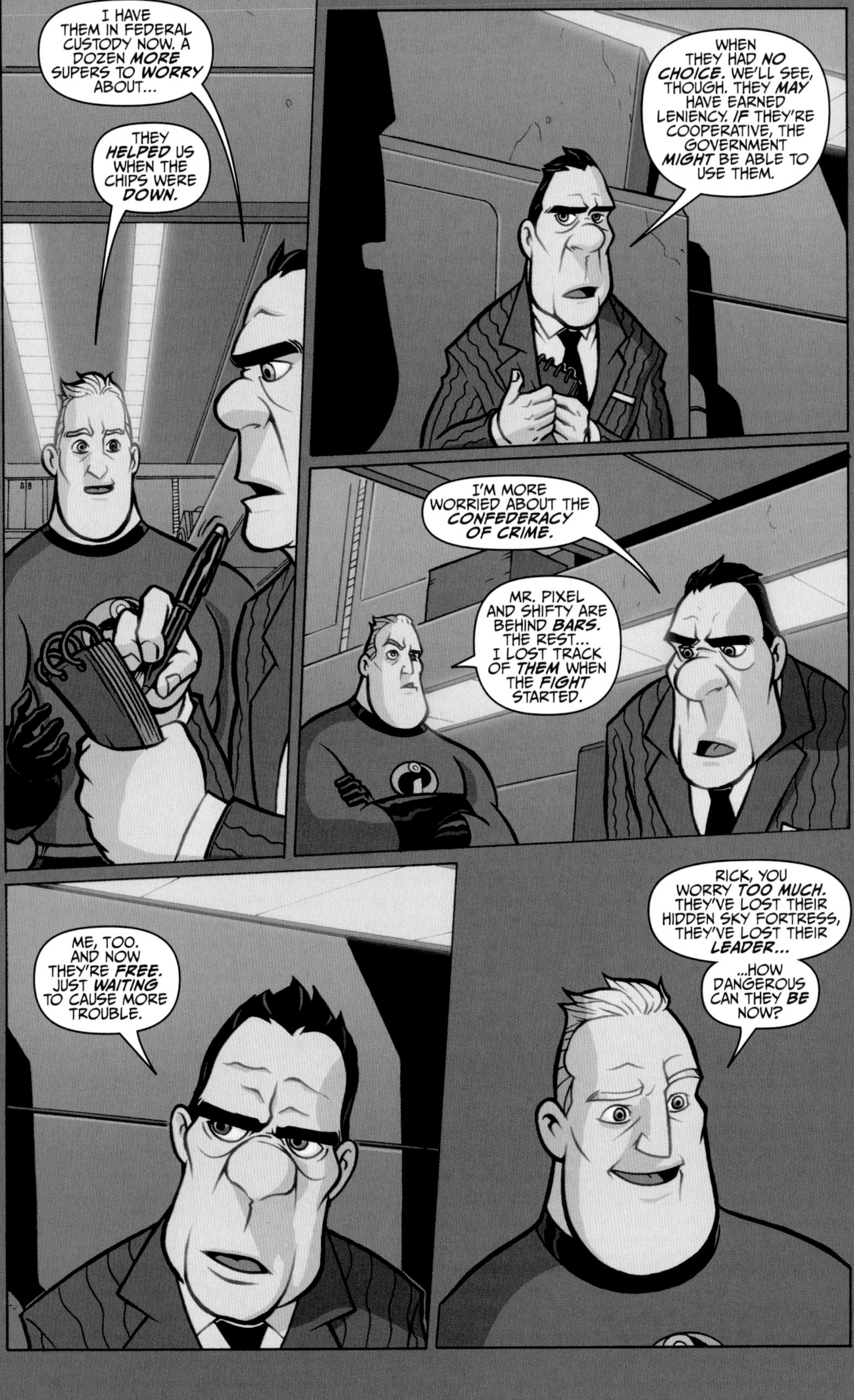
I HAVE THEM IN FEDERAL CUSTODY NOW. A DOZEN MORE SUPERS TO WORRY ABOUT...
THEY HELPED US WHEN THE CHIPS WERE DOWN.
WHEN THEY HAD NO CHOICE. WE'LL SEE, THOUGH. THEY MAY HAVE EARNED LENIENCY. IF THEY'RE COOPERATIVE, THE GOVERNMENT MIGHT BE ABLE TO USE THEM.
I'M MORE WORRIED ABOUT THE CONFEDERACY OF CRIME.
MR. PIXEL AND SHIFTY ARE BEHIND BARS. THE REST... I LOST TRACK OF THEM WHEN THE FIGHT STARTED.
ME, TOO. AND NOW THEY'RE FREE. JUST WAITING TO CAUSE MORE TROUBLE.
RICK, YOU WORRY TOO MUCH. THEY'VE LOST THEIR HIDDEN SKY FORTRESS, THEY'VE LOST THEIR LEADER...
...HOW DANGEROUS CAN THEY BE NOW?

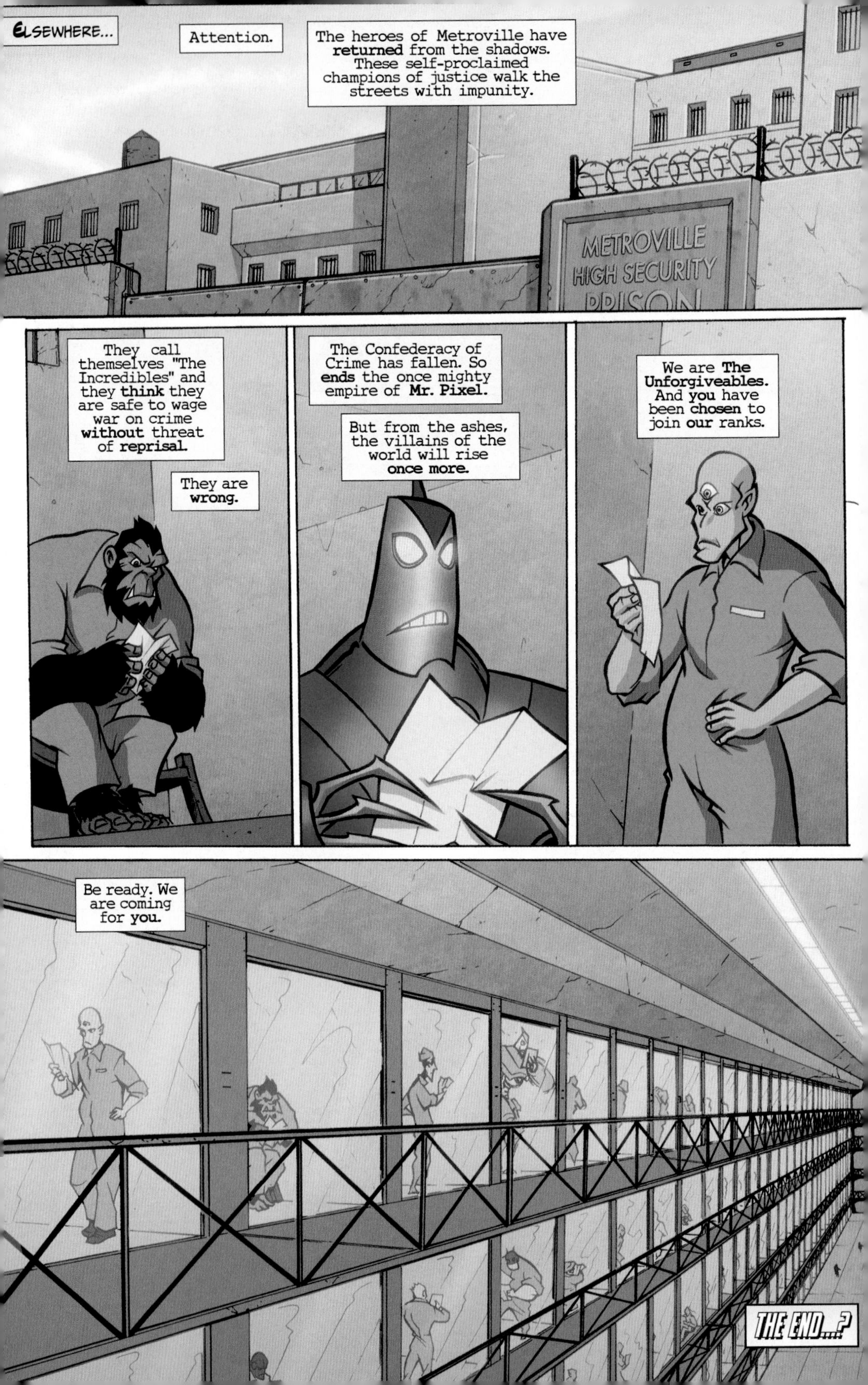
ELSEWHERE...
Attention.
The heroes of Metroville have **returned** from the shadows. These self-proclaimed champions of justice walk the streets with impunity.
METROVILLE HIGH SECURITY PRISON
They call themselves "The Incredibles" and they **think** they are safe to wage war on crime **without** threat of **reprisal.**
They are **wrong.**
The Confederacy of Crime has fallen. So **ends** the once mighty empire of **Mr. Pixel.**
But from the ashes, the villains of the world will rise **once more.**
We are **The Unforgiveables.** And **you** have been **chosen** to join **our** ranks.
Be ready. We are coming for **you.**
THE END...?

COVER GALLERY

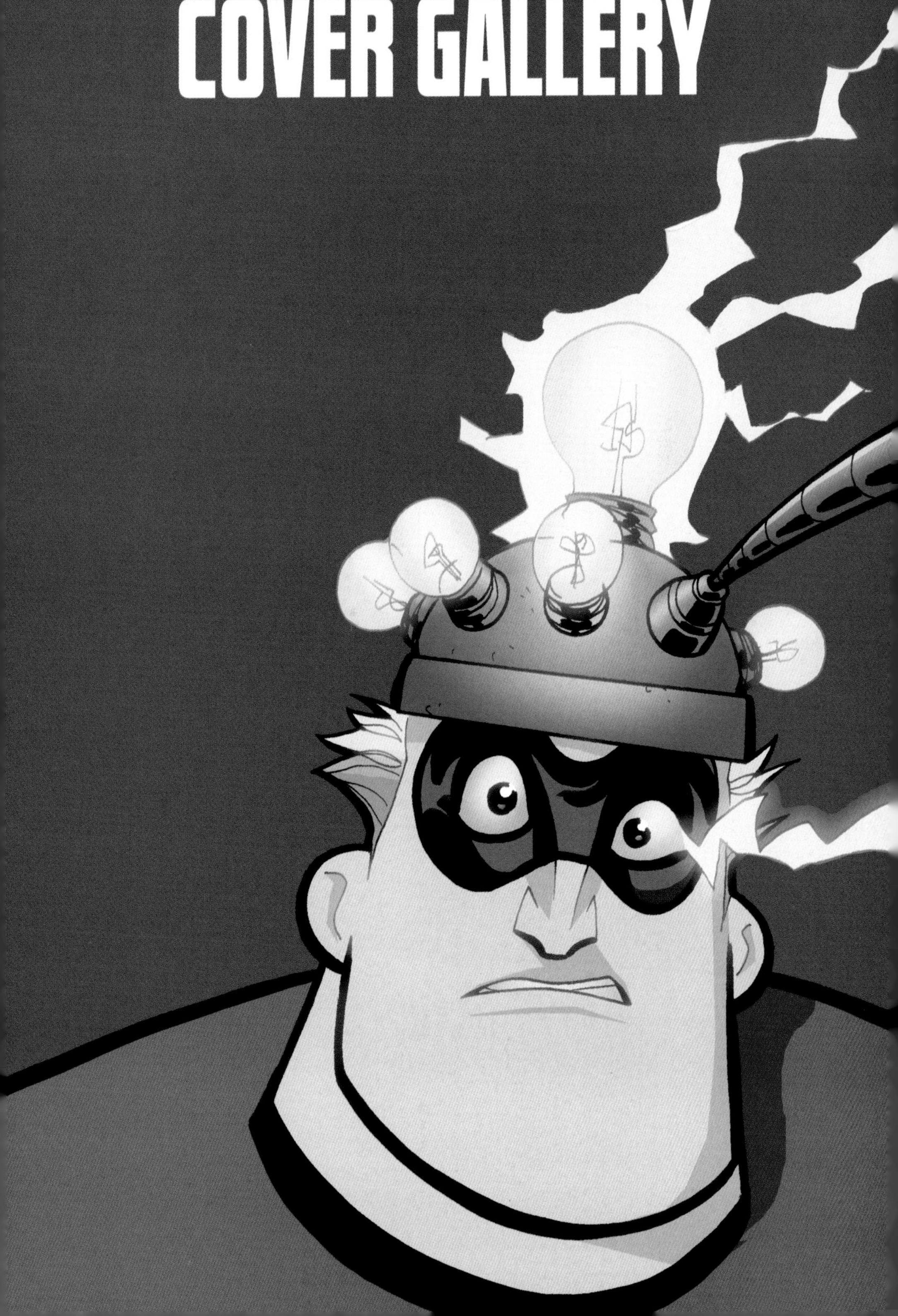

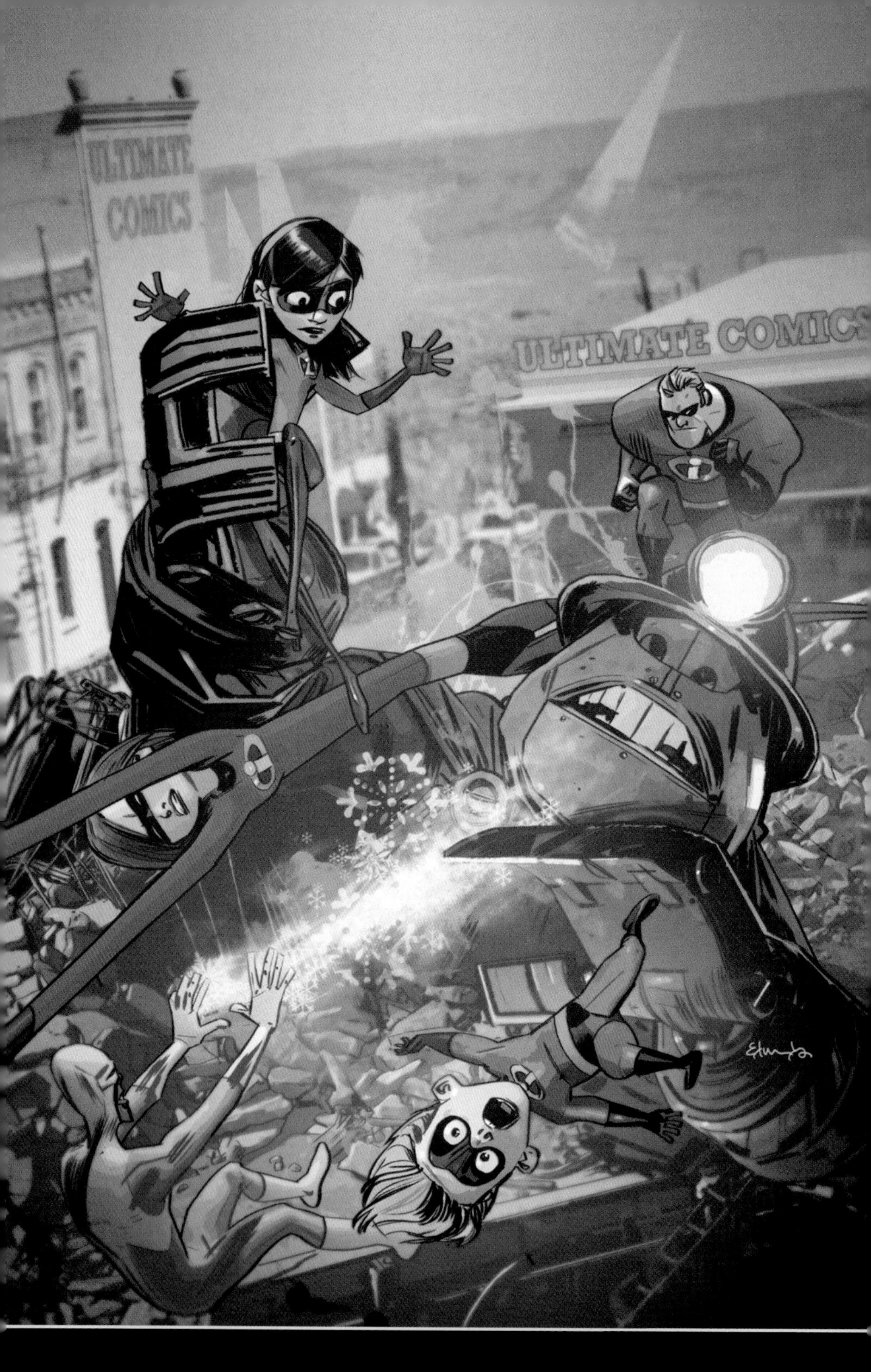
ULTIMATE COMICS
ULTIMATE COMICS

ULTIMATE COMICS EXCLUSIVE: TOMMY LEE EDWARDS

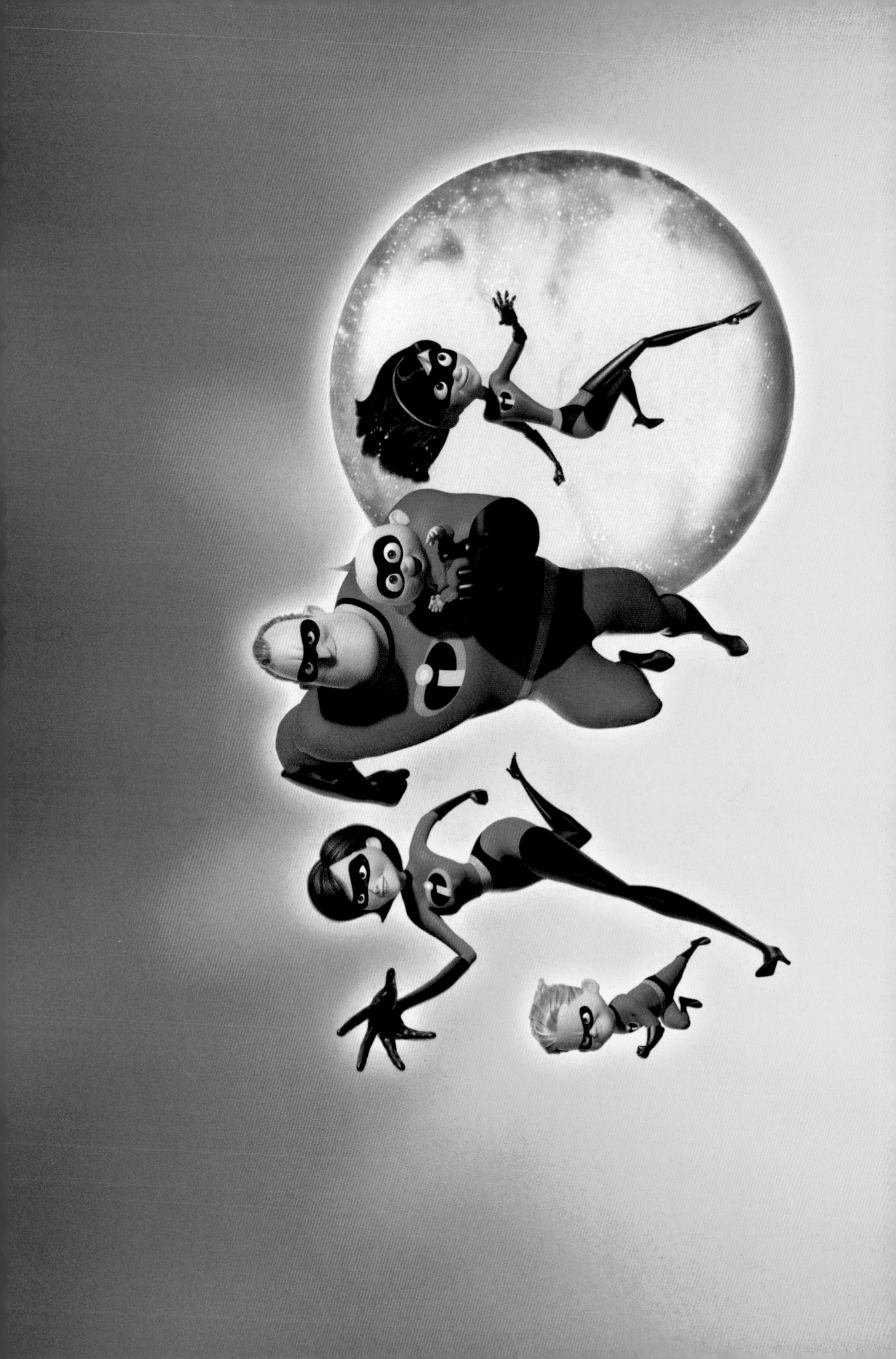

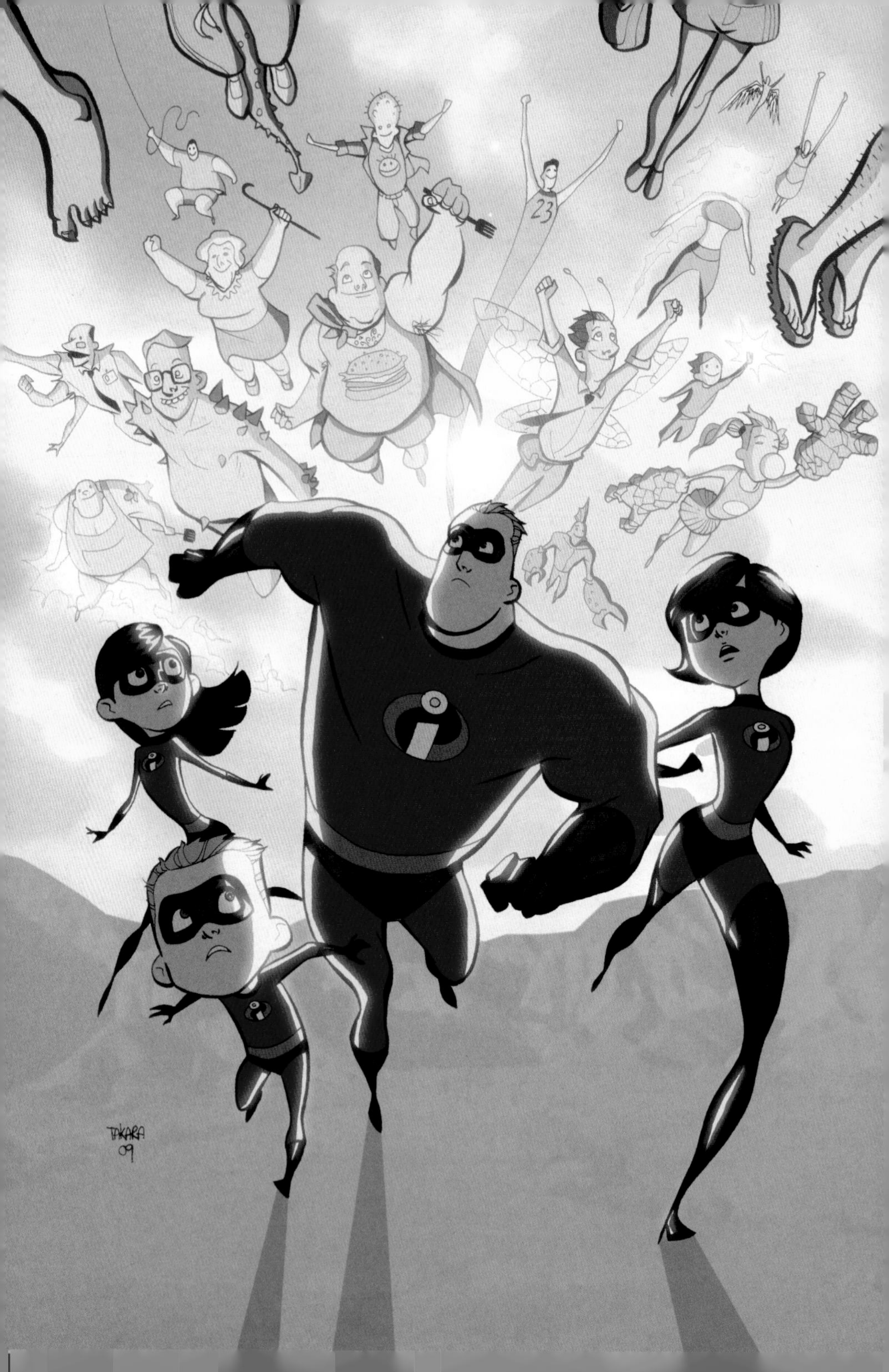
TAKARA
09

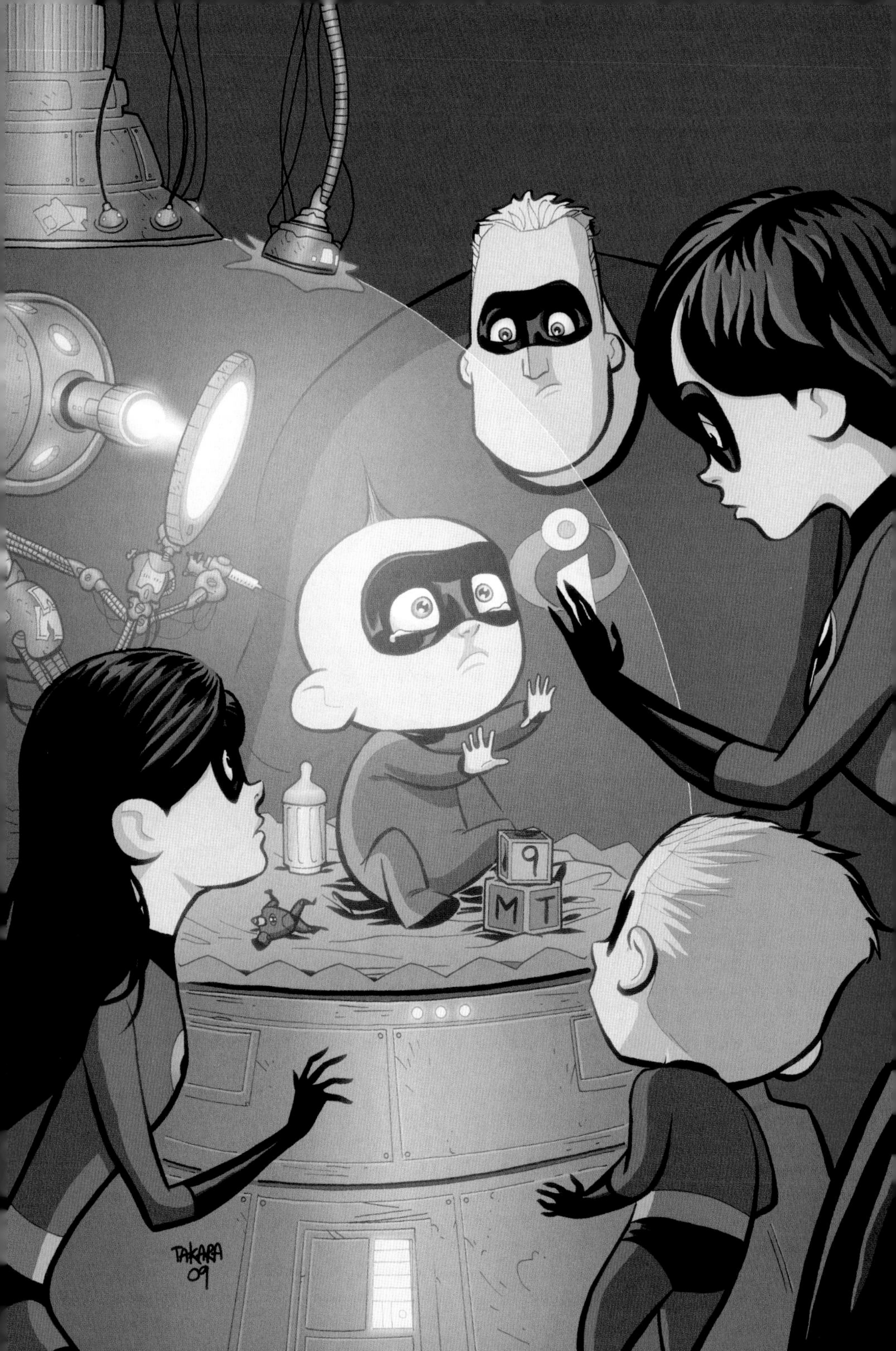
TAKARA
09

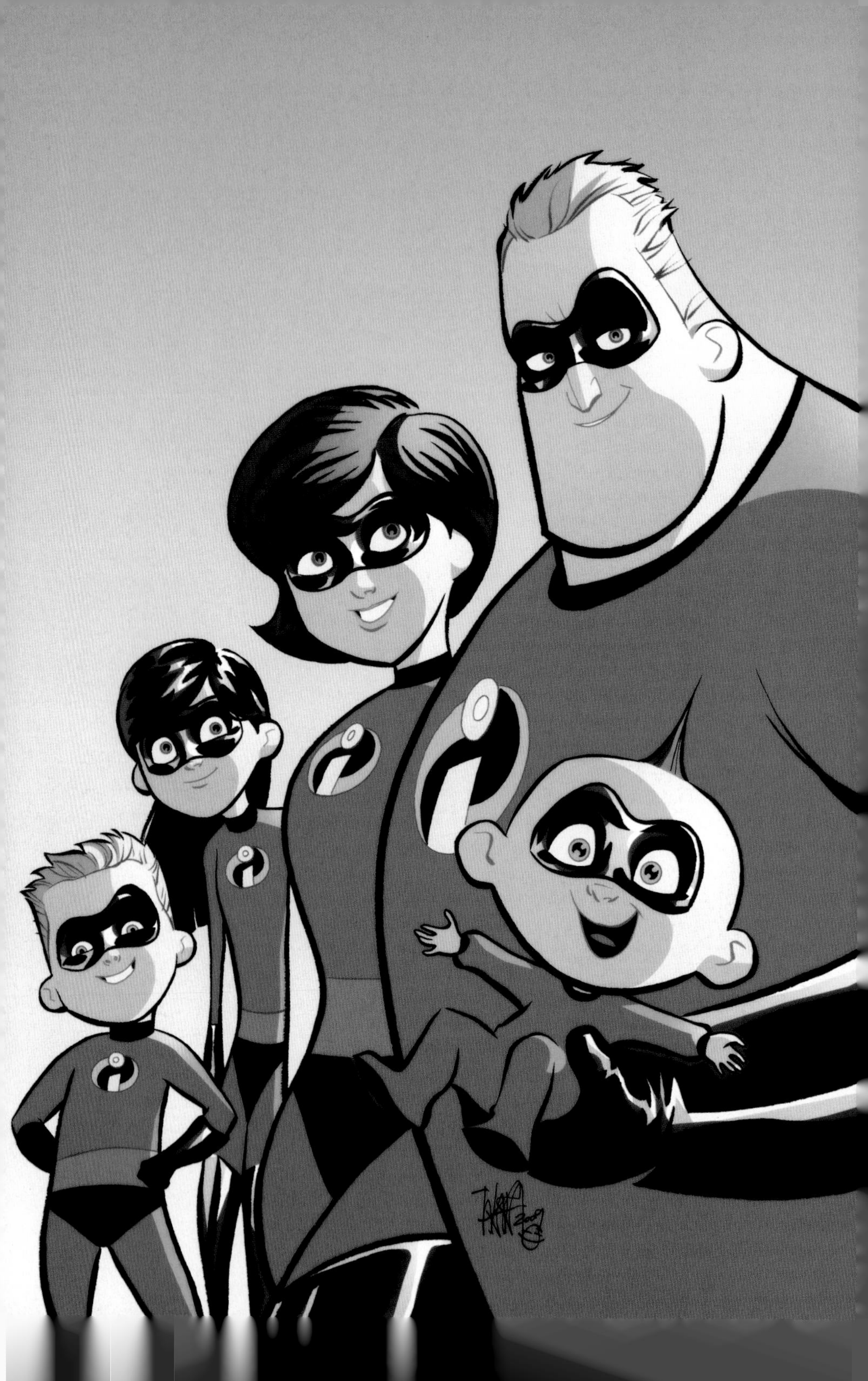

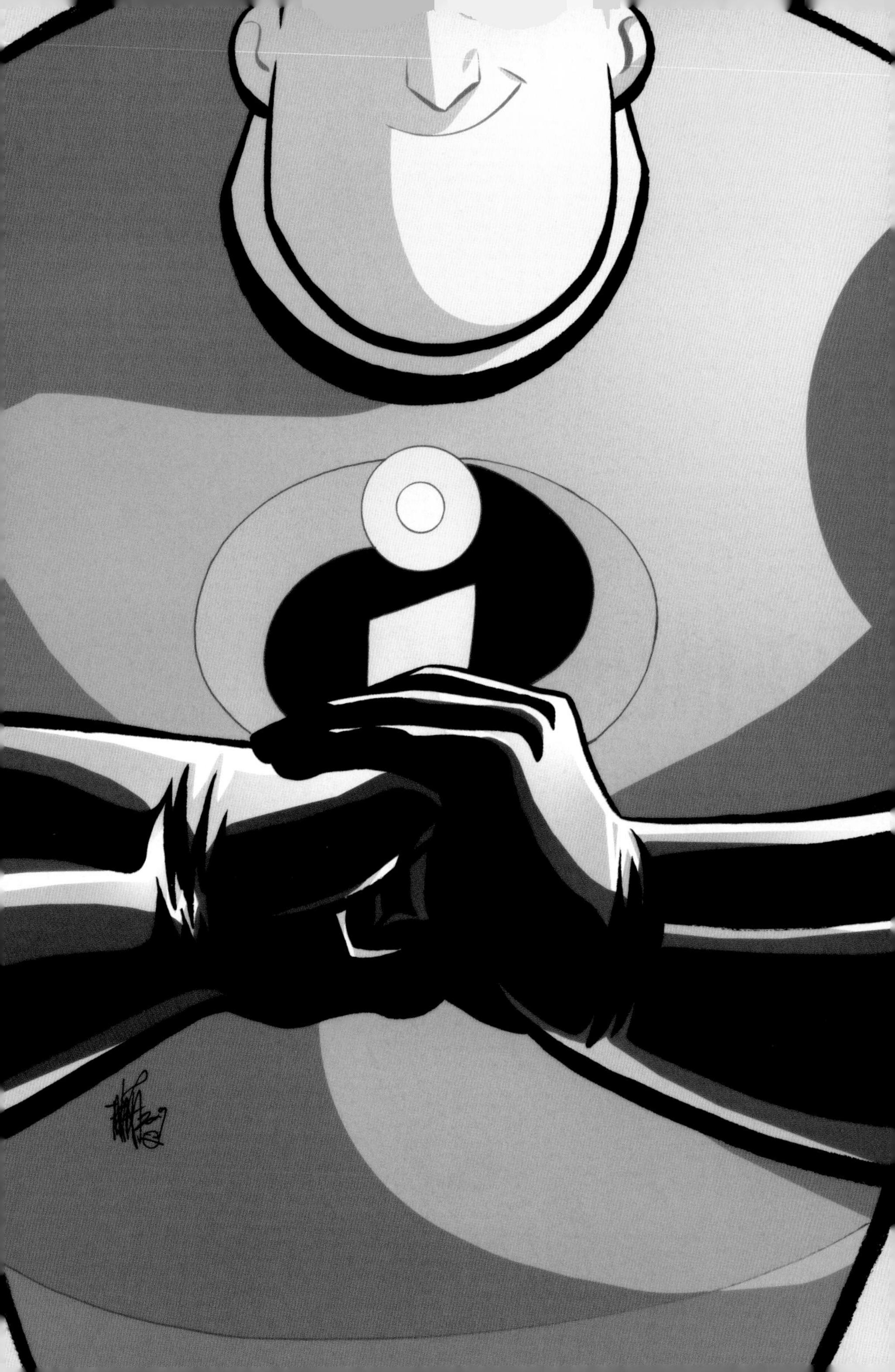

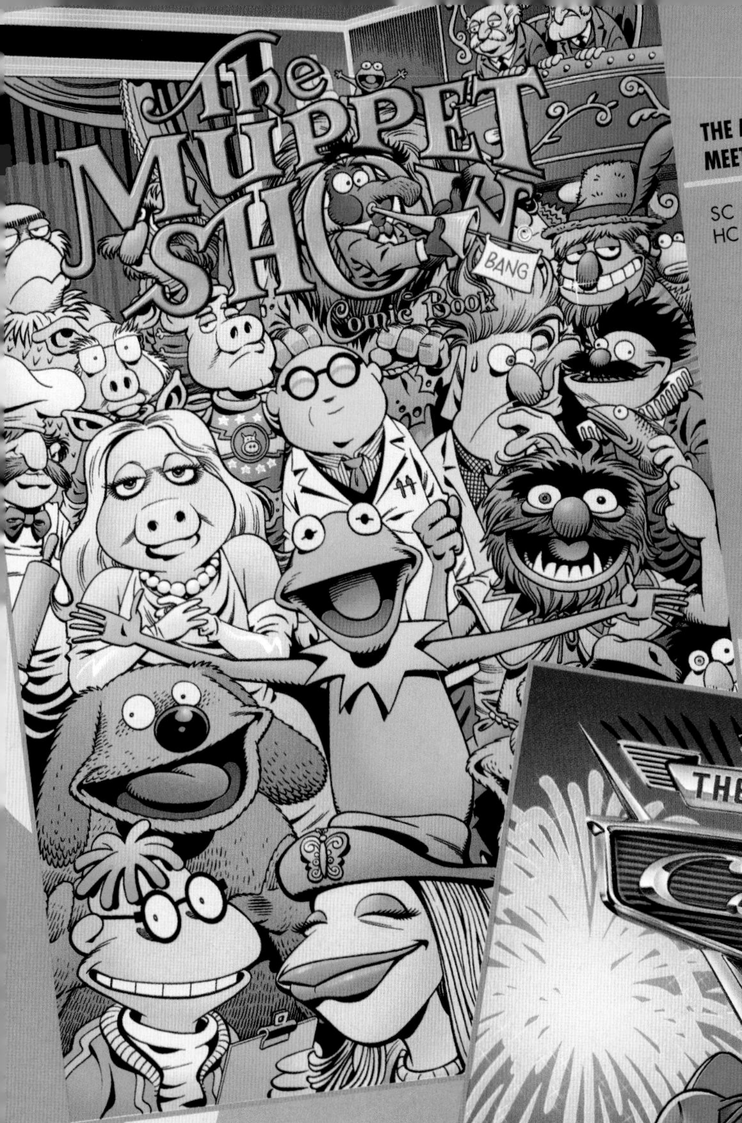
The Muppet Show
Comic Book
BANG

THE MUPPET SHOW COMIC BOOK: MEET THE MUPPETS

SC $9.99 ISBN 9781934506851
HC $24.99 ISBN 9781608865277

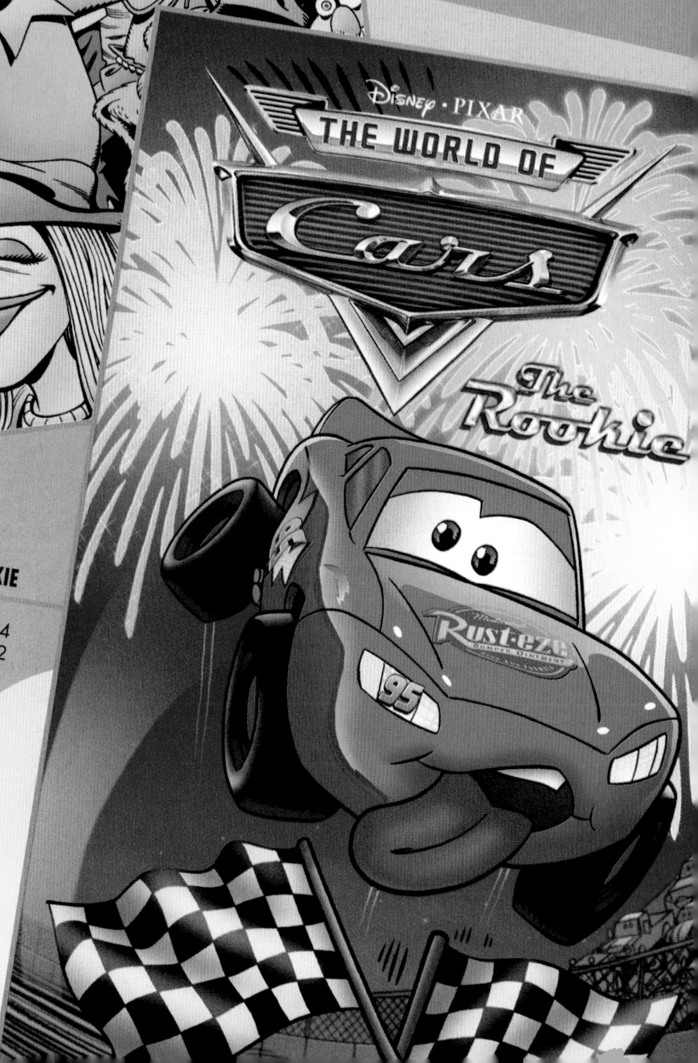
Disney • PIXAR
THE WORLD OF
Cars
The Rookie
Rust-eze
95

CARS: THE ROOKIE

SC $9.99 ISBN 9781934506844
HC $24.99 ISBN 9781608865222

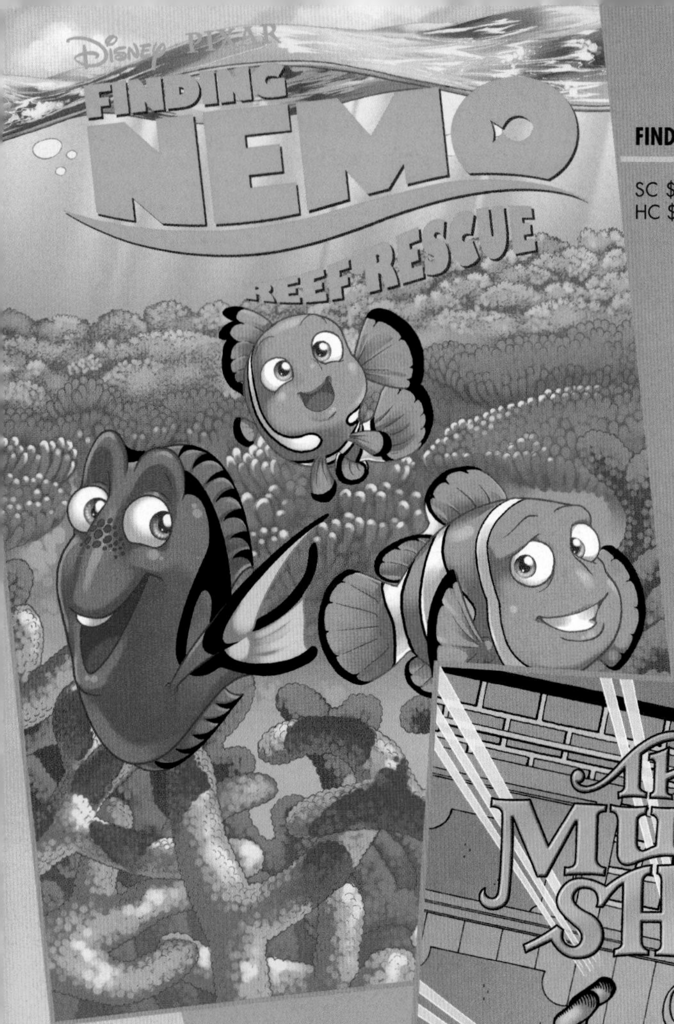
Disney PIXAR
FINDING NEMO
REEF RESCUE

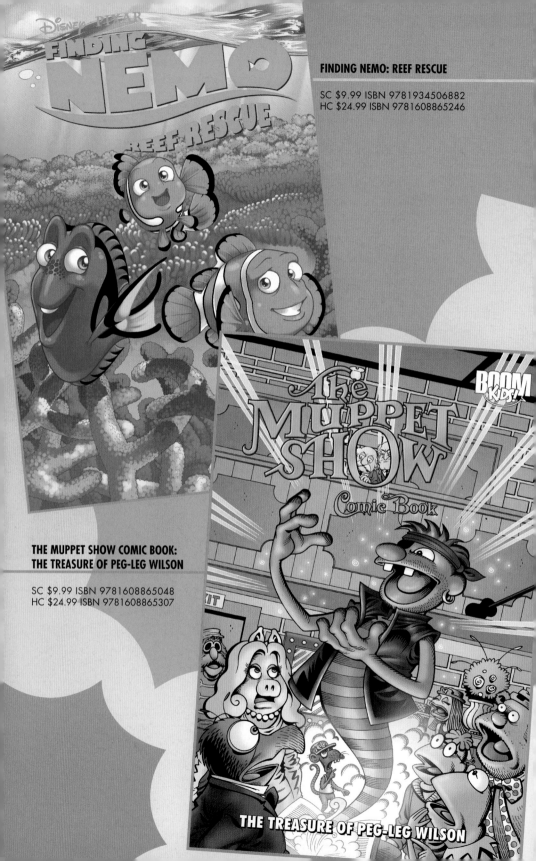

FINDING NEMO: REEF RESCUE

SC $9.99 ISBN 9781934506882
HC $24.99 ISBN 9781608865246

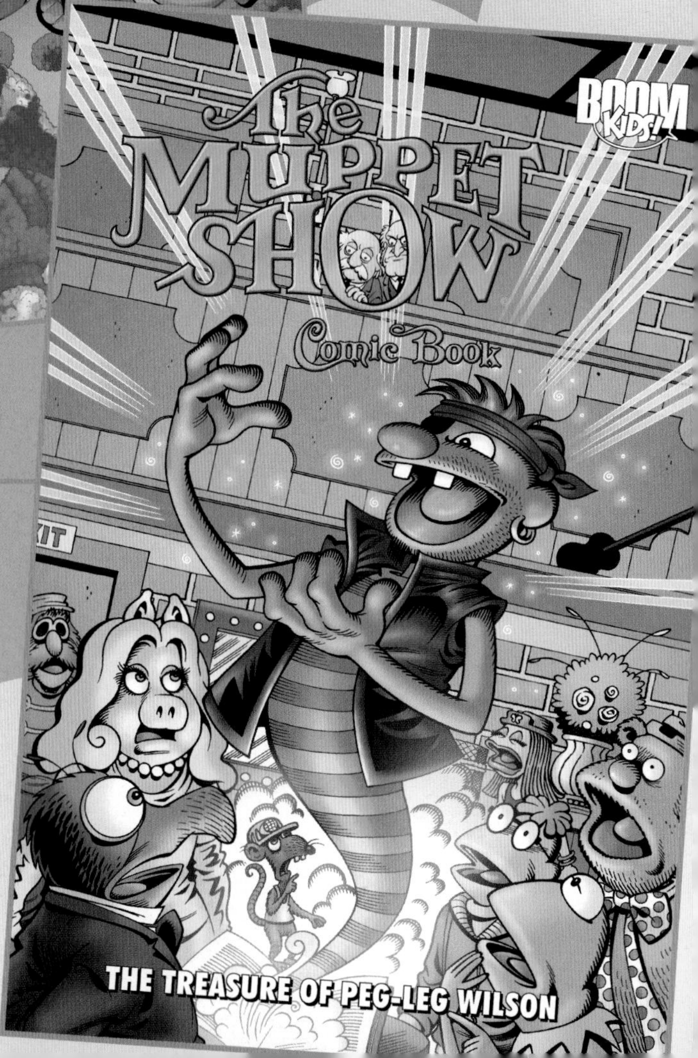
BOOM KIDS!
The MUPPET SHOW Comic Book
THE TREASURE OF PEG-LEG WILSON

THE MUPPET SHOW COMIC BOOK: THE TREASURE OF PEG-LEG WILSON

SC $9.99 ISBN 9781608865048
HC $24.99 ISBN 9781608865307